Deeds Not Words

by
Katharine D'Souza

For Jenny
Enjoy the Read
and your writing!

Katharine D.

"FORWARD"

Motto of the City of Birmingham

Chapter One

Caroline forced a smile as the potential for embarrassment made her stomach squirm. The appropriate etiquette for the situation eluded her. 'OK,' she said, 'what I can tell you is that the frame is older than the picture.'

She'd wanted to groan the moment the man placed the bin liner-covered object on her table. Now she couldn't bring herself to look him in the eye although she could sense his intense stare on her face. It was easy to be enthusiastic when much loved collections of medals or photographs were brought to the museum to be assessed by a curator. But she dreaded amateur oil paintings and this one didn't change her opinion. It took little skill to judge that the chipped plaster frame was worth more than the poorly executed artwork it held.

She tucked her hair behind her ears and blinked a couple of times while she considered how to break the news. Visual arts were not her field of expertise: she was a curator of antiquities; but these regular events at which the public were invited to bring in their treasures had not once tested her knowledge of ancient artefacts. Most people were interested only in whether their possessions might be worth something. Historical interest or significance was less relevant and Caroline found her colleagues quick with excuses why their time was too precious to attend the sessions. Most items turned out to be modern and mundane.

'It's old then, is it?' The man wrinkled his nose to move his thick lensed glasses back into place.

Caroline paused and lowered her voice. 'Not very.' It was a difficult balance to find, the point between allaying hope while still being positive about a person's treasured possession. The room's tiled floor and high glass and ironwork roof created excellent acoustics and she didn't want to broadcast her judgement to everyone. 'The frame could be up to one hundred years old. Possibly. Although…'

'But the painting, it looks like a Constable, don't you think? And he was working about two hundred years ago.'

'You're right: Constable's paintings are that old.'

'Oh, so you don't think this is a Constable then?'

She shoved her hands into her pockets and tried to swallow down the excruciation. The past yielded its secrets easily only when the details weren't worth knowing. 'Well, the picture is a Constable, but this version wasn't painted by him.' It was typical this should land in front of her; absolutely typical of the way her career was going.

Movement across her peripheral vision made her glance up at a young man whose black anorak and navy baseball cap bore sports-brand logos. With the cap pulled low on his forehead he slouched against the glass of a nearby display cabinet. He seemed to be watching her.

'I don't get what you mean.' Her attention was dragged back to the man in front of her who tilted the picture to examine it himself. 'My mum always called it "her Constable"; it's been above the fire as long as I can remember.'

'I see. Well, maybe it was hers in that she painted it? I'm sorry to break it to you, but I think it's from a paint by numbers kit.'

The man was silent.

Caroline flushed but kept talking. 'Look here, you can see the printed design under this pale blue paint. I mean, it's been very nicely done and displaying it in this ornate frame means it's a lovely decorative item…'

He shook the black bag open, shoved the picture back inside and left. His fast footsteps echoed around the room and Caroline dropped her head into her hands. From the table beside her a colleague leant over and whispered, 'Congratulations. You get the award for worst item of the afternoon'.

She moved a hand and glared at him. 'I could murder you, Bill. It was critical you said so much about that Wedgwood jug wasn't it? You could see it was a picture next in the queue.'

Bill ignored her and beckoned to the last woman waiting to see them. His smile faded as she unpacked several newspaper wrapped items from her bag and said, 'I've got this lovely collection of ornaments…'

Caroline turned away to hide her smirk at Bill's comeuppance and began to stack the reference books she'd brought from her office in the museum's basement. One day, she thought, one day I might actually need to refer to something. My fifteen years of study and experience will lead to a breakthrough; I'll make a discovery that will change current interpretations of history. She sighed. It was unlikely perhaps, but positive thinking was free if occasionally difficult to maintain. A glance at her watch showed there were still five minutes before the session was due to end so she sat down, smoothed her skirt over her knees, and looked around the room.

The gallery housed the museum's collection of glassware and ceramics. Glazed cases allowed visitors to view items from all angles: to study designs, firing techniques, or maker's marks. They also allowed Caroline to meet the eye of the sportswear-clad man who'd been watching her earlier. He lurked behind a display of ornamental maiolica dishes and she doubted he was the type to take an interest in fifteenth century Italian pottery. Despite his clothes, she also doubted he was any kind of athlete. First impressions could be unreliable, but two hours of interaction with the public had depleted her store of politeness. That bloke, she thought, is neither sportsman nor scholar. He's shifty.

She glanced at the porcelain figurines grouped on the table in front of Bill. No, there was no need to worry their owner was in danger of being mugged as soon as she left the museum. Mass produced fairies were unlikely to tempt an opportunistic thief. Caroline looked back but the suspicious man had moved. She stood to survey the rest of the room and jumped when she found he'd sidled up beside her.

'Oh,' she said. 'Hello, was there something you wanted us to take a look at? I'm afraid we've only a few minutes left.'

'I've got this.' He produced a dirty, cloth-covered bundle from his coat pocket and began to unwrap it. 'I want to know if it's worth anything.'

Typical, she thought, money's all that matters as usual. She faked the smile again. 'We can't give valuations, but perhaps I can tell you what it might be.'

The man stopped unwrapping and looked at her. 'You won't tell me what it's worth?'

'No. I'm afraid I don't know the market; you'd need to go to an auction house for that. We're here to talk about the history of things. I might be able to tell you a little about your object, whether it's rare or how old it might be perhaps.' Caroline leant forward as a flash of gold caught her eye from within the folds of cloth.

He hesitated. 'I only want to know if it's worth cleaning it up.'

'OK, well…' Caroline held out a hand and he pulled the cloth further apart without passing it to her. She could see an ovalish lump encrusted with mud. The shape of the item itself was masked but, in places, bands of gold-coloured metal were visible through the dirt and gravel.

Caroline leant closer. 'Where did you get it?' she asked. She'd seen items which looked like that recently, very recently in fact, in the museum's conservation lab where they were cleaning the Anglo-Saxon items discovered in a Staffordshire field. Of course she couldn't be sure this was the same thing; not unless he allowed her to examine it more closely.

He pulled it away though and wrapped it again. 'It's mine. I've had it ages,' he said. His acting skills let him down; it was a blatant lie.

'Can I just..?' Caroline reached out. 'Please, I'd just like a closer look.' But he'd been spooked.

'No, it's OK. I'll go elsewhere if you don't know a value.'

'Well, I'm sure I could give a ballpark figure.' She knew she sounded desperate and that Bill had noticed something was happening.

'No, I don't want to disturb it too much.' The man finished wrapping and turned to leave.

She called out, 'If you change your mind, get in touch. My name's Caroline Hipkins. Call the museum and ask for me. I'd love to help and you might have a legal obligation to...'

The man was out of the room before she could finish advising him about the law relating to treasure. Finders were not necessarily keepers.

*

As she flopped onto her chair in the office she shared with two other curators Caroline knew it was unlikely that item was a precious historical artefact. Most likely it was a bit of long lost costume jewellery the bloke had dug up in his garden. Even to imagine it could be ancient treasure was foolish - the kind of idiotic thought inspired by a long and irritating day.

And yet, the mud had the same tone and sandy character as the soil which clung to the recently excavated Staffordshire Hoard; the gold had the same rich sheen; the stones could have been garnets. She rubbed her eyes. It was madness, or jealousy. After all, at the morning's team meeting to discuss the displays to accompany the Hoard, her proposal to balance the military nature of many of the items with a display about domestic life in Anglo-Saxon times had been dismissed. Bill's suggestions about interactive battle games had not.

She glanced over to his desk on the other side of the room. His head was bent over his keyboard and his bald patch gleamed in the fluorescent glow from the overhead strip lights.

'Enjoy your trip to fairyland?' she asked.

He looked up and grimaced. 'There is a very good reason why I cannot normally spare the time for public interaction.'

She smiled. 'That you're a miserable sod?'

'Your problem is you're desperate to be liked. Bet you'd even have said something nice about the fairies.'

'Doubt it.'

'I fear they were made in China and not under one of the Dynasties.'

Caroline laughed. 'So you'll be making your usual excuses next time then? Leave all the hard work to those of us with customer care skills.'

Bill snorted. 'More like care in the community. What was in that dirty hanky the last man was showing you?'

She didn't want to tell him what she'd thought based on her first glance. The entire team had spent too much time looking at seventh century treasures; her mind was seeing them where they couldn't possibly be. Could they? 'Oh, probably nothing,' she said. 'He was a bit of a weirdo, wasn't he?'

The papers and books on her desk related to her rejected exhibition ideas so she pushed them aside and opened her notebook to a blank page. What she needed was a big, original idea that would impress her boss. She'd been working at the museum in Birmingham for two months since her return from London and knew he'd barely noticed her presence. If she planned to stay that needed to change. She chewed the end of her pen. The job was a step backwards but keeping it for a while would be the easiest option, the safe choice. It was better that way.

*

After a few unproductive hours Caroline decided to go home. She climbed the grand marble steps, which must have once graced public rooms but now led to the offices and studios used by staff, and indulged in a short stroll through the galleries. Amateur oil paintings may not have fed her aesthetic hunger that afternoon, but a private view of the collections on her way home meant she wouldn't dread returning to work the following day.

First she visited the room housing the ancient Greek and Roman artefacts that were her particular responsibility. It was a good collection displayed in the usual, conservative manner. Groups of items stood by old fashioned labels behind the glass of wooden framed cases. Everything was ordered, defined and safe. No grey areas, no unanswered questions. She frowned, recognising the room was dull almost to the point of invisibility. The few visitors she'd seen lingering there seemed only to be taking advantage of a sit down on their way to the lift.

Something would have to be done to link antiquities to the present day, to tell the stories which fascinated her so much she'd made caring for the past her career, but it could wait. Loose parquet tiles knocked against each other underfoot as she crossed the room and entered the public stairwell. There the dry, calm atmosphere of analysed and preserved history was dispelled by the roar of traffic on the road outside. Natural light filtered through a stained glass window featuring Birmingham's coat of arms: a woman with a paintbrush and a man holding tools. Art and Industry with the city's motto, "Forward", scrolled below them. Caroline turned her back and entered the fine art galleries to indulge in a quick view of her current favourite object: an oil painting by David Cox.

11

The subject was a cottage kitchen where one woman worked at a table and another sat beside a fire and concentrated on her knitting. The figure reminded Caroline of her nan occupied at the same craft. Although, a suburban living room warmed by the glow of a gas fire had little in common with the rest of the painted interior with its rough beamed ceiling and flagstone floor. Both women in the picture bent to their tasks with an enviable commitment and intensity of focus. The painting captured their sense of purpose and recorded a long-gone lifestyle.

The frame with its gilt foliage flourishes was over the top in Caroline's opinion. The restraint of a plain frame would be more in keeping with the scene's simplicity. No point saying anything though; most likely her thoughts would be at odds with the ideas of the fine art team, and there wouldn't be funds for anything as frivolous as replacing a perfectly good frame. She sighed, turned away, wished the front of house staff goodnight and headed home.

It was a short walk to her apartment in a modern block beside the canal. She wove a path through crowds of early evening concert-goers gathering at Symphony Hall and held her breath as she passed huddles of smokers gasping under the canopies of canal-side bars. The quality of the museum and the familiar, vibrant city had tempted her back to Birmingham, and she'd ignored the inner voice mumbling that it wasn't really a challenge, hardly even a change. Less enticing was that the move brought her back to the same city as her family. They weren't dreadful, just demanding. It was all very well for her mum and nan to assume she'd be available at their beck and call. What made them think she didn't have anything better to do?

All these concerts, theatres, bars and restaurants; who was to say she wouldn't be frequenting them every night? Some of her old school friends still lived in the city. She and Steph had once been regulars in the pubs and clubs; there was no reason why Caroline couldn't reclaim that busy social life. Of course she hadn't, and hadn't actually been in touch with Steph to suggest they meet up now she was back, but she had no desire to be drawn into the latest argument about whether or not her nan should downsize, declutter or do anything else to make the future easier.

Caroline shook her head to rid herself of the thoughts. Work had irritated her and she was hungry: those were the real problems. The apartment block was in sight as her grip on the strap of her handbag registered the vibration of her mobile ringing. It took a moment of rummaging before she retrieved the phone and groaned at the caller's name illuminated on the screen.

'Hi, Mum,' she said, wondering how Alice managed to time calls to coincide with her daughter's disloyal thoughts.

'Now don't panic, but I'm with your nan at the hospital. Can you come?'

Hunger and boredom forgotten, Caroline sprinted to where her car was gathering dust in an allocated basement parking space. The engine fired up on the second attempt and she cursed the fuel gauge as it hovered near empty. She'd forgotten the lack of petrol since last using the car. As she drove out of the city centre her mother's words echoed through her mind, 'She's had a fall, they've taken her for some x-rays.' That sounded serious.

Concern for her nan combined with the risk of running on fumes generated a tense, nauseous sensation in her stomach and she pulled in to a petrol station. As she fidgeted in the queue to pay she grabbed a bag of crisps and willed the cashier to speed up.

'It's buy one, get one free,' he said when she reached the front and thrust her credit card towards the chip and pin machine.

'What?'

'The crisps. You can have another pack free.' He'd obviously been on some kind of training course. Caroline frowned. Weren't petrol stations supposed to be staffed by

13

surly teenagers? Not eager young men in polo shirts branded with the company logo.

'I'm fine, really, just these and the petrol.'

From the queue behind her a man tapped her arm and proffered another pack. 'Can I have them then?'

'What?' Caroline was about to explode with agitation at the delay.

'Your free crisps,' the man said, 'I'll have them if you don't want them.'

She gaped at him. Did none of these people understand the concept of urgency? She snatched the bag. 'Yes, great, crisps all round. And pump two. As quickly as possible. Please.'

Chapter Two

After a battle with the pay and display machine at the car park and five minutes confusion as she translated the colour-coded map of the hospital into actual directions, Caroline located the ward. She found her mum hunched on a plastic seat in a corridor.

'How's Nan?' she asked.

Alice looked up. 'They think she's fractured a hip, she needs more x-rays tomorrow. Oh, but I've been so scared. What if she'd hit her head when she fell?'

Unwilling to engage with this worse than the actual case scenario, Caroline pressed for details of what happened. Alice managed to combine disapproval and anxiety in her strained voice. 'She was trying to get a box from the top of her wardrobe and fell from the stool.'

'Why? What on earth can have been so urgent she couldn't have waited for one of us to do it?'

Caroline could picture the dark wooden wardrobe. It stood about seven foot high before the edge of its carved door stood proud of the top and screened a teetering pile of boxes, only a fraction of the clutter which littered her nan's home.

A nurse approached. 'We're finished settling her if you want to go in. Twenty minutes until visiting time ends for this evening.'

Caroline left Alice to argue about the unfairness of the time limit and rushed into the four-bed side ward. Her nan was in a bed by the window, propped on pillows, the tube from a saline drip snaking to her arm. She looked smaller than she did at home.

'Oh, Nan, what have you done now?' There was no criticism in Caroline's tone and she reached to stroke an age-spotted hand.

'Don't let your mother cause a fuss and what have they written up there? Everyone keeps calling me Elizabeth.'

Caroline looked at the whiteboard mounted on the wall above the bed in between bits of medical equipment. Over the smeared remnants of carelessly erased ink was scrawled the name Elizabeth Dabbs. No one used that name. Her nan had been known as Beth for eighty years. Caroline nodded. 'I'll find a pen and change it but first tell me how you're feeling.'

'Sore. Sore all over.'

'Well I'm not surprised. What on earth were you doing climbing on a stool?'

Before Beth could respond, Alice marched up to the bed, 'They think you've fractured your hip.'

'I know that. That'll be why it's so painful.'

Caroline shook her head. The two women continually baited and bickered with each other and the drama of the situation had them both wanting to take charge. She tuned them out for a moment and looked instead at the other occupants of the ward. Each of the three beds contained an elderly woman. One was plugged into the patient entertainment system which loomed over her bed, colours from the screen flickering on the lenses of her glasses. The others were motionless, pinned into the cage of their hospital beds by tightly tucked blankets. One caught Caroline's eye and opened a toothless mouth to caw at her. Caroline looked away. She had enough to contend with from the women of her own family.

'I need to sort out some things I've got up there,' Beth said. 'Nothing for you to worry about.'

'Your entire house needs sorting out. What I don't understand is why you didn't wait for me or Caroline to come round and help, or why you decided to start with the top of the wardrobe,' Alice replied.

'They're my things. I don't want you two looking through them.'

'We're family; we'd be looking through them if you'd killed yourself falling from a great height like that!'

Caroline could see the nurse hovering in the corridor and interrupted. 'We've got to go soon, Nan. Is there anything else you need bringing in?'

'I packed her a bag while we waited for the ambulance,' Alice said. 'Although why you didn't just call the ambulance rather than calling me first to say you needed help, I still don't understand.'

Beth shook her head, obviously too tired to engage in this new argument. She rested back on the pillows and squeezed Caroline's hand. 'I would like my book please, love. It's on the coffee table. And my other slippers. The navy ones.'

*

Caroline drove them back to Beth's house in Edgbaston. Alice's car was awkwardly positioned on the drive having been abandoned for an ambulance during the crisis that afternoon. The women sat and looked up at the double-fronted red brick villa Beth had inherited and Alice had grown up in. With only two storeys, it was one of the smaller houses in the street but still large for a single occupant.

'She can't keep living here,' Alice said.

'You've been saying that for at least five years.'

Alice lifted her handbag from the passenger foot well on to her lap before inertia struck again. 'If she has broken her hip…'

'We don't know that yet. Don't start assuming the worst,' Caroline said, not adding that her mum had been assuming the worst for a lot longer than five years; probably since birth. 'I'll pop in and get her that book; I can drop it off after work tomorrow.'

Alice nodded. She'd arranged to be back at the hospital for the start of visiting hours the next day to make sure Beth got all the tests and treatment needed. She handed a set of house keys to Caroline. 'Make sure it's all locked up, won't you? I'll get home.'

Caroline waved from the doorstep as Alice reversed her car into the road. Then she turned and unlocked Beth's heavy, black-painted front door. The familiar scent greeted her: a mix of wood polish and mustiness with a hint of damp. Her flat had no scent, nothing to evoke memories as this did. Here the smell recalled regular childhood visits – days spent in this house at weekends or school holidays, occasional overnight visits when she and her brother Peter would be tucked into twin beds in a shared room because they'd convinced each other the house was haunted and were too scared to sleep alone.

The house was a collection of oddly shaped rooms with dark corners, creaking floor boards and wood panelling. She saw it as characterful now, not creepy. Once she'd made sure the back door was locked and bolted Caroline found the large print library book Beth had left in the living room and secured the front door behind her.

She was surprised to find it was only nine thirty as she drove the short distance back to her apartment. The stress of the evening made it feel as though months had passed. As she waited for the gate to the car park to swing open she glanced upwards. The building had a flavour of the architecture of seventeenth century Amsterdam, in an artificial essence sort of way. There were gables and each apartment was narrow. The comparison couldn't be stretched much further and the rent was stretching her salary. It was a good location to help her adjust with her return from London though. Going back to the suburb where she'd grown up would have been an admission of failure.

Several hours later than she'd anticipated when she left work Caroline closed her front door and dropped her bag on the kitchen counter. She opened the fridge and stood in front of it as though studying a work of art. The contents were as minimalist as the rest of the flat's interior. She sighed, let the fridge door slam shut and flopped on the sofa to dial her brother's phone number.

While she waited for the call to connect she kicked off her shoes and glanced at the room's bare walls. The flat was rented and had included the landlord's choice of furnishings. She'd taken down the cheap prints of Venetian scenes the moment she moved in two years earlier and they currently lodged behind the vacuum cleaner in the hall cupboard. Grubby outlines of where they'd hung against the cream paintwork were the only remaining décor.

When Peter answered, Caroline could hear music playing in the background. The drumming and rhythms put her in mind of some kind of ethnic folk music but she guessed it would be something altogether trendier and chose not to display her ignorance by commenting. Peter was five years younger and had moved to Brighton after art college. He lived a bohemian lifestyle she wouldn't admit she envied. After she'd updated him on the hospital situation, she said, 'I need you to send me a picture.'

'Caz, do I have to remind you that you hate my paintings? I quote: "anaesthetic for the eyes" and that was one of the more polite things you said.'

'Yeah, don't send one of the beach scenes. They're pure tourist tat. Something with buildings in. Or a dog. Send a dog.'

'I'd love to help with whatever it is you're on about, but I can't. I have an exhibition.'

Caroline paused, conflicted between pride and jealousy - Peter, whose paintings were unapologetically of the most commercial kind, had an exhibition? Meanwhile her boss wasn't prepared to allow her a couple of display boards to expand on her historical insights? She dredged her manners back to the surface. 'Wow, where? How many pictures will you be showing?'

'Only one of those touristy galleries, but they're giving me a whole room and good commission. All my dogs will be needed there.'

'Abandoning artistic integrity has been worth it, then? You might actually sell some paintings. Fair enough. I'll keep staring at blank walls. Actually, I saw a picture you'd have loved today.' She told the tale of the paint by numbers Constable.

'Poor bugger,' Peter said. 'But, I've just had the most brilliant business idea. I'll design a picture of Brighton Pier and sell outlines and watercolour kits. Now everyone can create their own Hipkins masterpiece! You're a star, Caz. Listen, I've got to go.'

Unbelievable, Caroline thought, my sole purpose is to provide the raw material for others to build success from. Much like the investment in the flat she'd bought with her ex-husband, Matt. Decorating that was her domestic dream come true. They'd bought paintings and redecorated to show them off, not just bunged up previously owned prints or posters. They'd created their home – comfortable and modern without the controlled order of Alice's house or the barely contained clutter of Beth's – and now it was gone.

She no longer knew where those pictures were, or any of the furniture. She'd taken her share of the increased value in the property as cash when she and Matt divorced. Possessions would have been painful reminders of the lifestyle they'd managed to sell so easily and which couldn't be more different from the way she lived now. Matt had used his share of the money to finance changes which bore no comparison to her life: back in Birmingham, drawn into family dramas and irritated at work. He was in the midst of an adventure, one she'd been offered a part in but judged as too risky. The single time she hadn't gone with the flow. With no scope to compromise, she'd taken a stand and he'd gone without her. She couldn't blame him and returned to the fridge to take out the slice of ham and jar of pickle that were going to have to serve as the evening's meal.

Times like this she missed Matt most. A complete foodie, he'd always kept their fridge well stocked so a delicious supper required only a flick through a recipe book. She smeared pickle onto the ham, rolled it into a tube and popped it in her mouth well aware that this was not the way a thirty-five year old woman was meant to behave.

Most of her peers lived in houses full of the clutter collected through their lives so far: children, pets, that sort of thing. Caroline didn't even have photograph albums, well, who did these days? What would be the point of hoarding prints up to a certain point, and then having digital? An inconsistent and incomplete record would frustrate her.

There were piles of photographs at Beth's - bundles spilt out of envelopes in almost every drawer you opened at that house. No chronological order, no logic to which were stored where: it drove Caroline's curatorial mind mad. She certainly didn't feel compelled to look after a collection of her own as well as at work.

'Not much character,' was what Alice said about the flat on every visit. It was meant to be a temporary solution but the ease of the journey to work overruled any incentive to move on.

Caroline had known colleagues who, when catalogues for specialist auctions arrived in the post, would flick through glossy pages to select which pictures or furniture they'd buy, should money conveniently become no obstacle. They'd choose decoration for their homes, imagining a life surrounded by things.

She could imagine nothing worse. Simplicity was her watchword these days. She tried to keep everything straightforward and easy - at home, at work, in relationships. If Beth was ready to start sifting the contents of her house Caroline wouldn't stand in her way. She'd offer to do the climbing and carrying though. It was ridiculous Beth had tried to do it alone.

She dropped the knife into the washing up bowl and wandered back to the silent living room. It was likely Peter had rushed off to a party or a date. No way he'd be home alone, bored and eating snacks for dinner with nothing but hospital visits and work to look forward to in the week ahead.

The thought of work reminded her of the mystery item secreted in the suspicious man's hands. What could it be? He obviously thought it was something of note to have been so cagey and she considered whether she should mention it to someone with more specialist knowledge, but then her experience was that the general public weren't capable of expert analysis. It was probably best forgotten.

The enthusiasm she'd once felt for artefacts had begun to elude Caroline. Sometimes, as she slipped on lint free gloves to handle a precious piece of ancient pottery, or summoned as much reverence for the spine of an old book as for the words inside it, she found herself wondering if it would really matter if she dropped or tore it. Would the world lose much if she were the last person to see or use the item? She wouldn't deliberately vandalise or destroy; but did have a growing sense of futility about her life. The past had been and gone; the future looked murky.

Opportunities and alternatives weren't easy to come by and the thought of chasing them alarmed her. This job is other people's dream and I'm qualified for nothing else, she thought. Too many things have changed recently. I can't possibly be craving something new.

The flat was stuffy and she slid open the door to her tiny balcony and leant against the chill of the metal railing to gaze at the canal below. Light from surrounding buildings illuminated the bright paint of narrow boats and reflected off smooth black water. In the apartment block opposite she could see into rooms whose occupants had lit lamps but not drawn curtains or closed blinds. The glimpse into other people's lives showed her that most of them were watching TV in various states of undress. She stepped back into her flat, closed her curtains and turned on her own TV.

*

'You left early last night,' Bill accused Denise.

'And I was here early this morning,' she replied and rubbed at the creases left on her trousers by her cycle clips.

Caroline bent her head over her desk and focussed on the paperwork she'd picked up. Bill and Denise had ignored the fact it landed in the pigeonhole they shared two days earlier; Caroline was too conscientious to leave it any longer. The Loans Officer had printed an email from another museum requesting the loan of a pair of vases and sent it down along with a bundle of forms to be completed. He clearly couldn't be bothered to do it himself. She sketched an abstract doodle down the margin of the top page and tried to tune out the bickering of her colleagues. She wondered if it was possible she'd be exposed to fewer arguments if she spent more time among small children rather than with her family and workmates. She respected Denise and Bill as fellow curators, was even beginning to consider Denise a friend, but didn't find either of them easy to share an office with, especially when they tried to draw her into their disputes.

'Well, you missed out yesterday, Den. Caroline and I saw some real treasures,' Bill said.

Denise didn't take the bait. When they'd been for drinks together after work she'd made it clear she thought she and Caroline should stick together against 'the old fogey' as she called Bill. 'Actually, Caroline,' she said, 'you missed out. A visitor was asking for you.'

Caroline looked up. 'A member of the public?' She immediately thought of sportswear-man with the mud encrusted item – had he changed his mind?

Denise riffled through bits of paper on her messy desk as though searching for something. 'No, someone who works for Dunnant's Antiques. I have his card somewhere. He was in doing research for a client and asked if you worked here. Our friends in Fine Art sent him down.'

More likely to be someone trying to add to her workload then. Caroline lost interest and only half listened as Denise said, 'He was ever so posh, had those upper class trousers…'

'Upper class trousers?' Bill asked. 'Is that a well-known sartorial category?'

'Caroline knows what I mean, don't you?'

Caroline smiled, put her paperwork down and guessed. 'Pinky-red cords? Or mustard coloured, teamed with a tweed waistcoat?'

'You see?' Denise gestured to Caroline while sneering at Bill. 'Anyway, his name was Olly Mortimer; he'll be in again soon and hopes to catch up with you then.' She leant over and handed a business card bearing the gold embossed Dunnant's logo to Caroline.

'Let's hope he hasn't changed his trousers, can't wait to see them,' Bill muttered.

Caroline couldn't speak. She placed the card on her desk and looked back at the form where text blurred before her eyes.

'Do you know him?' Denise asked. 'Tall, fair hair? He said he knew you at university. Scar on his left cheek.'

'I think I remember,' Caroline lied.

She stood up and left the room as Denise finished the message. 'He specifically said to mention the scar.'

Caroline ran up the marble steps and through the door separating the private rooms of the building from the public galleries. She navigated round a party of school children whose teacher was barely preventing from scattering to the far corners of the museum, smiled a distracted greeting to one of the room attendants and sat down on a wooden bench in front of the cabinet containing the Ancient Greek pottery which was the subject of the loan request. Not that she was working; she needed to think.

The memory was vivid: bright red blood on torn tanned skin; the perfection of a Greek god's visage marred by the accident. He'd been showing off, of course; the archaeological field trip granted him a stage set and the two of them had abandoned their allotted task to record details and measurements of some tumbled ruins. Olly posed on a fallen column and declaimed philosophy to an imaginary crowd. She reclined in the Cypriot sunshine with eyes closed to hide her admiration, her hands dropped to caress the rough, sun-warmed stones as though they could yield secrets through touch. Which meant she hadn't seen how it happened when he fell, just heard a scuffling before he yelled and swore and she opened her eyes to find him injured. His confusion could have been sunstroke or concussion and there was a frightening amount of blood.

One trip to the hospital and four stitches later, they went back to the frugal accommodation to wait for the rest of the group to return.

'Thank you,' Olly said. His blue eyes were sincere above the injury.

Caroline reached up to place the tips of her fingers on the grazed skin below the square of bandage on his cheek, investigating the damaged texture just as she'd run her hands over the stones of ruined monuments earlier. His skin was warm with life and energy.

He'd taken her hand and placed his lips against her fingertips leaving the barest caress of his skin against hers. His lips were firmer as he placed them against her wrist, the crook of her elbow, the base of her throat, her own mouth.

An intense image of Cypriot sunshine on tangled white sheets and bronzed limbs among the ruin of a single bed caused Caroline to flush hot. That feeling: that the past was irrelevant, only the present existed. Until, as she'd watched him play a lock of her dark hair through his fingers, the fact he had a beautiful, blonde girlfriend waiting at home couldn't continue to be ignored. Feeling guilty she'd joked, 'What am I, your bit of rough?'

He'd smiled and moved his hand to cup her face as he whispered, 'My Aphrodite.'

They'd both laughed and she knew she'd been an idiot to be seduced by him. She tried to take no offence that the afternoon of blood and intensity wasn't mentioned again. They had different groups of friends at university and hardly spoke until graduation day when he pulled her aside to wish her well. 'Take care, Aphrodite.'

She'd put her fingertips to his cheek again, the skin pale below the black mortarboard, the scar faded to a white line traced across his cheekbone. 'You try not to fall off any more pedestals,' she'd replied.

Now he'd reappeared in the present day. Getting Denise to mention the scar was a message, an indication that he was still trouble.

Chapter Three

On her way to the hospital Caroline nipped in to Beth's to pick up the navy slippers she'd forgotten. Alice had calmly confirmed Beth's hip was fractured and the consultant would decide whether to pin the bones or replace the joint. Her lack of emotion was a sure sign things were serious.

Knowing Beth wouldn't be home for a while, Caroline did a tour of the house to make sure the heating was turned down and the plants weren't dying of thirst. As she crossed each room to check the cold metal window latches were securely fastened she wondered why Beth remained keen to stay in such a large house. Temporary responsibility for it felt burden enough.

A terracotta plaque half hidden by a tangle of wisteria above the front door proclaimed '1900' – the date when a distant relative had built the house; but she'd forgotten the complicated details of great-, great-, great-, relations who featured in its story. Beth would have made the worst kind of history teacher, one who parroted names and dates with none of the storytelling or drama which could have brought the family history to life. Right from childhood Caroline had decided that ancient history was her passion, not banal incidents from Birmingham's recent past.

All she could recall was the house had been built by a man using profits from his manufacturing company, a common enough story in this part of the city, although the company can't have been that successful. Alice had always been reluctant to admit her childhood home wasn't in what could be considered the best part of Edgbaston and Caroline frowned at her mum's snobbery; not many families in Birmingham had passed a house down through generations. Beth had inherited some interesting bits of furniture as well.

As she toured the house and looked at it through critical eyes Caroline appreciated it was a good example of Arts and Crafts architecture. It featured dark wood panelling, beautiful floral patterned tiles, alluring inglenook fireplaces and many rooms with dual aspects through leaded windows containing stained glass insets. Even wearing an occasionally unfortunate 1970s décor, Beth's house was attractive in comparison to the mean, box-like rooms of the flat.

But it was too big. Considering Beth's needs on discharge from hospital, she could understand why Alice said Beth needed looking after. There had to be options though. To give up the house after it had been in the family for over a hundred years felt wrong. Perhaps a stair lift or a downstairs bathroom could be installed? But these things had already been discussed and Beth had not embraced any new ideas.

The final room Caroline visited was Beth's bedroom. She found the slippers tucked under the bed hidden behind a frilled valance. As she moved to the window to check the latch Caroline stumbled and nearly fell over a pile of items in front of the wardrobe. The contents of the box Beth had been taking down when she fell were still strewn across the rug.

'Honestly, Nan,' Caroline said as she knelt to smooth the rucked up edge of the rug which had caught her foot. All around the house were cupboards full of possessions, shelves piled with books and leaflets, drawers overflowing with old clothes. Why would Beth start with the boxes on the wardrobe if she'd decided to sort things out?

She set the box upright again, removed a hardback book which was unbalancing it, and began to gather the other items together, noting the presence of a number of jewellery boxes amongst yellowing paperwork. Before she had time to take in more details the harsh ring of the doorbell made her jump. A glance at her watch as she went downstairs showed it was six thirty, already after the time she'd intended to reach the hospital. Unable to think who would be calling on Beth, Caroline opened the door, prepared to make fast excuses to get rid of the visitor.

The man on the doorstep seemed startled to see her. 'Hello,' he said and raised his eyebrows questioningly. 'I'm here to see Beth.'

She assessed his shabby suit for clues about what type of appointment it could be. He wasn't one of the neighbours and was too young for Beth's circle of friends. She tensed, ready to see any kind of sales or con man off the premises. 'She's not here at the moment, can I help at all?'

'Oh, we spoke on the phone and she did say to call by this evening.' He paused as though considering how to proceed. 'Perhaps I should introduce myself? I'm Richard Garrold, Beth's nephew.' He offered his hand in greeting.

Caroline stared at his hand, then his face. 'Nephew? I didn't know she had any nephews. I'm her granddaughter, Caroline.'

The man pressed his lips together and drew his arm back. 'Ah, well, she perhaps wouldn't have mentioned it yet. She and my dad didn't get on. They'd lost touch. I've only recently made contact with Aunt Beth myself.'

'Oh. Well, there's bad news I'm afraid.' Caroline explained about the accident.

'Poor Beth! Well, I won't hold you up, but can I keep in touch to find out how she's doing?' He delved in the inside pocket of his jacket. 'Here's my card, perhaps you could call me? And tell her I send my best wishes. Do you think she'll be in hospital long?'

Caroline took the card which advertised that Richard Garrold was Managing Director of a Birmingham company called Farlane's. She looked back at him, scrutinising his face. Why wouldn't Beth have mentioned they had more family in the city? 'I'm not sure,' she said. 'Had she asked you to come over this evening for anything in particular?'

'No, um, it's fine. Tell her not to worry for now, and that I wish her a speedy recovery.' He turned back towards his car almost forgetting his manners in his eagerness to leave. 'It was nice to meet you, Caroline. I guess we're cousins once removed or something.'

'Something like that,' Caroline said as she watched him drop his car keys then grind the gears in his haste to get away. She turned to grab her bag and closed the front door firmly behind her, double locking it. Richard's appearance and quick retreat unsettled her and she checked up and down the road several times to be sure he'd really gone before she turned out of the driveway and towards the hospital.

*

Caroline found Alice looking out the window while Beth talked on a mobile phone. 'Are you allowed to use those in here?' Caroline asked.

'I can't see why not, all the staff seem to,' Alice said. 'And it's your brother's fault anyway. He rang to find out how she was and of course she insisted on having a chat.'

Caroline waved at Beth who nodded to acknowledge the greeting but carried on smiling at whatever Peter was telling her. He'd always been the favourite grandchild, probably because no one ever expected him to be anything but charming. He wasn't the one who had to be responsible, or run errands, or turn up for regular visits. Beth demanded nothing but occasional entertainment from him. Caroline put Beth's book on the table positioned over her bed and slid the navy slippers into the bedside cabinet.

'Don't know why she wanted those,' Alice said. 'She won't be walking anywhere for a few days.'

Caroline frowned. There had obviously been an argument. Hanging around the hospital all day would have been frustrating enough for her otherwise active mum without the two of them antagonising each other as well. 'What's the latest?' she asked.

Alice spread her hands. 'We've seen them all: radiographers, nurses, consultants, anaesthetists… They hope to take her in to surgery tomorrow morning and think they'll pin the joint in place. She'll be nil by mouth from this evening which will improve her mood no end.'

Caroline realised Alice's own bad temper was probably caused by stress and worry. 'Have you been here all day?'

'Your dad dropped me off at ten this morning. He'll be back to get me soon.'

Her own day at work had been another exercise in irritation, but at least she hadn't had to spend it in a hospital. She'd dealt with bureaucracy, difficult colleagues and spent any time at her desk hoping that if the phone did ring it would be the man she'd asked to call rather than Olly. She hadn't decided how she felt about seeing him again. 'Mum, do you know who Richard Garrold is?' she asked.

Before Alice could answer, they were interrupted by Beth who had finished talking to Peter but couldn't end the call. 'Here, you do it,' she said to Alice.

Admiring Alice's forbearance at the rudeness of the command, Caroline bent to kiss Beth's cheek. 'How are you feeling, Nan?'

'Nicely dosed up on painkillers, thank you,' Beth replied. 'Did you bring my book?'

Caroline pointed to it among the clutter of water jug, tissues and glasses case on the adjustable table. 'And I met someone while I was at your house this evening.'

Beth pursed her lips before saying, 'Tell me later, darling, I think your mum's just off.'

Alice gathered her possessions and prepared to leave. 'I'll be in again first thing, Mum. You get some rest before the surgery, OK?'

'If the nurses would leave me alone for five minutes I might get a chance,' Beth replied. 'They keep waking us up to make sure we're not dead.' She closed her eyes and Caroline could tell from the pale skin around her mouth and dark patches under her eyes that Beth was exhausted. Normally her over-enthusiasm and interfering was what sparked the disagreements with Alice, not this type of whingeing.

Alice bent to kiss Beth's forehead. 'Yes, well, I'll be back to check up on that myself tomorrow.'

'Dad not coming up?' Caroline asked. Alice didn't reply and Caroline nodded as she took over the visitor's chair by the side of the bed. As usual it was the women of the family who were left to do everything.

Once Alice had left the ward, Caroline lent forward and stroked Beth's hand. 'So who's Richard Garrold then?' she asked.

Beth's eyes moved below her closed eyelids but she didn't open them to look at Caroline. 'Oh, darling, I'm too tired to go through it all now. But listen, I need to change my will.'

'Nan! You're not that worried about the op are you? You'll be fine, I'm sure of it.' Caroline moved forward on the chair and gave Beth's fingers a squeeze. 'There's no need for you to be worrying about your will.'

'But it's not right,' Beth said. 'I need to put things right.'

Caroline began to feel uneasy. A long lost relative, the need to change a will? Perhaps Beth's fall happened in time to alert her family to a trick being played. She tried to soothe Beth by stroking the dry skin of her forearm and said, 'Not now, Nan. Let's worry about that when you're back on your feet shall we?'

Beth turned her head and opened her eyes. 'Your mum's been driving me mad today.'

'I can imagine.'

'But don't go thinking I want to write her out of my will. It's not that.'

Caroline smiled. 'Pleased to hear it, but I'm not going to talk about it anymore. You're too tired. How about I read a chapter of your book to you?'

Beth closed her eyes again and nodded. Caroline opened the book at the marked page and began to read aloud from a romance whose characters and intrigues made no sense to her while the settings seemed historically inaccurate. She glanced up occasionally to check she wasn't so loud as to disturb the other occupants of the ward. The woman opposite was still plugged into the TV and paid no attention. The bed in the far corner was empty. Best not to ask why, Caroline thought as she turned a page. And from the next door bed, the toothless woman still stared.

At the end of the chapter, Caroline checked her watch. Ten minutes until the end of visiting time. Beth appeared to be drifting towards sleep so, not wanting to disturb her too much, Caroline whispered, 'Time for me to go.'

'Don't tell your mum.' Beth's voice was low and Caroline had to lean closer to hear.

'About Richard?'

Beth responded with a tiny nod.

'OK, I won't.' The promise was easy to make, her mum had enough to fret about for the time being. It didn't mean Caroline herself wasn't going to do some investigating. Seeing Beth injured was bad enough, she wasn't going to stand by while anyone took advantage of her. There was no real need to involve anyone else at this stage though. She could easily discourage Beth from doing anything hasty about her will. Status quo was her preferred option in all things until she'd completed thorough research of all alternatives. Then she'd have a feel for the scale of the predicament and whether reinforcements were required.

'I'll be thinking of you tomorrow, Nan. Hope the operation goes well.' She slung the strap of her handbag across her body and bent to kiss Beth's cheek.

'Take care, love,' Beth murmured. 'Look about you.'

Caroline smiled. Beth always said that and the phrase seemed stronger for years of repetition. It hadn't lost the power to make her feel cared for. As the lift descended to the ground floor, she retrieved her car keys from her bag's zipped side pocket. Her fingers brushed against the two business cards she'd also tucked away there. Wondering what type of person still used business cards in this digital and austere age, her mind started to tease at the ideas both names had generated. She began to compile a list of queries to Google as soon as she got home. Firstly: Olly Mortimer's area of specialism at Dunnant's Antiques to see if she could guess why he'd appeared in Birmingham. She'd be interested to see a recent photo of him as well. Secondly: Farlane's. What kind of company were they and did Richard Garrold seem legitimate? And finally: hip surgery success rates.

She realised Olly had claimed first place on the list and flushed with guilt.

Chapter Four

Caroline ushered her tour group back to the museum's entrance then turned her phone on. It beeped as the text message she'd missed while she'd been answering questions about Anglo-Saxon Britain arrived. 'Surgery complete. Dr thinks was ok. Nan still sleeping. Mum x'. She fired back a quick reply with a promise to visit after work. Sometimes the lack of a social life came in handy. At least she wouldn't upset other people's arrangements. Her only plan for the evening was to continue her investigations into Richard Garrold. Last night's brief internet trawl hadn't revealed anything useful.

Down in the office Denise's head was bent over a book and Bill was typing with a two fingered racket at his computer.

'Yeah, it was fine, thanks,' Caroline said.

'Hmmm?' Denise didn't actually look up from her desk, just turned an ear towards Caroline.

'The lunchtime tour, it went OK, thanks for asking. About fifteen people, usual mix of folk who aren't listening and those who like the sound of their own voice. I can't quite believe it was my turn again. Lucky old me.'

Bill stopped typing briefly to frown at her. 'The public would rather look at you than me.'

'Not the point. I have just as much work to be getting on with as you.' Caroline shuffled the papers on her desk and picked up a new exhibition catalogue to flick through. The scent of glossy paper and expensive ink cleared her sinuses of the body odour of the man who'd followed too close behind during her tour. She couldn't decide which was worse: the people who wanted to use the tour as an opportunity to display their own knowledge or the quiet but socially inept ones. It was always the men who were difficult. The women were attentive, keen, and sensible. And older, always older. An interest in the past didn't seem to afflict many people her own age, although, they were probably all working during the day. Weekday events were aimed at retired people or holiday makers. People with nothing else to do than listen to or argue with Caroline. She sighed and, keeping her voice neutral, asked, 'Any messages?'

Denise smirked as she replied, 'Such as from our scarred antique dealing friend?'

'Not necessarily,' Caroline said and hoped Denise wouldn't notice her lifting the catalogue to conceal a blush. 'There was something interesting brought in to our assessment day and I hoped the owner might get in touch.'

The rattling from Bill's keyboard stopped again. He cleared his throat. 'Ah, well, actually…'

'Yes?' Caroline snapped the catalogue shut and put it down.

'That chap, um, I did take a call which may have been him.'

'And?'

'I've made an appointment to see him tomorrow.' Bill started typing again.

'You've made an appointment?' Caroline rarely raised her voice. Passions didn't often run high enough to warrant being unprofessional in her world. This was different. She stood up. 'You?'

'It might not be the same man,' Bill said and shook his head in a casual manner. He didn't look at Caroline.

'If you didn't think it was the same man, if you didn't suspect it was something interesting you would either have fobbed him off or dumped him on me.' Caroline was aware her voice was shrill. 'I appreciate that both of you have been here longer than me and you maybe think it's acceptable to expect me to do the lion's share of the less interesting work, but I'm not going to stand by and let you claim all the glory, Bill.'

'Hey,' Denise said, 'Are you OK? You're overreacting aren't you? What's going on?'

'It's nothing.' Bill pushed his chair back from his desk and finally looked at Caroline. 'It's probably nothing.'

'Of the hundreds of things we have to look through, this is the one which may turn out to be something.' She'd been happy to back down over who was going to contribute more to the public engagement programme knowing the others were further along with their research projects. But it wasn't fair that everything interesting should be taken away from her.

'You don't know that,' Bill said. 'Like I said, it's probably nothing.'

'And yet you're prepared to take the time to check when it should be my discovery.'

Denise intervened again, 'What's got in to you two?'

Bill and Caroline glared at each other, neither wanting to admit that they'd had a tantalising glimpse of something which could either turn out to be very, very special or utterly worthless. Reputations could be made – or lost.

Neither of them answered and in the silence the click of the door opening made all three turn to look at the man who'd entered the room.

'Sorry,' Olly said, 'I did knock a moment ago but perhaps you weren't quite able to hear…'

Her face already burning from anger, Caroline put a hand out to the back of her chair for support as Olly approached her. His greeting was smooth and confident.

'It's so good to see you again, Caroline,' he said as he took her other hand and leant in to kiss her cheek. 'You're looking well.'

He grinned and she wanted to kick him for being so smug. She knew she looked dreadful when her face went red and attempted to keep her voice steady as she replied, 'Olly, it's been years. What a lovely surprise.'

He looked to the others. 'I'm so sorry, am I interrupting something?'

'Not at all,' Bill said and turned back to his computer.

Olly raised an eyebrow as he met Caroline's eyes. 'Then I wonder if you'd be able to join me for a late lunch?'

*

She'd perhaps have been less flustered if Olly had been wearing the red cords. It would have given her an irrational reason to project her irritation on to him. As it was, his composure made her more embarrassed and Caroline didn't know how to behave. He'd already witnessed her unprofessional outburst and it wasn't as if they'd been regular companions who were comfortable around each other. She commented on the weather and shook her head in annoyance at the smiles he attracted from a couple of her female colleagues they passed in the corridor. He isn't that good looking, she thought and surreptitiously combed fingers through her hair as they reached the exit and he stepped forward to open the door.

As she passed him, Olly stroked the lock of hair she'd just tucked behind her ear. 'I'm glad you've kept it long,' he whispered. 'I always found your hair distractingly attractive.'

Caroline's mouth dropped open. His only comments to her so far had been polite small talk of the bland variety. She'd already begun to wonder what they'd have to say to each other over the course of a meal.

She stepped away from his touch and asked, 'So what brings you to Birmingham?'

He smiled and dipped his head as if to accept her rebuff. 'I've been working for Dunnant's for a few months now, based in Stratford. I'm doing a bit of research for a client in Henley-in-Arden who's selling some items. The museum has a couple of similar pieces. Your colleague who knows about ceramics has been very helpful.'

Caroline didn't doubt it. She knew exactly which of the fine art curators he meant and that the woman was even more of a push over than she was herself. 'Not where I'd have guessed you'd end up,' Caroline said. 'I imagined you'd be high flying somewhere.' She kept it to herself that her internet search had already turned up enough information to piece his CV together.

He widened his eyes to feign offence. 'Dunnant's are one of the country's top dealers, I'll have you know.'

'Are you sure you don't mean one of the county's top dealers?' She smiled to let him know she was teasing; the company did have a good reputation nationally. Their website listed him as one of their experts in Sculpture and Fine Arts. He'd added a History of Art MA to his first degree and had published a few articles on eighteenth century artists.

'I was working in London until a few years ago. My, um, wife wanted to move to the country, better for the kids, you know.'

Caroline hugged her arms tight across her body. She couldn't believe he'd dared to flirt with her if he was married. 'Actually, I'm not sure I do know what an 'um, wife' is,' she said.

'We, ah, separated. A few months ago.'

'Oh. Sorry to hear that.' Caroline regretted taking a haughty tone. Her emotions were a mess. After the tension of worrying about Beth's operation that morning and anger at Bill's conniving tactics, Olly's arrival had stirred up and flustered her. She glanced across at him. His bluff confidence seemed to have evaporated in the face of her leap on to the moral high ground. He walked beside her, hands in pockets and head bowed almost as if he needed her forgiveness. She stopped and placed a hand on his arm. 'I'm sorry I was snappy too.'

'No, no, it's fine. I obviously didn't turn up at the best time for you today. Look, let's sit down, get some food and start this conversation again.'

He led the way to a nearby bar Caroline hadn't been in before. Filled with young office workers in suits it had a confident, business-like ambience although the glitzy chandeliers and cocktail menus suggested it was geared towards after work hours. While Olly's outfit of chinos, chambray shirt and a navy linen jacket wasn't too far out of place, Caroline felt like a scruffy student. She'd dressed that morning knowing she had to take the tour group and had been pleased with how the bright floral print of her skirt toned with the short sleeved lime cardigan she'd pulled over her fitted white shirt, but she didn't fit in with the patrons of the bar. 'I'd have dressed up if I'd known I was coming out,' she said, not knowing what she would have worn instead.

'I'm glad you didn't know then. I like the outfit.' He smiled without a hint of a leer and pulled out a chair for her at a free table.

Choosing food and drinks smoothed over a few minutes but then silence fell between them. Caroline looked around the room and took a few hasty sips of her beer. She was trying not to remember that the single time the two of them had previously been alone was that afternoon in Cyprus. Other than that, the only time they'd really spent together was debating in tutorials or at parties thrown by mutual acquaintances. They didn't have a relationship. She wouldn't have called them old friends.

Their lunch was delivered swiftly and talking about food filled a few minutes. When that topic began to dry up, Caroline asked about Olly's job but he was understandably discreet about his clients. The conversation flagged.

'I heard from Tim that you were working in Birmingham.' Olly was obviously also trying to find their common ground. Tim had been on their degree course and Caroline occasionally bumped in to him at conferences. 'But you have family here too, don't you?'

'Yes, I've returned to my roots. The city changed a bit while I was away though.' She sipped at her drink again and wondered what he really wanted.

'Maybe you changed more?'

She looked up to find him gazing at her. The etiquette of the occasion kept slipping away from her. One moment they were polite, treating each other as strangers; the next this intimacy crept up on her in his flirtatiousness or her teasing, as if they knew each other far better. And now he seemed solicitous, as if he were a supportive friend.

She frowned. 'Well, we all grow up.'

'Tim said you were divorced. I'm sorry things didn't work out for you.'

Olly's eyes showed concern, but Caroline was annoyed that Tim had been gossiping about her. He'd never thought to share any gossip about Olly with her after all. No, their chats had been purely work related: dry museum talk. Clearly not something Olly had any time for.

'Thank you. I'm sorry to hear your marriage is having problems too. It's not easy, is it?'

'Especially not when someone as bad as me is involved,' he said.

Caroline raised an eyebrow. 'You didn't?'

'It seems I haven't grown up. I'm still very easily led.' A smile began to pull at the corners of his mouth. Caroline's eyes were drawn to the movement and the scar which still distorted the clean shaven skin nearby. Was he implying that she'd led him on all those years ago? That wasn't how she recalled it.

'Then I'm afraid I'd probably side with your wife,' she said, 'and your children.'

He quickly replaced his smile with a look of contrition. 'And you'd be right to,' he said as he laid his knife and fork down on his plate which was now empty except for the salad garnish. 'I was pleased to see you were taking no nonsense from that idiot in your office as well.'

She didn't know how much of the argument with Bill he'd overhead and she didn't want to discuss it. 'Oh, I'm sure that'll turn out to be a fuss about nothing. I'm feeling a bit stressed today – my nan's in hospital. I've got a lot on. Speaking of which, I should probably be getting back to work.'

'Thanks for having lunch with me. It was good to see you.' He paused and glanced at his watch. 'I've still got some research I'd like to do in the archives at the library but I think I'll have to come back another day. Maybe we could meet for a drink or something next week?'

She studied his face as she slid her arms into her jacket and scooped out the hair trapped behind her collar. His attitude bothered her. She wasn't entirely sure she liked him. She definitely didn't trust him. On the other hand, her diary wasn't exactly brimming with social events. 'OK,' she said.

Chapter Five

Beth opened her eyes and frowned as a nurse approached the bed. Caroline smiled at him and asked, 'How's she doing?'

'Not bad. We'll see if we can get you up for a bit tomorrow,' the nurse said as he adjusted Beth's drip.

Beth clutched at Caroline's hand. 'Up? I've just had major surgery. I can't go getting up.'

'We'll see,' he said, distracted by the notes he was making in Beth's file.

'Don't panic,' Caroline said. 'They know what they're doing.'

Beth turned to her, wincing as she moved in the bed. 'That man,' she said, 'you haven't told your mum, have you?'

'Which man?' Caroline was flustered. How did her nan know about Olly, or did she mean the nurse? 'Oh, you mean Richard Garrold. No, I haven't said anything.'

'Don't yet.' Beth's hand scrabbled at Caroline's. 'But listen, where I fell, in my bedroom... Did you go in there?'

'Yes, your slippers were under the bed. Sssh now, Nan. You need to get some rest.'

'The box from on top of the wardrobe – was it open? Had things fallen out?' Beth's words were slow and she closed her eyes again.

Caroline shook her head. 'The only thing I'm concerned about right now is you. I didn't get a chance to tidy up the mess you made when you fell.' She stood up to smooth the sheets Beth was plucking at.

'Can you go there tomorrow, love?' Beth opened her eyes to focus on Caroline again. 'Pack those things away for me? I don't want your mum to see them yet.'

'OK. Look, I'm going to go now. You need to rest, not get yourself upset.' Caroline picked up her bag and bent to stroke her thumb across Beth's cheek. 'I'll see you tomorrow.'

Beth's eyelids fluttered. 'Put that box away for me first,' she murmured.

Caroline frowned as she walked out of the ward. She considered going straight over to Beth's to investigate why the contents of that box were so important. It had been a long day though, and the thought of pursuing her research into Richard Garrold from the comfort of her own sofa had more appeal. She still had Alice's keys for Beth's house; there wasn't any immediate urgency to act. Whatever it was that was strewn across that bedroom rug would still be there the next day.

She drove home slowly and sketched what she knew of her family tree in her mind. They weren't a big family: herself and her brother Peter, their parents Alice and Ray Hipkins, an aunt and a couple of cousins on her dad's side. Alice was Beth's only child. Beth had been married to George Dabbs, Caroline's maternal grandad who'd died years ago. That was as much as Caroline knew. She'd never had reason to wonder about anyone else, had never considered there could be others.

But Richard Garrold claimed to be Beth's nephew and that his dad was Beth's brother. If they'd fallen out that did give a reason why Caroline hadn't heard of him. Then there was the story about Beth inheriting her house from family – so who had that come from?

She'd always considered her family as stable. They didn't go in for the dramas many of her school friends had been subject to. It was one reason Alice was so disappointed when Caroline announced she and Matt were divorcing.

44

'How can we fix things?' Alice had asked.

Caroline knew better than to expect Alice would understand. 'It can't be fixed,' she said. 'I don't want the changes he wants. It's too much. I can't keep up.'

Alice hadn't referred to it since. She'd welcomed Caroline back to Birmingham, created a role for her daughter as general dogsbody, and never once suggested she should have been less risk averse. Only Caroline berated herself with that accusation. She knew that if she wanted to be seen differently she needed to behave differently. That was the problem. She grimaced and let herself into the flat.

The previous night she'd discovered that Farlane's, the company on Richard's business card, were based in nearby Hockley and made engine components. Their website had an antiquated look - a single static page with no links or photographs. The firm's contact details stood out in black type against a white background. A paragraph about their capabilities used technical terms lost on her, but the site confirmed Richard's job title. A further internet search turned up a recent article from the Birmingham Mail referring to redundancies at the factory. The firm existed, but whether it was still trading was another matter.

Once she'd made a cup of tea and sunk onto her sofa, Caroline reached for the laptop without enthusiasm. Everything she'd found out so far suggested something had happened in the past. Perhaps it would be better left buried? But Beth claimed to want to change her will, which raised two issues: first whether Beth was being tricked into something and second how it would affect Caroline's own family. Beth not wanting Alice to know was definitely suspicious.

The laptop finally booted up and Caroline opened her email to clear out the junk which accumulated there. She deleted without opening the very special offers from companies she'd once had cause to deal with and the random suggestions from Amazon of products they thought relevant because she'd once bought something with the same word in the title. The email from Peter couldn't be so easily ignored.

'Good to hear that the op went well but wanted to let you know that Mum's tried to get me to persuade Nan about moving into an old folks' home. She seems to think Nan'll listen to me. Thing is, I don't think it's a great idea but you're on the scene so I'll leave it to you to sort out. OK? Busy, busy here. Speak soon, P x'

Caroline groaned. Why did everyone assume she was available to take on their dirty work? She closed the email without replying. No need, she thought, he's too 'busy, busy' with his exhibition or out partying to read it.

Her fingers paused over the keyboard while she considered what else she could find out about Richard. He'd looked to be in his fifties and she couldn't imagine the boss of a failing firm was too internet savvy. She was unlikely to be able to spy on him through any social networking sites. A quick query confirmed it and she closed the search engine before the temptation to type Olly's name in instead overwhelmed her.

The internet wasn't going to supply the answer to what she really wanted to know: what had Richard Garrold said to Beth in order that she'd want to change her will? Beth herself was the only one who could answer that and her current poor health didn't fully explain why she was reluctant to talk about it.

Before Caroline could decide on any further research avenues, her phone rang.

'How was she when you left?' Alice asked.

Caroline sighed. 'Exhausted. Not surprising really.' At least Peter's email had forewarned her of the tack her mum was about to take.

'I saw the surgeon and he was confident she'd recover well. We'll have to talk to her though.'

'Talk to her?'

'Make her see sense about the house. It's a disaster waiting to happen. There aren't facilities on the ground floor if she can't manage the stairs any more. The maintenance would cost a fortune if it was being done properly, which it's not. She can't spend another winter heating two rooms and letting the rest of the house rot away.'

'Nan loves the house, Mum.'

It was Alice's turn to sigh. 'I love the house too. I grew up there, remember. But the fact is that neither you nor I would want to live there so it'll be sold when she dies.' Alice paused and there was a noise against the handset as if she'd put her hand to her mouth at the thought. She sniffed. 'Better that she spends her last years in comfortable accommodation, not struggling to hold on to a house.'

On a practical level the argument made sense. 'I agree,' Caroline said, 'but it's not what she wants. And before this fall she was doing fine.' She glanced around the flat where her laundry from two days ago was still hanging from a clothes airer and a stack of used plates, mugs and glasses littered the kitchen counter. Until this week, Beth had been doing better at managing her home than Caroline could claim to be.

'Well I've made us some appointments this Saturday to look at alternatives. You're not busy, are you?'

Caroline paused long enough to swallow her irritation. 'Let me check my diary.' She grabbed a book and riffled its pages near the receiver. Of course she was free this weekend, but did she really want to spend her time wandering around old people's homes? 'Yeah, I can do that,' she said, cursing herself for being so considerate.

'Good. Pick me up at ten thirty then. The first appointment's at eleven. Oh, and will you visit your Nan tomorrow evening? I'll go over during the day and text you if there's any news, but your dad and I are going out tomorrow night.'

Friday night on the geriatric ward; Caroline couldn't wait. She ended the call and flung the phone down on the sofa. Even her parents had a better social life than hers. No wonder she'd jumped at the chance to see Olly again despite her suspicions about his motives for getting in touch. There were plenty of people she'd been at university with whose names she couldn't recall and who she had no desire to see again. He ought to fall into that category of acquaintance. Except he didn't.

She let her fingers stray back to her laptop, found the Dunnant's website and clicked through to the page listing details of their staff. Olly smiled at her from the photo next to his profile. She studied his expression. There was confidence in the set of his mouth and the upward tilt of his chin, while the crinkled skin by his eyes betrayed a glimmer of that cheeky twinkle. He was too attractive for his own good. And hers. She slammed the laptop screen closed and flicked on the TV.

Chapter Six

Caroline stared at the email she was writing until the words began to swim across her computer screen. She was aware Bill was preparing for his appointment. He stood, lifted his tweed jacket from the back of his chair, cleared his throat and stuffed a pen, notepad and magnifying glass into his pockets. He left the room without saying anything.

The door slammed behind him and Denise asked, 'Are you really mad at him?'

Caroline paused before replying. Bill had been at the museum for years and he and Denise had worked together for a long time. Caroline had no desire to cause trouble. 'Wouldn't you be?' she asked.

'Well, maybe in our line of work the item is more important than the discovery.'

Caroline didn't need to be told this. Personality counted for very little. If a major new discovery was made there would of course be public interest in the owner, particularly if a lot of money was at stake. The media loved any story about a fortune being made. But the academics or curatorial staff would be quickly forgotten; except within their own field. There were papers which could be written and presented, curriculum vitae could be enhanced. Prestigious appointments could be chased.

Caroline rubbed her eyes and wondered if she cared enough about her career to want to risk the working relationships in her current team. Ultimately the job didn't mean that much to her any more, but she hated being taken for a pushover. 'I'll apologise,' she said.

Denise smiled. 'You know he wouldn't, if the situation were reversed.'

'The situation wouldn't be reversed.' There was no point Caroline pretending her ambitions extended to that kind of duplicity. Accepting this job was an attempt to achieve a quiet life for a while. It was supposed to be easy, a job she could do with her eyes closed. And yet, to ingratiate herself with new colleagues and bosses, she found herself doing too much. She allowed them to take advantage. Well, it would stop now. She looked back at her screen and deleted the last paragraph she'd typed. There was no point being too helpful.

The door handle crashed into the wall as Bill stomped back into the room. Caroline glanced up in time to catch the glare he directed at her, as if whatever had happened was her fault.

'Good meeting?' Denise asked. 'It was very fast.'

'Waste of time,' Bill replied and dumped his things back on to his desk. He slung his jacket over the back of his chair from where it promptly slid to the ground and scattered his change across the lino. 'Bugger it.'

'What a shame,' Denise said, her tone a little too cheery to be sincere.

'He didn't even bring the thing, just a photo. As if I can judge authenticity from a photo on his mobile phone.'

Caroline pressed her lips together to suppress a smile and caught Denise's eye. To gloat would not be appropriate. 'You're not sure then?' she asked. 'I couldn't really tell.'

'What is this thing you're both being so secretive about?' Denise asked. 'You're behaving as if it's the Holy Grail.'

Bill snorted. 'Jewellery, probably jewellery.'

'Or adornment for armour,' Caroline added, 'maybe some kind of religious artefact. Embellished metal, at any rate. Currently covered in mud.'

'Oooh, treasure.' Denise rubbed her hands together. 'So when do we get to see it?'

'Possibly never,' Bill said. 'I may have scared him off by pointing out it could be Crown property if he dug it up somewhere.'

Caroline sighed. It had been obvious the man needed careful handling. Her suspicions about his criminal intent meant she would have treated him with caution and ensured she got enough evidence before giving him too much information. Bill had clearly blundered in. He sat down and started typing. Then he paused. 'He's cleaned it up a bit,' he said.

'And?' Caroline asked.

'It could be genuine. Gold with etched decoration. Lozenge shape, maybe three inches long with punched holes.'

'Where did he find it?' Caroline had forgotten any upset she'd felt. Now she was intrigued.

'I didn't get any useful information from him. He clammed up completely. He knows we're interested though, knows he could be on to something. So we'll just have to wait and see what his next move is.'

*

It was raining as Caroline parked in front of Beth's house. She sat in the car a moment looking at the building through the blur of raindrops on the windscreen. The decorative brickwork on the chimneys wasn't ostentatious, merely elegant; the small leaded panes of the windows were charming compared to the huge picture windows of her flat. It was perhaps a shame the area was no longer as affluent as when the house had been built, so much so that Alice now referred to it as Five Ways rather than Edgbaston – rewriting history now she no longer lived there – but Caroline held on to her sense that this was what an ideal home looked like.

She pulled her hood over her hair and made a dash for the front door. Once inside, the stale, damp scent of a neglected house wafted towards her. It had only been a few days, but in Beth's absence the house was cold and its décor seemed dated. Regular visits since childhood meant Caroline had never looked at the house with a critical eye; she just accepted it. It was Nan's house, full of Nan's things.

Now the silence made her feel she was trespassing. As she climbed the stairs to Beth's bedroom, Caroline looked around. The stairwell was hung with framed family photos and a few watercolours which, now she studied them rather than looked past them, Caroline thought quite good. The representation of light and deft composition of the scenes marked out an artist of talent. Unlike the photos, which were placed almost randomly at awkward heights on the wall, the paintings seemed to have been positioned carefully where they would receive enough light to illuminate them while protecting them from direct sunlight or where they would be in a line of sight as the viewer turned the bend on the stairs.

Caroline opened the door to Beth's bedroom and switched on the light. The forty watt bulb in its fringed satin shade didn't dispel the gloom cast by the grey day. She righted the wooden stool Beth must have brought from the bathroom to stand on and knelt to look at the few items which had spilt out of the box onto the pink rug.

The hardback book she'd removed turned out to be a scrapbook which at initial glance seemed to be full of yellowed newspaper cuttings. There were three velvet-covered jewellery cases and a few flimsy envelopes which held letters addressed to Miss Susannah Garrold at an address in Ladywood postmarked with dates from a hundred years earlier. Caroline's fingers itched with the temptation to slip one from its envelope. She wouldn't dream of reading a letter addressed to Beth had she found one, but was it really immoral when the recipient of the letter was dead?

She selected one on which the address had been typewritten reasoning it was more likely to be something official rather than personal. The stiff paper was awkward to unfold and the ink was faded but a phrase from the middle of the letter leapt out at Caroline. 'Following your recent arrest and incarceration, we can no longer continue to employ you...' Eyebrows raised, Caroline scanned the rest of the letter. It seemed that in early 1913 Susannah worked as some kind of tutor for a family in Edgbaston and this was a letter of dismissal following a criminal act. No wonder Beth hadn't mentioned Susannah before; she'd obviously been in some kind of disgrace. Conscious of Beth's instructions to put the things away, and the lack of time she had before the hospital visiting hours ended, Caroline packed the items carefully back into the box on top of some other packages still lodged there. Then she sat back on her heels and considered the box as though it was one of the archaeological sites she'd excavated.

Having the same surname as Richard Garrold obviously meant Susannah was a relative. Caroline knew she was looking to excuse her curiosity as her fingers strayed to the edge of the scrapbook. Beth's instructions had only been to hide the items from Alice, not that Caroline herself shouldn't look. It felt too much like prying though. This wasn't research in an archive or unearthing strangers' remains. These were her nan's possessions which had been stored in a private place and which Beth obviously wanted to keep secret. The intrigue was fascinating. Perhaps Beth was ashamed to have a criminal in the family; Caroline was desperate to know more. It would have to wait. She needed to get to the hospital.

Caroline closed the dusty flaps of the box's lid and slid it into the space between the wardrobe's clawed feet. Beth would be able to reach it without risking her neck but it wouldn't draw attention. She stood up and straightened the blanket she could remember watching Beth crochet many years before and which now lay across the eiderdown, turned off the light and closed the bedroom door firmly behind her.

At the top of the stairs, Caroline paused. She leant forward to look more closely at the watercolour hanging there. In the bottom right hand corner she could make out faded initials in grey paint. S.G. Susannah Garrold's name immediately filled the blanks in Caroline's mind. Could it be her handiwork?

Aware of the time, Caroline put the thoughts aside and hurried to the hospital, stopping on her way to buy Beth a plastic tub of prepared exotic fruit. Once at the bedside she peeled the film lid off and held out her offering. Beth leant forward and stabbed a chunk of pineapple with a fork. 'That's more like it,' she said with her mouth full.

'Something a bit different, at any rate,' Caroline said.

Beth was still pale except where the bruises from her fall bloomed on her thin arms. Caroline had also brought chocolate to tempt her sweet tooth. She wasn't sure whether she was trying to soften Beth up in order that she could ask questions about the Garrolds, or trying to salve her conscience about nosing in Beth's possessions.

Beth skewered a slice of kiwi fruit and chewed in silence for a moment. As she prodded in the tub to select her next morsel she asked, 'Did you call by the house?'

'Yes. I tidied the things in your bedroom.'

'Thank you, love. Did you hear I managed to walk a couple of steps today?'

It was a clumsy attempt to divert attention but Caroline didn't want to push Beth too fast. Bill's experience was a lesson in how wrong that could go. 'Mum said. How did your hip feel?'

'Ooh, it was painful. They said I did well though.' Beth leant back and winced as she tried to find a more comfortable position against the pillows. 'They'll change the dressings again tomorrow,' she said and gently patted her hip through the layers of blankets and sheets.

Caroline jumped up to help Beth get comfortable, adjusting the hand knitted cardigan slung round her shoulders so it wasn't rucked up behind her back. 'I love this cardi,' she said. 'Great colour.'

'I've still got some of the wool, I think. I could knit you something when I get home.'

Home. Alice hadn't mentioned whether or not she'd had a discussion about that with Beth, and Caroline hadn't yet decided what view on it she was going to take, not until she'd seen some alternatives. It was time to change the subject back again. 'So, who are the Garrolds then, Nan?'

Beth closed her eyes. 'It's ancient history,' she murmured.

'My speciality,' Caroline said. 'And Richard Garrold asked me to call to let him know how you are. It would be nice to know who I was talking to.'

There was a pause before Beth replied. 'Didn't he say? He's my nephew.'

'Yes, and it was the first I've heard of us having any relatives on your side. I couldn't help noticing the name Susannah Garrold on some of the things in that box you dropped too.' Caroline kept her voice soft and non-confrontational. 'Look, I won't talk to Mum about it if you still don't want me to, but tell me about Richard. What does he want?'

'Just my help. That's all. Tell him I'll call him as soon as I get home, will you? Let him know I'm OK for now though.'

'All right, Nan. I'm only looking out for you, you know. I wouldn't want any long lost relatives to bully you in to anything.' Caroline took the bar of Dairy Milk from her bag and peeled back the wrapper. Beth's eyes opened and she took the row of chunks Caroline snapped off and handed to her.

'Thanks, love. You're a sweetheart.'

Caroline actually felt as though she were a swindler, beguiling Beth with sweet treats while raking around in her past and snooping in her personal possessions. She popped a chunk of chocolate into her own mouth and let it dissolve against her tongue.

'You won't mention it to your mum, will you?' Beth said.

'No. Of course not.' I'm caught between the two of them, Caroline thought. Tomorrow it'll be mum I have to dupe.

Chapter Seven

As instructed, Caroline arrived in Harborne to collect Alice at ten thirty on Saturday morning. She parked across the bottom of the drive rather than pulling in alongside her parent's gleaming saloon car. No need to invite comparison with the scratches and pigeon droppings adorning her own car's paintwork. She swept a few crumbs from the passenger seat and grabbed her bag.

The house's exterior was unchanged from her childhood days although what looked shockingly modern when they'd moved in from a Victorian terraced house nearly thirty years before now appeared dated and stale. The front door was turned away from visitors on the side of a porch which presented an unwelcoming blank wall to the kerb. The brickwork was pale, green tiles hung over the upper storey and the windows formed perfect squares, outlined now in pristine uPVC rather than the original, draughty aluminium. The architectural style of the 1980s was not one Caroline imagined would get a revival any time soon. She hated the house from the moment they moved in when she was six, and had dreaded major life changes ever since. Her divorce had been a necessary precaution, an easy preference to the alternative. She took a breath and let herself into the hallway.

Inside, the house was unrecognisable from her childhood. Alice had instigated several changes of décor since the original beige walls and oatmeal carpets. The current inspiration fitted the profile of a boutique hotel. Striped chocolate and gold wallpaper was offset by gilt framed mirrors while underfoot a cream runner softened the oak laminate flooring. Caroline kicked off her shoes and dropped her car keys with a rattle into a glass bowl on the console table.

'That you, chick?' Ray's voice called from the living room.

She pushed the door open and found him ironing a shirt with the board set up in front of the TV. 'Hi, Dad,' she said and lifted a hanger holding a freshly ironed white shirt from the door knob. She twirled it, pretending to inspect the collar, cuffs and vent in the back. 'Hmm, yeah, you've still got it.'

He swiped his left hand across his forehead in pretence at relief. As a teenager, she'd shared laundry chores with him to earn extra pocket money and he'd spent hours critiquing her ironing technique, ensuring every school shirt met his exacting standards.

'Now then,' he said, after placing a kiss on Caroline's cheek, 'how did you think your nan seemed? Your mum's worried about her.'

Caroline paused. This required delicate handling. 'You haven't been in to see her recently yourself?'

'Ah, well, no. I wouldn't want to interfere.'

He may have passed useful knowledge about how to iron shirts on to her, but it was obvious to Caroline that the skill their dad had passed on to her brother was how to pass the buck. 'Well,' she said, 'I don't think she's doing too badly.'

'Good, good. Your mum's nearly ready.'

Ray unmuted the TV so they could listen as a chef demonstrated how to bone a joint of lamb. Caroline perched on the sofa to avoid disturbing the upholstery. The sofa cushions were obviously freshly plumped and were not littered with a profusion of handmade tapestry cushions and embroidered throws to add comfort.

Alice's interior design was nothing like her mother's.

Just as Caroline was about to query whether Ray intended to retrain as a butcher, Alice appeared at the door.

'Come on, we'll be late.'

'See you then, Dad,' she said instead and went back to the hall where she had to wait while Alice applied lipstick and ran the brush she kept in the drawer of the console table through her hair. She looked Caroline up and down, but said nothing. Who knew there was a dress code for visiting old people's homes, Caroline thought.

Alice tutted as she got into the car. 'I told your dad to leave space for you on the drive.'

'He did,' Caroline replied. 'I chose not to use it.' It was petty, she knew; but always satisfying to rebel in however small a way against Alice's plans.

*

Their first appointment was at a newly built property run by a private health care company. Well-tended foliage decorated the car park. At the front door, Alice pressed the intercom and the door immediately buzzed to admit them. Alice turned to Caroline and smiled. Nothing pleased her more than efficiency.

They were met in the hall by a woman in a beige skirt suit and powder blue blouse who introduced herself as Miriam, the matron, and claimed to be delighted to meet them. 'Come through to the sitting room. Let's have coffee,' she said, almost as though they were there on a social visit.

The sitting room itself was well equipped for just that. Groups of high-backed armchairs surrounded coffee tables distributed around the large room. Only a few had occupants. An elderly woman who had appeared preoccupied with her knitting muttered, 'Not another one,' as Caroline passed. It wasn't clear to whom she referred. Caroline hesitated, wondering if she should respond to the woman, but it didn't seem to be expected.

Miriam had laid out some brochures on the table she steered them to and drew Alice's attention to them. She'd been quick to identify the decision maker in her visitors. Glossy pages were illustrated by pictures of groups of elderly women and the occasional man playing cards, being served tea, or taking part in an exercise class. There was no photo which showed the room as it currently appeared in reality: sparsely populated and with a TV playing to a glazed audience of one in the corner. Caroline suppressed a desire to open the windows.

'We have various levels of care available,' Miriam said, 'from temporary, convalescent support, through residential units with warden support to full nursing care for those with disabilities or dementia. What sort of thing does Granny require?'

Caroline flinched at the woman's use of the overfamiliar name. Beth was Nan to family members only, and never Granny. Her reaction to Miriam and her establishment moved from an unspecific dislike to full hostility. Unfortunately Alice wasn't similarly afflicted. 'Well, we haven't had a social services assessment yet, but my mum has been living independently until now. She's had a fall and I fear her mobility will be restricted meaning she can't stay in her own home.'

'So it's support with everyday tasks she'll need, not nursing care?' Miriam asked. 'Obviously we would need to assess her ourselves.'

Caroline detected a slight cooling in Miriam's enthusiasm. Obviously they weren't turning out to be the high fee earners she'd hoped for. The coffee arrived and was served by a young woman in a nurse's outfit. Her elaborate gestures with the milk jug suggested she would have preferred to be working as an air hostess. Caroline was the only one to thank her.

'My mother is reluctant to accept she needs help,' Alice said. 'What my daughter and I need is to be informed about her options so we can guide her.' She took one sip of her coffee, pursed her lips and set the cup and saucer firmly aside. As a critique, it was devastating.

Miriam stood up. 'Of course. Perhaps you'd like to view our facilities?' She bustled out of the room followed by Alice while Caroline gulped down the rest of the weak coffee, anxious not to offend the nurse on waitress duties. Miriam showed them a tiny, one bedroom flat with miniature kitchen and bathroom facilities. 'We like to encourage our residents to socialise, not sit in their own rooms.' She watched as Alice opened a cupboard in the kitchen. 'Nutritious meals are available to all in our dining room downstairs; there's no real need for a resident to cook. It's enough to make you want to move in yourself, isn't it?' She emitted a tinkling laugh and Caroline couldn't look at Alice for fear of hysteria.

Next Miriam showed them a bed sitting room with en-suite bathroom where those who required more nursing care could stay. Even Alice couldn't summon enthusiasm to ask any questions. Caroline waited outside in the corridor lined with hand rails and floored in easy mop vinyl. An elderly man appeared at glass panelled door at the end of the corridor. He banged on the glass and gestured to her, indicating that the door was locked. Unable to bear his increasing distress she stepped in to glance at the room and bumped straight into Alice who was turning to leave it. They exchanged grimaces.

'I don't think I need show you the dementia ward,' Miriam said. 'Not really what you're after at the moment.'

'No,' Alice replied. 'Do you have any questions, Caroline?'

'None,' Caroline said. She was desperate to leave before she was overcome by the heat or had to look in the eyes of any of the unfortunates who had to live there.

'Right. Well thank you, Miriam, for showing us around. I think we've got a clear idea of the set up. We'll be in touch.'

'Please do,' Miriam said, her tone empty of enthusiasm.

Back in the car, Caroline snapped her seatbelt into place and restrained a shudder. 'You've got to be joking, Mum. There's no way Nan could live somewhere like that.'

'No, maybe not.' Alice consulted her diary. 'Well, our next appointment is to see a retirement flat. There is a manager on site but it's more about independent living.'

Caroline started the engine and pulled out into the main road. Her own flat suited her needs for the moment – it was secure, convenient, low maintenance – but it would take a very special flat to be the right fit for Beth, if moving out of her own house even turned out to be necessary.

The block of retirement flats had been built at a road junction along from a parade of shops. After failing to find the entrance to the car park, Caroline abandoned the car on a nearby road and they walked to the front door.

'Handy for the shops,' Alice said.

Caroline was less impressed by the local amenities. 'When did you last know Nan get a Chinese take away?' Beth's current home stood on a tree-lined, residential road. The nearest decent shops might be a ten minute walk away, but they included a butcher's, the GP's surgery and a café. Close proximity to a betting shop and an off licence was less likely to impress her.

'I'm only saying,' Alice said and peered at the panel of buttons next to the door until she located the doorbell for the manager.

It took about a minute and a half for the door to be answered, during which time Alice stood straight backed and with hands clasped. It was almost as though she was timing the response as evidence, of what Caroline was unsure.

'You must be Mrs Hipkins,' the manager said when she finally got to the door. She was dressed less formally than Matron Miriam, a fact Caroline was sure would be added to Alice's collection. 'Come on in, I'm Fiona.'

She ushered them into a wide hallway lined with pin boards. In addition to printed notices about evacuation in the case of fire and the next residents' meeting, handwritten signs offering items for sale or proposals for coffee mornings were pinned up. Caroline noted them with a smile. At least people were allowed to express themselves here.

'You must be Mrs Hipkins' daughter?' Fiona held a hand out to Caroline. 'Come on through to the communal lounge, but it's quiet at the moment.'

'You don't have a programme of organised activities then?' Alice looked at the uninspiring furniture and stained carpet with obvious disdain.

'Of course,' Fiona said. 'But we have many younger residents. Most of them happily do their own thing during the day so we have evening socials.'

'Younger?' Alice asked. 'I thought this block was for over-sixties.'

'That's right. But at least half are fit and youthful, just like you. You'll fit right in.'

Caroline choked back a laugh as Alice's mouth dropped open and her face flushed. Fiona had already turned to move towards the kitchenette in the corner of the room but Alice had frozen to the carpet. Guilt at her reaction to Alice's humiliation forced Caroline to speak. 'I think there's a misunderstanding, Fiona. We're here to look at a flat on behalf of my nan. She's in her eighties.'

Fiona turned slowly, her hand to her mouth. 'Oh, Mrs Hipkins, I'm so very sorry. I don't know what to say…'

'I'm fifty-five,' Alice said and glared at Fiona, 'and not ready for one of your flats, thank you.'

'You do look youthful, that's why I…'

Caroline caught Fiona's eye and shook her head. When you're in a hole, and the water's flooding in, stop digging, she thought. Fortunately the telepathic message got through.

'Perhaps I should let you have a look around the flat?' Fiona said.

She hurried off down a corridor with Caroline keeping up and Alice walking behind at a stately pace. Fiona produced a bunch of keys from her pocket which put Caroline disturbingly in mind of a jailer. 'Do you have keys to everyone's flats?' she asked.

'I have a skeleton key,' Fiona replied. 'For security, you know.' She glanced over Caroline's shoulder before leaning in to whisper, 'I'm so sorry. She doesn't look over sixty, I just thought, oh, I don't know.' She pushed the door open, holding it wide to invite Caroline and Alice inside. 'I'll leave you to it for a moment. Everything's self-explanatory really.' The door closed behind her.

Caroline led the way into the sitting room. It was relatively spacious. There was probably room for a small dining table, a sofa and maybe an armchair. She stepped into the kitchen. Its fittings were modern and clean. There wasn't much workspace but it had everything she expected to see. On her way back to the bedroom she passed Alice who was standing in the doorway to the sitting room, arms folded and expression grim. Caroline ignored her and checked the bedroom and bathroom. Both were unexceptional. Fine.

'Well?' she asked.

Alice turned to her. 'Not quite what we're looking for.'

'Come on, Mum. She made a mistake. There's nothing actually wrong with the flat apart from being painfully boring.' The walls were magnolia, the carpets beige. Caroline couldn't go so far as to be enthusiastic about it. She certainly couldn't see Beth living there.

'Let's go,' said Alice.

After a brief, and strained, exchange of pleasantries with Fiona, they were back in the car. Caroline buckled herself in but didn't start the engine. 'Don't you think this is a bit premature, Mum?'

'We've got to be prepared.'

'Yes, but Nan's been living on her own without any problems up to now.'

'Not entirely. I go in every day.'

Caroline started the engine. 'Do we have any more of these appointments?'

'No, that's it for today.'

'Well, neither of those places would be suitable.' She drove back to the main road and waited, the click of the indicators signalling her intention to turn right. Alice craned her neck forward to look right, then left, then right again, obscuring Caroline's own view of oncoming traffic. She placed a hand on Alice's arm to push her back against her seat. 'Mum, I'm driving, remember?'

'Sorry, darling.' Alice sighed. 'I just don't want your nan to have to suffer because we weren't ready to meet her needs.'

Caroline nodded but didn't respond. So that was what was behind Alice's behaviour, guilt because she hadn't been ready to help her dad. His sudden illness started while Alice was pregnant with Caroline and Alice had been unable to take charge of the situation.

*

By the time she got back to her own flat, Caroline was in no mood go out again. Denise from work had mentioned she and some friends were seeing a film that evening and Caroline was welcome to join them. It was kind of her, but utterly not what Caroline needed. No, an evening in front of the TV would suit. She texted her apologies.

Curled on the sofa with a glass of wine, she flicked through the channels and found nothing to watch. She thought again of Beth's home and how items to occupy her hands or mind were placed by each chair: a bag spilling knitting needles and bright skeins of wool by the armchair in the living room, a newspaper folded open to the crossword on the dining table, books on the coffee table or bedside cabinet. Beth might be retired and living alone, but she was not short of stimulation or occupation.

Caroline had once been used to a more exciting life, in which weekends with Matt had been packed with activities such as visits to friends around the country or hosting parties of their own. Caroline recalled one particular Saturday when they'd decided to go to Paris, just because they had nothing else planned.

'Pourquoi pas?' Matt asked as they'd lain in bed contemplating the day ahead. Of course it was easier from London; Paris was a train ride away. An expensive train, but frugality was not one of Matt's characteristics, while his impulsive exuberance had been an obvious attraction – until it became too exhausting to live with.

His proposal had been a surprise. They were turning thirty, living in London and loving the lifestyle of restaurants, exhibitions, gigs and parties. Their flat in Clerkenwell allowed for an easy commute to Caroline's job at the British Museum and Matt's in the City. If it weren't for Matt's job, they'd never have been able to afford to live there. They met up after work in stylish bars and planned holidays to destinations featured in Sunday supplements. Caroline's choices took them to Petra or Peru; Matt preferred city breaks or exotic beaches. It was under the fronds of a palm tree that he'd popped the question, causing Caroline to choke on her rum punch. 'Marry me,' he murmured, one hand reaching lazily for hers.

She sat up on the sun lounger and swung her legs towards him. 'Really?'

He removed his sunglasses and smiled. 'Yes, really. I want to do this for the rest of my life.'

She thought he meant being with her, that her company was the thing he wanted to commit to. Romance, or rum, had gone to her head. She said yes. It didn't make much difference; their lives continued much as before. She kept her maiden name. She had a professional reputation after all. And they agreed they should move and establish a home.

Somewhere though, there had been a misunderstanding. When she looked back and tried to identify where the relationship had begun to go wrong, Caroline couldn't find the point. During which conversation should she have been clearer? When did she make one assumption, while Matt made another? She was thinking suburban houses and babies while he was in no hurry to change their lifestyle, a fact she didn't appreciate until he was offered the job in New York.

'Isn't it great?' he asked. 'What a fantastic opportunity.'

Not in her eyes. But in the end, what she'd hated most was what her reaction revealed about her. She was conventional, cowardly, keen to fit in with society's expectations.

He'd tried to persuade her. 'We can still have a baby in a flat in New York. And they're offering me a massive raise to go – you won't have to worry about finding work.'

It wasn't about the job, or the baby and it was a relief she hadn't yet got pregnant. It was the realisation that he was always going to be looking for the next challenge and she didn't want to keep up.

Caroline put her feet up on her sofa in Birmingham, sipped her wine and realised that these days she was so far behind her life had gone into reverse. The reappearance of Olly hadn't helped. She hadn't even managed to move on from a teenage crush. She forced herself to concentrate on the news headlines. It was important to be informed about what was happening in the world. It was not important to daydream about old flames who made her heart beat faster, especially those whom the evidence of the past recorded as unreliable.

Chapter Eight

By Tuesday, it was apparent the week was going the same way as the last. Denise called in sick which meant Caroline would have to spend the morning herding a school party around the Ancient Egyptian displays. The uncharitable thought crossed her mind that Denise might be faking it.

She scan read the email the teacher had sent in preparation for the group's arrival. Helpfully, he'd detailed key points from the curriculum he wanted to focus on. Some chance, Caroline thought. All the kids'll let me talk about will be mummification and fighting. It's all they'll remember, anyway.

Bill grunted a greeting as he entered their office. They hadn't spoken much since their argument over the mystery object but she put her annoyance aside; there was something she wanted to ask him.

'Have I remembered right that your dad lives in a warden-controlled flat?' Caroline remembered Bill mentioning it during a recent department trip to the pub.

'Yes, in Bearwood.'

'How does he like it?'

Bill frowned as he looked at her, 'It's OK I suppose.'

Realising the question must appear random, Caroline explained, 'My nan might need to move out of her home and I don't know anyone who lives in those kind of flats. I just wondered if it was working out for him.'

'I see. Well, yes, Dad's fine there. He wouldn't have managed in the house after my mum died. He has meals delivered to the flat and I go round to do the cleaning once a week, but other than that he still does his own thing.'

Caroline smiled. The thought of Bill in rubber gloves scrubbing his Dad's bathroom was incongruous. She wouldn't have guessed him capable of cleaning his own home. After asking for the name of the company which ran the flats, she thanked him and returned to her work. The ice had been broken though, and Bill was keen to continue chatting. 'Dad does get a bit bored. He's been retired nearly fifteen years but he's never got the hang of not working.'

'What did he do?' Caroline was too polite to draw the conversation to a close.

'Worked for an engineering firm. He was a tool setter.'

'Oh, which firm?'

'Not one of the big ones. A small, family-run outfit called Farlane's. I don't think they're still going.'

She looked up and forced herself to blink at Bill, not stare. 'Farlane's?' The coincidence unsettled her. Could there be more than one firm with that name? She glanced at her watch. It would have to wait; the school party were due.

They were gathered near the entrance foyer, thirty children exchanging lewd comments about the nude male statue which dominated the room. Caroline took a deep breath. They were barely teenagers. She raised her eyebrows at the teacher and led them to the Ancient Egyptian collection on a mezzanine gallery running around the walls of the antiquities room.

Once there she delivered her standard spiel about the historical context of the exhibits and the influence of ancient cultures on the present day without too many interruptions. She pointed out key items in each display case and ignored the boys loitering at the back as they leant over the balcony in danger of plummeting into the room below. The few ordinary visitors who were looking at the Greek and Roman artefacts down there glanced up with irritated expressions and Caroline adjusted the pitch of her voice so it wouldn't carry to them. She fiddled with her security pass, immediately fearing the complaints she'd have to field, or worse, hecklers. Even the kids might come up with questions she couldn't answer. Her shoulders began to tense and she had to pause and take a breath to steady her voice. Once the tour finished, the teacher glanced at his watch and asked the group if they had any questions for Caroline.

'Miss,' one boy yelled, 'why is it the mummies don't stink?'

His friends sniggered.

'Well, they developed the preservation technique because it was so important to them that the bodies would last forever in the afterlife. The embalming process means there's nothing to decay and create a smell. And it's worked, hasn't it? Isn't it amazing that we're here talking about this mummy almost two thousand years after he died?'

Their faces remained blank. Clearly the concept of making something which would stand the test of history was not impressive.

'Miss, you see this?' A girl pressed a finger against the glass of a display case. Her fingertip left a smear. 'It says here girls didn't have to go to school.'

'That's right,' Caroline replied. 'Women did have some power and respect in their society, but only boys from the richest families went to school. Girls would be taught skills at home though: cooking, weaving, that sort of thing.' She immediately regretted the way she'd phrased it. Her choice of words made it sound as though female roles were less important.

'I want some of the bling, Miss. How much?'

Caroline turned to a knot of girls crowding the jewellery display. Necklaces made of shells, faience and carnelian beads in shades of turquoise and purple undimmed by time gleamed behind the glass. 'Not for sale, I'm afraid.'

'Look though - Egyptian GHDs!'

Caroline sighed. It didn't matter if she unwittingly undermined female roles in society. These girls had already accepted the gender divide. She joined them to explain how the metal hair tongs would have worked and point out the kohl pots essential to any ancient Egyptian noblewoman's make up kit. The very least she could achieve would be to send them away with an understanding that history had some relevance to them; that knowledge from the past was worth preserving even if it only related to make-up tips. Those stood the test of time where belief systems and cultures did not.

Finally the hour was up and the teacher stopped tapping at the screen of his phone and took charge of the kids. 'Say thank you, everyone,' he said. 'And no, we haven't got time to go to the gift shop.'

Caroline slumped against the balcony as they trooped away. From her vantage point she could see into a cabinet of Roman artefacts in the room below. She focussed on the one object she'd select were the museum a shop: a dark green, perfectly square, moulded glass bottle. She'd rearranged that display case recently to bring different items out from the stores, but this bottle retained its place. As she'd slipped a gloved finger through the elegant handle and cradled its base she'd imagined tipping it to pour oil much as its original owner must have done thousands of years ago. The rim was chipped but it was otherwise perfect. It was beautiful, practical and utterly covetable. Millennia might have passed, but fundamentally little had changed.

Silence fell as the door closed behind the last of the visitors. She sniffed at the chilled air and picked up the scent she associated with the past, a smell with dry stone as its main component. Alice had remarked that the room smelt dusty on the one occasion she'd visited. She was

71

probably right. Everything was crumbling. Caroline lifted her gaze to where the walls of the balcony were lined with a plaster cast of the frieze from the Parthenon. This she was less fond of; it was a reproduction after all. It told a good story though with its parade of dancers, musicians and horses headed to a festival in honour of Athena: goddess of wisdom, craft and war for just cause. A goddess well worth worshipping, Caroline thought. A party I would very much like to attend.

*

When she got home, Caroline called the mobile number listed on Richard Garrold's card but it went through to his answerphone. She left a message that Beth's surgery had been deemed successful and she was improving, before leaving her own number so he could call for more information. She was keen to ensure he didn't get to Beth without her knowing about it.

Her last conversation with Beth hadn't revealed much more information about the Garrolds. Caroline had tried to be subtle about her questions. 'I was admiring those watercolours in your hall. Lovely aren't they?'

Beth nodded. 'Mmm, listen, could you drop my book back to the library, love? And get me another?'

'I'll ask Mum. She'll know which ones you've had. Those pictures though, they're all scenes of Birmingham, aren't they? All by the same artist?'

Beth glanced around as if hoping a change of topic would present itself.

'Are they by Susannah, Nan? Is she a relative of ours?'

Beth paused before she answered. 'Yes, she was my aunt.' She didn't elaborate.

'It's a nice collection; they might have some value.'

That got Beth's attention. 'Do you think so?' She was quiet again as she considered this.

Caroline let the pause hang for a while before she mentioned that she'd left the message for Richard. The ward was silent, the other occupants either asleep or away from their beds. A squeak of rubber soled footsteps against lino could be heard in the corridor and the pressure relieving mattress Beth lay on clicked and sighed as it released air to adjust her support. Eventually Caroline spoke again. 'That comment you made, about changing your will, it's something to do with him, isn't it? Has he asked you for money?'

Beth pursed her lips. 'She was an interesting woman, my Aunt Susannah. Very generous and forgiving. I hope I can follow her example.' She smiled at Caroline. 'Don't worry. I know what I'm doing, and once I get home I'll sort everything out. Things should be equitable, don't you think?'

The mention of 'home' brought the conversation back to a topic Caroline wasn't keen to discuss. It had become obvious that Beth wouldn't be able to live alone, at least during a period of convalescence. Perhaps it would be better to wait until after the consultant's next assessment before broaching the subject with Beth herself though. Caroline thought she'd been pushy enough for one day.

'You won't take any snap decisions will you, Nan? Think things through, talk to us about them. Please don't think I'm worried about the money – it's not that I expect you to leave everything to Mum, or to me and Peter. I'm just concerned about this bloke appearing from nowhere and you suddenly talking about changing your will. There's too many con men around these days.'

'Oh, that's no con man. Richard is definitely a Garrold; he's like all the other Garrold men.' As though aware she'd said more than she intended, Beth had then successfully changed the topic to gossip about the health of the woman in the neighbouring bed for the rest of Caroline's visit.

Caroline couldn't forget Susannah though. It wasn't only the salacious thrill of having a criminal in the family; the fact the Garrolds had never been mentioned was weird no matter how she looked at it.

'Have you ever heard Nan mention relatives called Garrold?' Caroline asked Peter when he finally returned her call that evening.

'Garrold? No. Hipkins and Dabbs are the only names I've heard in our family. But, you know me: I leave all the family stuff to you and Mum.'

She had noticed. What she was surprised, and now feeling guilty about, was that she'd never asked Beth about her relatives. If Susannah was such an interesting woman, why was this the first time Beth had mentioned her? 'She never talked to you about when she was little or mentioned that we had cousins on her side, not just in Dad's family?'

'Have we? First I've heard. Where's this coming from? Please don't tell me she's starting to lose her marbles.'

'No, nothing like that, I know she likes to chat with you, thought she might have mentioned something. I met this bloke at her house who says he's some kind of cousin of ours – a Richard Garrold. And, well, Nan said something to me about wanting to change her will.'

There was a pause before Peter spoke again. 'Have you mentioned this to Mum?'

'No.' Beth hadn't asked her not to tell Peter, but it even that felt like breaking a confidence.

'I wouldn't. You need to find out what's going on. One thing I do know is Mum's expecting to inherit the house, or the proceeds from selling it at any rate.'

Caroline grimaced. Talking about Beth dying made her nauseous; as for discussing the money, that was extremely poor taste. 'But people don't anymore. If Nan does go to live in whatever other kind of accommodation, the money from the house will have to fund it. No one gets to inherit houses these days the way Nan says she got it. Not unless Mum and Dad move into the house and look after her there.'

Peter laughed. 'God, can you imagine! Poor Dad, he'd be living in a warzone.'

'More to the point, he hates that house.' Caroline glanced around her flat and tried to imagine living in Beth's house herself. No, she couldn't see it happening. 'I can see his point. It was designed for a big family; it wouldn't suit any of us.'

'I can't have this conversation. It's too morbid. You should find out about this Garrold bloke - make sure he's really who he says. Ultimately, it's up to Nan what she does with her money though.'

'I know. Listen, it would be great if you'd come and visit her you know. You'd really cheer her up.' Caroline didn't admit she'd also like the burden shared.

'Well, um, I'll see what I can do. I'm pretty busy. I'll be in touch.'

As Caroline ended the call and dropped the phone on her coffee table she almost wished she hadn't bothered mentioning the Garrolds to him. His sole contribution had been to instruct her to do things she already planned and it wasn't only morbid to be thinking about what would happen after Beth died; it was mercenary and insensitive. She wasn't personally relying on any inheritance or hand-outs, even if her mum was.

As for Peter, well it was easy for him to forget the past. He wasn't here, drawn in to family problems as she was. With his exhibition to prepare for he was understandably more concerned about the future.

Protecting Beth was the most important thing. Caroline flipped open the lid of her laptop and mused while it booted up. She needed to meet with Richard Garrold and ask him some straight questions. In the meantime there was another name to investigate. The 1911 Census was the most recent available and it was possible that, as Beth's aunt, Susannah Garrold would have been alive then. Caroline navigated to the website where she could view the entries and searched on the name. No records were found. A wider search for the surname Garrold in Birmingham brought up three entries at one address: William aged 42, Annie aged 41 and Thomas aged 22. Caroline gazed at the screen. It was a strange way to meet relatives.

Chapter Nine

Olly pushed his chair back and stood to greet Caroline. 'Sorry I couldn't give you more notice,' he said as he bent to kiss her cheek. 'My plans for the week changed at the last minute.'

Did his face linger a little too long near hers, or had she imagined it? She blushed and looked down at the documents he'd been engrossed in when she arrived. They were in the Archives room of the Central Library and he'd covered a table with probate records, barely legible spidery handwriting hinting at their age. She reached to lift one and he lightly smacked the back of her hand. 'Client confidentiality,' he said. His voice was loud in the hush of the room and the man at the next table looked up.

Caroline suspected most people there were tracing family trees or looking up esoteric bits of local history, not tracking extremely valuable items as Olly was. 'I thought all these documents would be online by now,' she whispered.

'Not all of them. Anyway, didn't Prof Davies always say we should go back to primary sources wherever possible? Touch things, smell them, get under the skin of the past.'

He'd spoken in a low voice and his references to touch, scent and skin made Caroline's nerve endings tingle. She took a step back and a deep breath. 'Fair enough,' she said. 'Good point. I'll just take a quick look at something if you're nearly done?' She left him to tidy his papers and went to the Enquiries desk to ask where she'd find the early twentieth century trade directories.

Discovering the Garrold family in the 1911 census had uncovered a mystery. She'd had to register with the website and enter her credit card details before she could view the full record, but it had been worth it. William Garrold was the head of the household and gave his profession as Factory Owner. He'd been born in Glasgow. He listed Annie Garrold as his wife; they'd been married for twenty three years and she'd been born in Birmingham. They had four children of whom two were living when the census was taken. Only one, Thomas, appeared on the census return though. His occupation was shown as Factory Manager.

Caroline smiled when she read they also had a live-in housemaid. It was a snippet she knew Alice would enjoy should she ever get to share the story. However, the note William Garrold had written across the bottom of the form snuffed out her smile. The first four lines of the official paperwork had been completed in neat handwriting – regular sized letters in bold black ink confidently detailed the extent of William Garrold's household. Below those carefully recorded details though, in the same handwriting although perhaps less controlled, was the message, 'My daughter has attempted to make a protest by staying away from home on the day of this count. She does live here at my expense.'

Caroline gasped. She read the message twice to be sure she'd properly understood. The fury in William Garrold's words still burned despite the hundred years since they were written. Even the depersonalising process of scanning the record into pixels on her screen removed none of the emotion. William Garrold had refused to allow his daughter her protest. He advertised her existence whether she liked it or not. It was clear he was not a man to be crossed.

A quick internet search informed Caroline it was likely the missing daughter had been a suffragette, refusing to be counted as a citizen until she was granted a vote. 'Good for you,' Caroline whispered to her screen. 'Could that be you, Susannah?' It seemed many suffragettes had managed to get their political message onto the forms, scrawling notes such as 'Women live here too' or 'No vote, no census,' across the official documents. Not so in the Garrold household. There it was clear William was in charge and he did not support the suffragette cause.

It was another dead end with no proof of a relationship to these Garrolds. While it had been tempting to search for a record of Susannah's birth in the online indexes to discover if William and Annie were her parents, Caroline had decided to stop. It felt too close to snooping. Much better, and probably faster, to ask Beth some direct questions and save the cost of ordering strangers' birth certificates. And Caroline longed to hear more about Susannah. Had it been her suffragette activities that landed her in jail? That would have been a measure of commitment well worth respecting.

It seemed less intrusive to investigate the history of Richard Garrold's company in the library archives. She'd convinced herself of the necessity at any rate and slid the 1911 Kelly's Directory from the shelf where it sat in a tight line of rebound books. As she flicked through the pages she felt a nostalgic sorrow for all these small, specialised firms, founded with such hopes and most long gone, swallowed up by mergers or made obsolete by changing times. How had the demand for a product as specialised as picture rod joints ever supported an individual firm?

Once she'd located the index of advertising manufacturers, she slid her fingertip down the yellowed page until she reached the letter F. There they were: Farlane's Fasteners, iron foundry and castings, page 325. She flipped forwards to the page on which they'd taken out a full page advert.

The ornate font and basic layout of the design were typical of the era; the words boasted of the firm's ability to manufacture a range of bolts, nuts, rivets, screws and all requisites. Customers were invited to contact William Garrold for immediate delivery. Caroline raised her eyebrows. The man's self-importance leaked even into his adverts. This was proof the Garrold family had owned Farlane's back in 1911, whatever the company had now become. It corroborated that Richard Garrold had some legitimacy as the owner of a family company, even if the link to Beth wasn't yet proven. Caroline forced herself to pause. Garrold was an uncommon name, but not an extremely rare one. Was it too much to assume a relationship between a William Garrold in 1911 and Richard Garrold today if they turned up in the same place? She wasn't trained to assume. She was trained to seek proof.

'You know most people do their shopping online these days.' Olly had approached without her noticing and read the advert over her shoulder. 'Farlane's Fasteners? How wonderfully alliterative.'

She made a show of closing the book to highlight his double standard in snooping at her activities and slid it back into its slot on the shelf. She could always come and take a photocopy another time if the details were of any relevance. 'Just a little research, you know,' she said and stepped sideways to increase the distance between them again. He didn't appear to apply the same personal space boundaries as other people. Or perhaps she was being oversensitive?

He smiled at her. 'What I do know is that reading dusty old books can certainly generate a thirst. Shall we go for that drink?'

Caroline led the way across town using the shortcut through the convention centre. Their footsteps seemed loud on the stone floor of the enclosed walkway through the middle of the building. As usual, a few other people were using it as route from the city centre to the canal basin, but everyone except Olly seemed in a hurry to get somewhere. He looked around at the bland passages and exhibition spaces waiting to be branded with marketing materials for the next conference to one side, while the wall of Symphony Hall's auditorium loomed on the other. Caroline wondered what she could say about it; in a way the building reminded her of the oddness in their relationship. At university, they'd both been impressed and fascinated by history and culture – now she remained in that world while Olly had taken up commerce in hunt of profit.

'This is nice,' he said.

She assumed he meant the building. 'Yeah, Birmingham's been smartening itself up recently, I suppose.'

'Speaking of image, that's another nice outfit you're wearing.'

Caroline laughed. 'Very smooth.' Unlikely to be his true opinion of her cropped black trousers and tunic though. Perhaps it was harsh to judge him so quickly, but from what she'd seen of his girlfriend twenty-odd years ago, it was most likely that his taste still ran to women rather more groomed and preened than she was. His own clothes were smart and tailored, less offensive than Denise's description of a rusticated toff had implied. Perhaps he saved those clothes for times when he had meetings with clients.

'I meant it,' Olly said. He paused to pick up a brochure about the current concert season from a rack of leaflets and she wasn't sure she'd heard his quiet words correctly.

They walked down the steep staircase and were met by a sudden cool breeze as the automatic doors slid open to give them access to the canal-side terrace. Olly clutched his jacket closed. Caroline didn't react. She was desensitised to that particular sensation having experienced it several times every day during her commute. She kept walking, and held her head a little higher confident in the proof of how she belonged to her city. No matter what veneer of manners, experience and money he put on along with the subtle, crisp cologne she'd caught the scent of when he greeted her, she had at least one thing in her favour: this city, with all its advantages, was hers.

'You could almost be in Amsterdam,' he said as they crossed the illuminated bridge over the canal.

Caroline glanced around. 'You say that as though Amsterdam would be preferable.' Only this bridge was decked with lights and floral displays, dressed to appeal to tourists – she'd lost count of the number of times her journey across it had been interrupted by requests to take photos for visitors. They'd indicate which button she should press, and then pose with arms draped round each other while she framed their holiday smiles against a background of dark water and red brick. The very British, Victorian heritage of the area was what would dominate the pictures, not the incongruous fairy lights or bright windows of the bars and restaurants which occupied the newer buildings, their architecture faking the industry on which the area was founded.

Once they were seated in a bar whose interior was done out to look like a warehouse, Olly asked, 'Am I allowed to ask what you're working on? Should I clear my diary to ensure I can visit the Farlane's Fasteners exhibition?'

She smiled, comfortable with the gentle teasing. 'No, that's personal interest really. At work, the main thing for our team is still the Anglo-Saxon stuff. Can't believe how much interest that find's generated from the public.'

Olly nodded. 'It being local is critical, I suppose. Those of us in the field might like to cast our interests wider, but I can utterly understand the public being interested in what happened where they are.'

Caroline sipped her glass of wine and savoured the immediate ebbing away of tension as the warming liquid slipped down her throat. 'Especially when it could hint at marauding hordes fighting and looting – it's action movie stuff and the sums of money involved get attention too.

I'm afraid my ideas aren't guiding the work though. I just toe the line.'

'Somehow I don't see you as a line toe-er.'

She looked up and briefly met his gaze. 'You don't? Um, I don't know why. I don't think I've ever been particularly innovative or been the creative force behind anything.' She took a gulp from her glass and hoped he wouldn't ask for more details of her career. On reflection, all she had actually done in recent years was stagnate. Matt had offered an opportunity to start a life entirely new, but she'd chosen instead to cling to the familiar and let her world shrink. No wonder she was jealous of Peter's exhibition: not only did his artwork bring joy and colour into people's lives, but his work was being recognised, celebrated. Everything she did was dry and cold in comparison. It was about preservation, not creation. Even Olly got out and about and helped people get what they wanted. His role might be to realise the cash value of their possessions, but it was movement, change.

She flinched as the tips of his fingers touched the back of her hand. 'Please don't tell me you've given up being wayward?' he said.

'Wayward?' Her wine glass rocked as she unlaced her fingers from its stem to pull her hand away. 'What do you mean?'

'Oh, come on, Caroline, don't be offended. We used to have fun together. You weren't like the uptight, Sloaney-types who were only at university to find a husband. You were the cleverest one in our seminar group. I loved how you'd challenge all my lazy thinking and do it with a cheeky smile.' He paused and she noticed he'd edged his chair closer to hers. 'And then there was Cyprus…'

The warmth of the wine drained away, replaced by a cold lurch in her stomach. What certainty and confidence she may have once possessed had been eroded over recent years. Now Olly's undermining raid on both her career and her personality was unwelcome. Her voice was cold as she said 'Cyprus?'

'I have very happy memories of Cyprus.'

Caroline folded her arms and leant back in her seat. To some extent she agreed with his comment; she had happy memories of Cyprus herself, if she didn't consider the events there in any kind of external context. 'You behaved badly in Cyprus,' was all she allowed herself to say.

He smiled. 'As did you, I seem to recall. Fun, wasn't it?'

'I think I see why you and your wife are separated. Infidelity doesn't fit with most people's expectations of marriage.' Desperate for another gulp of wine, Caroline kept her arms firmly tucked against her sides. Her divorce from Matt had been too difficult, such a traumatic re-evaluation of her own expectations, that she couldn't begin to consider a relationship as just fun. She couldn't remember how that worked. His suggestive reference to the casual intimacy they'd shared made her panic. By joining him for a drink had she agreed to something? She'd heard that dating etiquette had changed but had taken his invitation at face value: old acquaintances, one drink. Reasons to leave began to form in her mind. As did reasons to stay.

Olly had leant back from the table but after a moment he broke the silence. 'I don't think I took enough time to consider my own expectations of marriage to be honest. I was probably never suited to it.' He wrung his hands together and looked at her with pleading eyes. 'Look, I hope I haven't offended you. It's really good to see you again and I promise I'll try to behave more appropriately. I'm feeling rather off keel what with the move and the separation.'

It was a feeling Caroline could sympathise with. She reached for her glass again and drained the remaining mouthful. 'Shall I get another round in then?'

As she waited at the bar, she texted Alice to ask how Beth was. The reply arrived before the drinks did: 'She hasn't had a good day. Can you visit tomorrow?' Caroline tapped out a quick confirmation and carried the drinks back to the table. Olly was gazing out at a group of women on a hen do. Decked in pink, fur trimmed cowboy hats, feather boas and inadvisably short skirts they dithered as they decided which bar to visit first.

'It's not even the weekend,' he said as she placed his glass of wine down on the aluminium topped table.

'Are you suggesting people can only indulge in fun on specified days?' Caroline raised an eyebrow as he turned to look at her instead. 'It wouldn't seem to fit with your philosophy of life.'

'There you go: that's exactly the type of challenge I expect from you. Putting me firmly in my place.'

She shook her head. 'I'm not serious. I'm a complete killjoy myself. What on earth are they thinking, dressing up like that on a week night?' She put a finger to her lips and ducked back into her seat as the door swung open to admit the hens. They whooped and screamed as they colonised the table next to Caroline and Olly. Caroline pulled her seat forwards to allow a particularly large woman space to manoeuvre and was rewarded with an honorary hen award – a feather boa was draped around her neck and lipstick kisses smacked onto both cheeks. She gave them a closed mouth smile and returned the boa while wishing the bride-to-be well.

Olly laughed and clinked his glass against hers. 'If you're quite finished, may I be nosy? Who were you texting while you were at the bar? A muscle-bound boyfriend who's on his way to deliver me a black eye?'

Caroline blushed. 'No, um, my mum actually. I was after an update on my nan.'

The corners of Olly's mouth softened and a frown drew his eyebrows together. 'I hope she's soon on the mend.'

Caroline thanked him and a thought occurred to her. 'You wouldn't know anything about watercolour paintings, would you? In terms of value, that sort of thing.'

'Of course. Are we talking about a known artist, something at the Museum, perhaps?'

'No, just a collection I was wondering if my nan should have valued. For insurance purposes, you know.'

Olly nodded. 'Well, with your exquisite taste, I don't imagine you'd be considering it if the paintings had no worth. I'd be happy to take a look if you'd like me to. No fee, obviously.'

'I wouldn't want to put you to any trouble. I mean, if you're going to be in Birmingham for work again sometime, perhaps I could take you to the house. I wouldn't want you to make a special journey.'

He pulled a leather bound diary from his jacket pocket. 'I haven't finished my research yet, but I'd happily come over to help you anyway.'

'I'd have thought a firm like Dunnant's had junior staff who'd be sent to trawl the archives.'

'Ah, caught red-handed. I may have volunteered to complete the job so I could look up an old friend at the same time.' He looked at her and smiled. 'But this provenance I'm working on for one of our clients is particularly important.'

Caroline didn't doubt it. The estimates against many of the items in the Dunnant's sale catalogues made for eye-watering reading. That concept though: provenance. It really could make or break an artefact. Should Beth's paintings turn out to be by Susannah Garrold then Susannah's own reputation would be critical in their evaluation. If she turned out to be an amateur working on her hobby, much as Beth herself turned out knitted clothing or homewares with embroidered or crocheted embellishment, then the paintings would be worth only what someone would pay for their decorative value.

Caroline needed to look at them again. They hadn't struck her as amateur. The artist's talent had shone through.

As for that man with his muddy treasure, well she'd still like a good look at the item, let alone think about where it had come from or what it might be worth.

Chapter Ten

Caroline perched on the metal-legged chair she'd drawn up to the side of Beth's hospital bed. Alice occupied the armchair on the other side. Neither was comfortable but heightened concern meant they wanted to stay close to Beth without disturbing her sleep.

'Why didn't they find out before it got serious?' Caroline whispered across the blanket.

Alice glanced towards Beth's face before replying. 'Her raised temperature could have been from the surgery and anaesthetic. They didn't investigate until she complained how bad the pain in her leg was when she was trying to walk.'

An ultrasound test that afternoon had found a blood clot in Beth's calf. Caroline stroked Beth's hand, unable to do anything else. The skin was puckered by surgical tape and bruised blue around the cannula which led to the drip now delivering anti-clotting and blood thinning drugs in addition to pain relief.

'The doctor was reassuring,' Alice said. 'They do think they've found it in time.'

A glance at her mother's face showed Caroline her fears weren't unfounded. Alice was worried too although she was trying to be calm about it. 'Look Mum, I don't think Nan's going to wake up for a bit. Why don't we go and get a drink? We can come up again before visiting time ends.'

A subdued mood hung over the hospital café where Caroline queued behind people in dressing gowns and bought two polystyrene cups of greyish tea. She carried them to the table and didn't blame Alice for setting hers aside untouched. She played with her own, letting the flimsy white plastic stirrer heat up in the scalding liquid so it bent under its own weight when she lifted it.

In a way it was liberating to misbehave at a table without her mum issuing an admonishment not to play with her food. As children, Caroline and Peter were regularly lectured on the importance of manners when they'd eaten in public, and Alice was prone to repeating salient points should her adult offspring fail to meet her standards for behaviour. That evening though, she was too distracted to notice.

Caroline abandoned her drink and reached out to touch Alice's arm. 'Don't worry. I'm sure the doctors and nurses are doing all they can.'

'It's just all so unnecessary,' Alice said. 'And what if…'

'No 'what ifs', OK? Let's concentrate on what's actually happened.'

Alice glanced at the table and a frown flicked onto her forehead as she surveyed the mess of stirrers and cup lids Caroline had abandoned there. She gathered them together and crumpled a paper napkin to mop the spilt drops of tea from the plastic surface. 'I just want to be doing something,' she said.

'I know, Mum.' Caroline had things she wanted to be doing too, such as asking Beth about Susannah and finding out what Richard Garrold wanted. It would have to wait. In the meantime, as long as she didn't give anything away, she could always see if Alice knew anything. 'Is there anyone else we should tell, you know, about Nan being in here? Any other relatives of yours?'

She'd tried to sound casual but Alice snapped her head up and glared at her.

'You make it sound as if we should get a crowd in to say their final farewells.'

'No, no, nothing like that. I just thought – I mean, I'll pop to the house to water the plants so I thought I'd let her neighbours know and I wondered if there was anyone else.'

Alice slumped back into her chair. 'No. It's just me. And you and Peter. I wish there were others really.' Her voice was weak; the formal, competent mask had slipped.

*

Caroline let herself into Beth's house and bent to scoop up the envelopes which littered the doormat. A flick through them revealed nothing urgent so she placed them on the hall stand, glancing at herself in the mirror framed in the panel above it as she hung her jacket on a hook set into its side. It was a nice piece of furniture, functional yet attractive. It was homely, not like the sleek modern designs in her furnished flat or those opposite whose illuminated interiors were revealed in uncurtained windows every evening. Beth's things weren't dated or overly formal as some antique furniture could seem either. Her home was comfortable; just right.

In the kitchen Caroline took a watering can from the cupboard under the sink. As the echoing can filled with water she studied the garden. The lawn was desperate for a mow. She realised Beth's gardener wouldn't have been able to get access in the last week. She added his name to a mental list of calls she ought to make, shook splatters of water which had overflowed the can from her hand and turned off the tap. Richard Garrold had made his way back to the top of that list.

She visited the plants in the dining and living rooms and admired their ceramic pots as she splashed water around their stems. Getting the information she needed from Richard could be tricky. Clearly he wouldn't just tell her why Beth might want to change her will, so an indirect method of collecting information would be required. She could ask about his family; that would come across as understandable curiosity. The firm as well – she could perhaps mention her tenuous connection via Bill's dad to get some information. It all depended on whether he'd answer the phone to her though, or whether he'd force her to record voice mail again.

Once all the plants had a drink, Caroline revisited the rooms to tidy up a little. She didn't want to admit to herself that she was now thinking of Beth's absence as a longer term thing but reasoned it was sensible to switch plugs off at the wall and pack away the pieces from Beth's craft projects in progress.

A pair of knitting needles from which a baby's jacket was growing had slipped from the soft ball of cream wool Beth had stabbed them into when she set the work aside. Caroline picked it up and stroked the light-as-air wool, admiring the lace-like pattern in the stitches, bemused by how Beth could create such beauty from a single thread of yarn. She tucked the bundle gently into the tapestry bag beside the armchair, careful to ensure none of the stitches were in danger of slipping off. As she zipped the bag, the gentle ring of knitting needles chiming together evoked memories of evenings she and Peter had spent there, sprawled in front of the television while Beth constructively occupied herself and the click-clack of her knitting provided a reassuring soundtrack.

She wondered who the baby's jacket was for. Beth had been kind and sympathetic about Caroline's divorce, as if she appreciated that her granddaughter's disappointment far overshadowed her own desire for a great-grand-child to be produced. If only Alice had been so sensitive. Caroline brushed a few strands of carpet fluff from her knees as she stood up and another childhood memory flashed into her mind: clothes covered in fibres when the carpet was new back in the early 1980s. Peter was learning to crawl and she'd also reverted to it as a form of motion. It had been a failed attempt to claw back some attention for herself.

She sighed as she returned to the hallway and wondered if she'd ever hold the leading role in her own life again. A second viewing of the watercolours as she climbed the stairs didn't boost her self-esteem. If this artistic ability ran through her family – with Susannah, Beth and Peter all being talented and creative – why did she have to content herself with talking about or preserving artefacts and artworks rather than getting to create anything? A careful scrutiny of the works reinforced her opinion. The paintings were well executed. The subtlety in the way light illuminated the columns of Birmingham's Town Hall in one picture, the viewpoint chosen and items included in a study of working narrow boats, each painting bore the hallmark of a trained artist at work. It would be interesting to hear Olly's expert opinion.

Caroline looked away from the paintings and down to the worn stair carpet. A curator is someone who cares for things, the things in my case being inanimate objects, she thought. In theory selecting which items to exhibit and the way they were juxtaposed put her opinions in front of an audience and guided their thinking, as did her accompanying text. Every exhibition had to stand in the context of its times – the prevailing politics or world view. What else could explain all those dusty display cases of anthropological exhibits in the worst of the old Victorian museums? Now the main consideration was what would get footfall in, what would make money. The answers to those questions didn't often coincide with her interests.

She stomped up the remaining stairs. Modern art seemed too frequently to trade on sensationalism and even exhibitions of old Masters needed a populist slant to be successful. Yet there were all these artists, like Susannah or, in her own small way, Beth, creating beautiful, practical items with no need for fanfare. Caroline stopped, one foot raised for the final step onto the landing. She took a quick, mental tour of the Museum's rooms. Ancient history, natural history and the industrial revolution were all covered. There was an enviable collection of fine and applied arts. But there was little reference to the everyday, small scale production of items to assist or beautify the daily routines of ordinary people. The craft works undertaken by ordinary women: Beth and the women like her down through the ages were absent. When the male Pre-Raphaelites were busy with their paintings, stained glass and the celebrated ceramics the Museum was replete with, the work of their womenfolk was generally consigned to a footnote even when the quality of their works equalled the achievements of the men.

Caroline frowned. She hated how written histories often overlooked women. As far as she was concerned warriors and kings soaked up too much attention, so perhaps the time was right for some re-evaluation? Maybe this could be her niche, her cause, her specialist subject? She stood for a moment, hands on hips. She could do it for Beth; for Susannah. It was an idea, the beginnings of an idea to redress the balance.

Chapter Eleven

As she walked past the David Cox paintings, Caroline placed a hand against the bunch of keys clipped to her waistband and silenced their jangling in the otherwise quiet room. A glance at her favourite picture confirmed the woman still worked at her never to be completed garment, still the star of that particular scene. The heavy door beside her creaked open and a woman pushed a buggy containing a screaming child into the room. Caroline didn't return the woman's smile. She turned back to the picture. It had been gifted to the museum by a Victorian industrialist, and painted by another man. It couldn't feature in her exhibition proposals. There had to be something else she could build her ideas around.

She stalked inspiration through the other rooms of the museum. The notepad and pen she carried weren't getting much use. Those male industrialists with education and opportunities had driven much of the city's history, while their sisters, mothers, daughters and wives stayed home and supported them. That wasn't the picture which interested Caroline. After all, those women weren't only being supportive. They were being productive and some were effecting changes of their own.

As she passed the room where items from the Anglo-Saxon Hoard were displayed, Caroline glanced inside. The crowds had reduced since the initial excitement generated by the new find but it remained one of the most popular exhibits. It was a term-time weekday though and the preponderance of the grey-haired in the Hoard gallery meant the young man stood out. It was him. Caroline back tracked and stepped into the room.

'I imagine you have a particular interest in these items,' she said as she leant over the display cabinet the man was studying.

He flinched and began to back away, one hand immediately against his coat pocket a betrayal that he had the item concealed there. 'I'm just looking,' he said. 'Looking's not a crime.'

'Of course not.' Caroline tried to reassure him with her tone of voice. 'After all, this is a fascinating collection, don't you think? So many items found in one place, although, it is possible other items have been found around that area – either before, or even since perhaps...' She let her words tail off and waited for the man to respond. Without the item between them, she looked at his face properly for the first time. He was young, probably in his twenties, and in need of a shave and a haircut. He looked around the room, focussing anywhere but on her.

'And if something was found,' he said, 'it would have to be handed over, right?'

'That's right. But if it was classified as treasure, there would be a reward payable to the finder and the landowner.'

'The landowner?' His forehead creased as he finally met her eye.

Caroline nodded. 'Of course, they're entitled to a share. People should always get permission from the person who owns a place before they go looking for things, don't you think?'

The man bit his lower lip and didn't respond.

'Look,' Caroline said, twisting the lanyard which strung her security pass around her neck, 'I don't know what it is you've found, but I would advise you it'd be best to discuss it with us properly. If you act in good faith now

95

then there's no chance of you being prosecuted because you didn't report the find.'

He flinched. 'Prosecuted' had been the wrong word to use. She moved on quickly. 'Without advice you don't stand any chance of making a significant amount of money if it turns out to be something. Am I right in thinking you feel a little out of your depth perhaps? We can help you.'

It wasn't working. The man had backed away as she spoke and turned to run from the room as she finished. She glanced up to check the location of the CCTV camera monitoring the room. It blinked a red light at her and she smiled knowing a front-of-house security guard would be watching.

She left the gallery, swiped her pass to access a corridor leading back to her office and considered whether she should share the encounter with Bill before deciding against it. There was nothing new to tell after all, only more supposition, no evidence, and he clearly considered colleagues as competitors. There was one thing he might be able to help her with though.

'Bill,' she said as she slipped back behind her desk, 'do you think I could visit your dad to take a look at his flat? If I ask the manager I'll get the official take on things. I'd rather hear it from him.'

'You want to visit my dad?' Bill's frown and tone of voice conveyed how outlandish the idea was.

Caroline smiled to imply her innocence. 'Unless you think he'd mind?'

'Mind a visit from a young woman? The old dog'll be bragging about it to all his mates. Go for your life.' He scrawled a phone number on a scrap of paper and passed it over.

Caroline ignored Denise's raised eyebrow, smoothed the paper and tucked it into her handbag. She would ask about the flats, of course, but if their conversation should turn to his former job at Farlane's, well she doubted he'd mind chatting about that as well.

'Have either of you put any ideas together for the meeting with the exhibitions team yet?' Bill asked, his voice casual.

Denise stretched her arms above her head and yawned. 'I've got ideas coming out of my ears,' she said. 'What I do not have is time to develop them. How about you, Caroline?'

'Not yet,' Caroline said. 'I'm thinking a few things through.' From the corner of her eye she was aware of Bill's gaze on her and she bent to the papers on her desk and hid her smile. It felt good to have a goal again.

*

Once Bill and Denise had gone out on their lunch breaks, Caroline made two phone calls. The first was to Bill's dad, Geoff. He was, as Bill predicted, delighted to agree to her request. She decided to assuage her guilt at abusing his good nature by finding out his favourite beer or chocolates and take him a present while she used him to collect information about Farlane's.

Her second call was to Richard Garrold. As anticipated, he didn't answer and she'd already decided on the careful wording of the message she left. 'Hi Richard, I just wanted to give you an update on Beth. Perhaps I'll call again later.' It was guaranteed to make him wonder at the least, and hopefully to make him worry enough to be sure he answered her call next time. The strength of her own concern about Beth struck her. It put the competition with her colleagues into perspective but the only practical action she could take was to protect Beth from Richard.

She felt more detective than historian as she turned her thoughts to Susannah, justifying it as research for the potential exhibition. She'd need to collect enough information to put a convincing proposal together and the story of an individual was always effective as a way in to a subject. An initial online search of published titles suggested not much had been collated about the actions of suffragettes in Birmingham. Caroline was sure they'd make a good case study for the exhibition on women's lives.

She started with the paper trail. It was recent history so there'd be no digging in fields for lost treasure; she wouldn't have the challenge of surmising what a different culture might have meant by their symbols or rituals. There'd be no barriers to interpretation but the time period wasn't her area of expertise. Still, the investigation would be all about evidence and given that only around one hundred years had passed since the events she was interested in, Caroline expected to find a lot to work with. The Victorian era had been a period of expansion in many things after all. Bureaucracy was one of them and the Edwardians had been so straight-laced they'd continued the trend.

She made a list of the information needed and sources to try. A published history of the Suffragette movement would be the best starting point, although, as in most things, she didn't doubt the majority of the coverage would focus on events in London. The key players in Birmingham would have to be identified, the organisations they formed themselves into investigated, any publications or pamphlets which had been preserved would need to be tracked down.

Caroline crossed the corridor to the museum's library. She flicked the light switch and illuminated ranks of stuffed metal shelves and overflowing stacks of pamphlet boxes. The room was full of information but all of it related to history older than the twentieth century. The archives at the Central Library would be the best place to start.

As Caroline walked across Chamberlain Square, she imagined how it would have looked in Susannah's day. The Museum and Town Hall would have been well established at that time, but the faded sepia photographs which lined some of the Museum's hidden corridors showed a road used to run through the now pedestrianised space. A severely gothic building had stood where the concrete library now loomed above the top of the square. The Chamberlain memorial fountain would have been in place but there had been less need to exhort passing merry-makers not to enter the water. She smiled as Big Brum, the bell in the clock tower above the Museum, chimed a quarter hour. That sound would have rung out across a very different city a hundred years ago.

When she reached the enquiries desk in the archives room, Caroline was pleased to find Yvonne, a librarian who'd helped her before. 'You'll never guess,' she said, 'I haven't made an appointment and I've all kinds of questions to trouble you with.'

Yvonne smiled. 'You Museum lot treat us as if we're your personal research team. But thank god you're not after yet another family history search. I blame the BBC: everyone's at it since the latest series of that 'Who The Hell Are You?' programme.'

'Don't tell me: everyone's looking for the war hero in their family tree.'

'That, or a link to royalty. Just being Joe Bloggs from Birmingham isn't good enough these days.' Yvonne sighed and gathered up the slips of paper in front of her, tapping them against the desk to form a neat stack. 'So what can I do you for?'

Caroline paused before replying. It was tempting to admit to Yvonne that it was almost family research she was on the trail of; it would give her someone to discuss the possibilities with, but she refrained. 'Suffragettes in Birmingham – what do you know?'

'Funnily enough, you're not the first to ask.'

Caroline froze. Surely Richard Garrold couldn't be investigating Susannah as well. Her voice pitched too high as she said, 'Oh?'

'A girl was in last week looking for information for a school project. Quite sharp, actually. She'll probably end up in your line of work.' As she spoke, Yvonne was tapping at the keys of the computer on her desk. 'Yes, there were three items we got out of store for her, and of course you can look in the newspapers from the time if you give me some dates.' She scribbled the reference numbers for the items on the retrieval slips and passed them to Caroline. 'Sign your life away and I'll get those three things down again.'

Caroline signed in the box and added the Museum initials in lieu of an address. Not Richard on the trail then, a coincidence; but it unsettled her. Perhaps she wasn't cut out to be a detective. Ancient history had never felt as threatening as the recent past was turning out to be. If this were only about work it would be easy to take it less seriously, but Susannah and the troubles in the family had piqued her interest. This was a story she wanted to hear.

She sat down to wait for Yvonne to fetch the items and realised she'd taken the chair Olly had been in when she'd met him in the room a few days before. The ghost of his proximity chased a flush up to her cheeks and reinforced the impression that she was doing something she shouldn't.

She pressed her hands against the cool wooden table top. Sneaking around only encouraged her to behave like a teenager. Any rational adult would just ask for the information she needed to protect her family or advance her career, not keep secrets from colleagues and relatives or flirt with an old flame. It was a relief when Yvonne returned with the books and Caroline was able to concentrate on her research.

The main facts of the struggle to get votes for women were known to her from history lessons at school. Their teacher had not been shy about sharing her feminist agenda and insisted on the moral imperative all women had to use their votes. Her words came back to Caroline every time she approached a ballot box: 'Your sisters fought and suffered to get you that right – how could you live with yourself if you didn't use it?' Caroline knew it was the right thing to do, but it was rare the politician she voted for actually made it into power. She couldn't help wondering if other voters were living in a different world from her own.

She turned the pages of a social history book to find the chapters about women's suffrage. From the middle of the nineteenth century there had been various campaigns to recognise women as equal citizens to men and deserving of the same rights. The book reproduced black and white photographs showing groups of placard-bearing women dressed in high-necked, full-length black dresses and neat hats. Caroline read about the genteel women, from well-to-do families in Edgbaston and other affluent suburbs, who'd been involved in the Birmingham Women's Suffrage Society and wondered if perhaps this was where Susannah fitted in. Their tactics sounded tame though: petitions had been raised, public meetings held. It wasn't the story Caroline hoped to find.

She recalled Beth's words: that Susannah had been an 'interesting' woman, someone Beth admired. That didn't suggest someone who sat passively at meetings or contented herself by collecting signatures on petitions. Susannah surely had a more dramatic story else how would the secrecy surrounding her and the rest of her family be justified?

Chapter Twelve

Caroline told herself she was there for purely practical reasons as she opened the door to Beth's house. Hoping to trick passers-by into assuming the house was occupied rather than empty she attached timer switches to lamps in a few of the downstairs rooms and varied the hours when each would go on and off. After bundling the packaging from the plugs into a black bag, she emptied the rest of the bins and left the dustbin in position for the bin men to collect the following day. She then spent time ensuring each house plant was healthy and not showing signs of neglect in Beth's absence.

Only once she'd completed those tasks, did Caroline let herself slide the cardboard box from under the wardrobe in Beth's bedroom. Even so, her guilty fingers fumbled as she untucked the flaps she'd closed over its contents. Once the box was open though, curiosity and analysis overrode her conscience about snooping.

The hardback book turned out to be Susannah's scrapbook and, as she turned its pages, Caroline knew she'd found the truth of the story. The hard covers were printed with an old-fashioned posy of flowers tied with ribbons against a lacy background. The design was faded and foxed but still provided a marked contrast to the yellowed newspaper cuttings pasted to the thick pages inside. Each article had been neatly clipped out and smoothed into place, and a scan of the headlines showed that the chronological collection reported intensifying activity by suffragettes in Birmingham, from protests to arson attacks.

Caroline closed the scrapbook and tucked it back into the box to read later. Now her thoughts were confirmed, there was no way she could resist looking at the rest of the contents, regardless of what Beth would say. The sturdy cardboard box had once contained tins of soup and would be up to the job of transporting the collection back to her flat. As she lifted it she smiled at the fact that, although the manufacturer was still in business, they'd been through several changes of logo and font for the brand name since their product had been packed in cartons like that one. So much had changed.

She folded the flaps in so they locked over the treasures inside and carried the box down to her car. As she passed she glanced at the watercolours hung in the stairwell and couldn't help grinning. If the other items built on the promise of the scrapbook, Susannah could yet be the star of Caroline's planned exhibition.

Once she arrived at the hospital though, her exuberant mood faded. Beth was awake, but unable to sit up. Her eyes seemed to have grown huge until Caroline realised it was more that her cheeks had hollowed out. Weight had dropped from Beth's body over the last few days. Caroline brushed a gentle kiss on her forehead and took a light hold of her cool, bony hand. 'Oh, Nan,' she said, 'you don't look so good.'

'Don't,' Beth replied, her voice stronger than seemed possible from such a frail body, 'don't talk about it. I've heard nothing but from your mum. Tell me something interesting. What's going on outside this place?'

Caroline shared the latest news headlines and some snippets of celebrity gossip she'd picked up from the radio - which soap star had been arrested for fighting in a nightclub and an actress who continued to deny her looks could be attributed to plastic surgery - but nothing seemed to engage Beth's attention for long. She asked no questions and showed no reaction to the worst of the international news or the most salacious of the rumours. When her supply of conversation ran out, Caroline sat quietly and stroked Beth's hand. While she was desperate to confess to having looked into Susannah's life, the reality of Beth's poor health left her feeling her preoccupations were irrelevant.

After a few silent moments, Beth moved her hand to attract Caroline's attention. 'Will you do something for me?'

'Of course,' Caroline replied. 'What do you need?'

'My solicitor. Her number's in the address book in the hall. Call her and get her to come in to see me.' Beth's voice was steady but her eyelids drooped as she issued the instructions.

Caroline moved her hand to Beth's shoulder. 'Oh Nan, you're not still on about changing your will are you? It really doesn't matter. You mustn't worry about it now.'

'I have to worry about it now. You have to get that woman to come and see me or I risk dying without doing the right thing.'

'You're just having a set back, Nan. You'll be well again and home soon.' Caroline knew her words weren't convincing. There was nothing wrong with Beth's reasoning – she was calm and lucid, yet the possibility remained that she was being misled. They were both going to have to be honest. 'This is about Susannah, isn't it? And Richard Garrold?'

Beth sighed. 'Richard is family and ought to appear in my will, yes.'

'So he has asked you for money then? Nan, are you sure...'

'That house, that house I live in, it belonged to the Farlane family. And you, your mum, Richard and I are all members of that family even though marriage and inheritances split us apart.' Beth took a few shallow breaths before she continued. 'Susannah left the house and

104

its contents to me and Richard's side ended up with the business. It was the generation before mine who broke things up. It's up to me to bring things back together.' Beth closed her eyes firmly and shifted away from Caroline's touch. 'So send me my solicitor, all right?'

Caroline nodded and withdrew her hands into her lap. 'I looked at that box of Susannah's things, Nan. Why did you never tell us about her?'

It was a few moments before Beth replied. 'I suppose she seems like a heroine – the militant suffragette, arrested for standing up for her rights. She was an amazing woman: determined, clever, principled.' Beth turned her head to look Caroline in the eye. 'She tore her family apart, and I won't follow in her footsteps. You'll find her will in that box. Bring it to me next time you come to visit.'

*

Caroline drove home thinking that principles were all very well, but they didn't make for an easy life. Susannah's arrest intrigued her though; the story was getting stronger. She was walking towards her apartment, balancing the box with one arm and searching in her bag for her keys when she realised someone was leaning against her front door.

'Hey, Caz,' Peter said. 'Let me help you.' He took the box from her and grinned.

She raised her eyebrows as she unlocked the door. 'I didn't know you were coming to visit.'

'Flying visit. To see Nan, and, um, I'd rather stay with you tonight if that's OK. Mum called to ask me to visit and seemed to think I'd do all kinds of other things while I was here.'

Caroline closed the door behind them. 'Which you'll be able to avoid if you don't show your face in Harborne?'

'Correct. I will of course spend as long as possible with Nan before I have to head back south tomorrow but, until then, I thought a few hours with my favourite sister would be delightful.

'Your only sister,' Caroline replied, shaking her head. 'I've just been with Nan. She's really not good.'

She cleared the stack of newspapers and discarded letters from utility companies from her dining table for Peter to put the box down, then began to unpack Susannah's possessions before she'd even taken off her coat. First she placed the scrapbook carefully flat on its back. It had been standing upright in the box and the drop when Beth fell must have led to the front cover tearing partly away from the spine. It would need careful handling when she came to read the contents in detail.

'What's all this then?' Peter asked as he returned from flinging his overnight bag into the spare bedroom. 'Bringing work home?' He reached into the box and she slapped his hand away before lifting a pile of letters and cards most of which seemed to be addressed to Susannah.

She glanced at the message on one of the postcards: 'I will send the cake recipe as soon as I am able'. The signature was indecipherable. She turned the card over to see a black and white photograph of a half-timbered building standing near a lake. The caption named it as 'Boathouse and pool, Handsworth Park 1906'.

Peter had moved into the kitchen area and opened the fridge door. He soon slammed it again. 'So, shall we go out for a drink then? Maybe some food, maybe even dancing?'

Caroline ignored him, set the correspondence aside and unpacked a series of small, velvet-covered boxes. At a glance, each contained a medal of some sort, one with an embroidered handkerchief tucked over it. What she was looking for was the will. Everything else was fascinating and she anticipated investigating each object, analysing the reason why it might have been preserved. Teasing out each item's story and the meaning behind it, looking for connections and reasons why these items made the collection rather than anything else was the kind of work she loved. At that moment though, Beth's demands were going to have to come first.

'Caz? A drink?'

'Hmm?' she replied.

Peter returned to her side. 'Seriously, what is this stuff?' He picked up the pile of letters and began to riffle through them.

Caroline grabbed them out of his hands. 'Careful!'

'Well, excuse me!' Peter mockingly held up his hands. 'If this stuff's so valuable perhaps it shouldn't be outside the museum.'

'It doesn't belong to the museum. It belongs to Nan, well, it's stuff that belonged to a great-great-aunt of ours, part of this other side of the family we knew nothing about.'

'Oooh, a family drama. This sounds better than Emmerdale.' He snatched one of the letters and held it out of her reach taking it to the sofa where he flopped full length onto the cushions and began to read.

Caroline continued to shuffle through the papers until she found the will. Two sheets of thick, watermarked paper entitled 'Transcript of the Last Will and Testament of Miss Susannah Garrold, 1944'. She slid onto a chair without pausing to pull it back up to the table and shrugged her coat off as she began to read. The legal language detracted from any character Susannah herself might have expressed and the idiosyncrasies of the typewriter used to produce the transcript made it hard to read. The 'a' key had left only faint impressions on the paper and the black inked ribbon had begun to run dry part way through the document so the type faded towards the bottom of the page. Caroline skimmed through sentences which revoked all former wills, nominated executors and gave disbursements for debts and funeral expenses before she got to the part which read, 'I give and bequeath unto my niece Elizabeth Garrold the freehold property in Edgbaston left to me by my mother in 1918 and the contents therein with the condition that she on her death pass it to her closest female relation.'

Caroline leant back in her chair and wondered if Susannah's lawyer had advised about the wording of her will. Her head filled with questions: how to define the nearest female relation? Was only the house subject to the condition, or the contents as well? Why did lawyers insist on using archaic language and no punctuation?

No wonder Beth was troubled about her own will if she had terms like this hanging over the home which all living members of the family would consider belonged completely to her. If the property was to be passed to a female relative would that mean it couldn't be sold to pay for nursing care should Beth need it, and would the condition be passed on to that next woman in line? Susannah had certainly been determined to make her opinions felt.

She heard the sound of Peter throwing the letter he'd selected aside and turned to him as he sighed, 'Boring! It's just from some dry, old woman to some long dead woman about a meeting they're going to. Trust the skeletons in our closet to be so dull.'

'You have absolutely no idea, do you?'

'None. And I care even less. However, speaking of closets, I haven't had a good night out in Brum since I came out of mine - fancy hitting some bars with me? You might pull.'

'Pull? In a gay bar? I'm not a lesbian you know.'

'No? Well, what I meant to say is: I might pull.'

Caroline exaggerated the irony in her tone. 'Fabulous though that would be to watch, I'll give it a miss, thanks. And anyway, you were never in a closet. I knew you were gay before you did.'

'And I will never forget how supportive my family have been.' He jumped up and crossed the room to hug her. 'So, can I have a shower?'

She brushed him off and wandered into her kitchenette to flick the switch on the kettle and drop a couple of slices of bread into the toaster. She could hear him whistling in the bathroom and frowned, annoyed he was making an event out of visiting his sick grandmother. He had no appreciation of how serious the situation was, but Caroline knew his visit the following day would delight Beth.

She dug around in a drawer until she found a spare key for him to take and wandered back to the dining table to gaze at the words on the transcript of Susannah's will. Being an historian meant she was used to assessing decisions and actions by the standards of the time in which they occurred, not according to her own morals, but this was different. This had resonance in the present day, for her own family.

Her training and practice was to base conclusions on the evidence in front of her. Extrapolation was dangerous; to imply or impute without evidence would be unprofessional. But this was about Beth and Alice. Caroline knew she had to protect them. Susannah's story was fascinating; to an impartial observer that was obvious, but what had Beth meant about the family being torn apart? The link to Farlane's Fasteners and the remaining Garrolds would have to be remade to understand what was going on.

She turned again to the pile of letters and cards and began to categorise them. Anything which appeared from a scan of the opening paragraphs to be about the suffragettes went in one pile; the others were filed in date order. All must have been kept for a reason – the collection was too small to be the remains of life in which nothing was thrown away, so whoever had assembled the collection must have judged each note to have some significance. She wondered who had collated it.

The most recent of the personal letters was dated from November 1943. It regretted to inform Susannah of the death of a woman who must have been one of the suffragettes as the writer continued: 'now only you and I remain from our band of sisters'. Having noted both women's names, Caroline refiled the letter onto the suffragette pile.

A waft of aftershave announced Peter's return to the room and he leant over her shoulder. 'Well, I'll leave you to your exciting evening then.'

'Take a key,' she said. 'And don't wake me when you come in.'

She immediately felt like a dry old woman herself and regretted speaking. The door slammed behind him and she abandoned her systematic review of the documents and turned instead to the one which looked most intriguing.

The address had been typed on a white envelope and the postmark gave the year as 1918. The letter inside was handwritten and Caroline recognised the author immediately. The bold, large letters matched those she'd seen betraying Susannah on the census form: William Garrold. It was a brief letter in which the omissions startled Caroline as much as the content.

'Susannah, You are aware that your mother's will bequeathed you the Farlane house in Edgbaston and that my lawyer has been unable to adequately contest this on the basis that destruction of her father's legacy was not my wife's intention by this gift. If you persist in defying the needs of your family by taking up your inheritance, you may consider that you are as responsible for the destruction of your brother's livelihood as is this war in which he serves and yet you call immoral.

From hereon I must ask you to correspond only with my lawyer and I can assure you that you will not be subject to any further inheritance from your remaining parent.'

Caroline read the letter twice before refolding it so William Garrold's words couldn't shout at her again. Her great-great-grandfather was not a man she could warm to. She'd felt a twinge of sympathy when she'd discovered from the 1911 census that two of his children had died as infants, but reading this evidence that he had disowned his daughter while his son was fighting in World War One left her fuming. To disagree with a daughter's politics was one thing, but to treat her so cruelly when faced with the very real prospect that her brother might not survive the war was beyond comprehension. Caroline shook her head but the words remained loud in her mind.

Of course William's son, Thomas Garrold, had come safely through the war. He'd served in the navy as an engineer before returning to Birmingham. As Beth had told the story to Caroline and Peter in the past, her father had waited until his forties to propose to his childhood sweetheart, so she and her brother had been born to relatively elderly parents. It was one of the few times Caroline heard her mention her brother. She'd assumed he'd died years before and there was nothing more to tell. The terms of Susannah's will had not included a bequest for her nephew either. It seemed there were further family secrets to uncover. Thinking back to Beth's implication that Susannah had not been a heroine, Caroline paused and wondered if stirring up the past was necessarily the right thing to do. Perhaps ignorance really was bliss. As long as Beth was looked after and not taken advantage of, maybe the past should remain under a shroud.

Peter wasn't interested. Their mum was bound to want to maintain the status quo and with Beth ill perhaps this wasn't the best time to be revealing details which had been hidden for so long. Caroline sighed and began to repack the box. The contents were intriguing but not urgent. One of the velvet medal boxes rattled as she lifted it. She eased the lid open to check the contents were secure and found that rather than containing a medal, two large copper old penny coins slid into her hand. Such low denomination coins seemed strange objects to have preserved until she turned one over and saw, stamped in crudely formed letters across the raised image of the King's profile, the words 'Votes for Women'. Surely defacing currency like that was treasonous?

Caroline smiled. The suffragettes might have broken the law but she rather liked their style. The thought of some crusty old man finding the message in his pocket amused her and she looked forward to a full investigation of the collection of suffragette memorabilia when she had more time.

Chapter Thirteen

Once she'd dropped Peter at the hospital, Caroline pulled into Beth's drive to find Olly already there. She parked next to his car and he opened her door for her. 'I could have picked you up on my way,' he said.

'No need, I have other things to do while I'm out,' she replied. 'I'm sure you're busy anyway.' His formal gallantry put her immediately on edge. She fumbled with her bag and the pint of milk she was carrying and dropped her keys which he bent to retrieve.

'This one?' he asked as he shook the bunch to select the correct one for Beth's door.

Caroline nodded but stepped in front of him and swapped him the milk for the keys. She'd added Beth's to her bunch of museum keys and they were too precious for a stranger to handle. 'Let me, there's an alarm.' She felt better for managing to delegate something but by the time she'd silenced the beeping and swept the post from the mat he was already in the living room.

'It was just these pictures out here I thought you could help with,' she said.

He turned slowly away from the sideboard he'd been looking at although she noticed he continued to run a finger over the joints in its construction. Checking for quality, he's on duty, she thought.

'Of course,' he said and joined her at the bottom of the stairs, 'let's take a look.'

She climbed a couple of steps to the first of the watercolours. It showed the Gas Street canal basin although almost unrecognisable from its present day guise. Working boats were moored by factories from which puffs of smoke rose into a clear grey sky. Flashes of colour from the livery on the boat in the foreground toned with red brickwork to bring some warmth to what had obviously been a chilly day. Caroline glanced at Olly, her height advantage on the stairs allowing her to spot that his hairline was receding and the skin around his eyes creased deeply as he scrutinised the picture.

He turned to look at her, and she blushed at being caught staring. 'May I take it down?' he asked and reached for the frame.

Caroline nodded. 'Of course, um, bring it into the kitchen. There's more light there.'

He lifted the picture away from the wall, cradling it with one arm as he reached behind to free the wire from the picture hook. 'How many did you say there were?' he asked and glanced back up the stairs.

'Five, all Birmingham scenes.' Caroline followed him down the stairs and through to the kitchen where he laid the frame on the table and bent over it. He took a magnifying glass from his pocket and used it to study the initials sketched in the bottom right hand corner and the details of the man and horse's features. He then lifted the picture and turned it over to examine the back of the frame where some fragments of what must have been a white label remained.

'It's a shame the label's gone,' Caroline said.

'Too much to hope for,' he replied. 'Can I look at the others?'

She nodded and stepped back to allow him to return to the hall. 'I'll put the kettle on. Tea or coffee?'

His voice was faint as he called, 'Coffee, please.' Down the stairs.

She let the tap run for a moment before filling the kettle. It was promising that he was distracted and hadn't given an opinion yet. If he thought the pictures worthless he'd surely have said so straight away. She prised the lid off the ceramic caddy into which Beth decanted her instant coffee and spooned granules into two floral china mugs from the cupboard above the kettle. Beth's kitchen was laid out for utility but adorned with homely touches such as the row of caddies which matched the crockery and table mats. Not to Caroline's taste, but she was envious of the thought and care Beth had invested in her home.

She waited for the water to go off the boil before pouring it. Olly had been coming in and out of the room and placing the other pictures on the table and she decided to wait until he was ready to speak rather than disturb his thinking.

Eventually all five paintings were gathered and she moved to his side to view them.

'It's a shame there aren't six,' he said.

'Six?'

'Hmm. An even number might make for a more attractive collection.'

'I see.' Caroline chose to interpret this as a positive thing. If the paintings weren't good he couldn't possibly wish to see more of them. She handed him a mug and he smiled as he took it.

'Any particular reason you didn't ask one of your colleagues to look at these for you rather than me? You must know plenty of people with as much, if not more, knowledge of art,' he said. He held the eye contact without blinking.

'Yes, but maybe I don't want everyone at work knowing my nan's business.' She spoke quickly and looked away. She hadn't even considered asking anyone else.

'And she's interested in their value, yes? For insurance or with a view to selling?'

Caroline sipped her drink. 'I don't think she knows what she's got here. I need to tell her that before she makes any decisions.'

Olly nodded. 'OK. Well, if they're not already listed on her insurance, they should be. As for value, well, let's think.' He tapped a finger against his lips as he mused. 'The artist, S.G.? What are your thoughts?'

'I think it's my great-aunt, Susannah Garrold.'

'She was talented and I'd guess trained. We can find that out. The marks on the backs of some of the pictures suggest they were exhibited, which we can also look in to. Without knowing anything more about the artist I'd be cautious and value them at around two hundred each, but the collection together maybe fifteen hundred. Factor that up several times if the artist turns out to be someone.' He looked at Caroline. 'You're disappointed.'

'No. Well, obviously it would be nice if it were more.' Her hopes had faded and the vague plan she'd been formulating about selling the pictures to get rid of Richard Garrold and whatever he was asking Beth for had begun to seem silly. Fifteen hundred minus commission for selling them didn't sound a significant figure. This wasn't going to be a solution.

'I am being very cautious, for now. It could be an awful lot more. We really should try to find out about the artist.'

'When you say 'we'?'

'You don't think you're going to get me off the case now, do you?' He raised his eyebrows and smiled at her. 'And I'd love a proper look at the furniture in the front room while I'm here, if I may?'

*

Caroline was still considering what Olly had told her as she pressed the buzzer on the intercom to Bill's dad's flat. After he'd studied the sideboard in more detail, pulled out its drawers and looked underneath it, he'd asked 'Do you think a receipt for this might still be around?' Provenances again, and a hint it was potentially worth even more than the paintings.

116

She had no idea if Beth was aware her furniture might include valuable antiques as well as hand-me-downs. Concerned about what might or might not be insured, Caroline had double locked the door then opened it again to make sure she'd set the alarm correctly before leaving the house.

The intercom clicked into life and a distorted voice invited her to 'Come on in.' The block of flats catered for the over-55s but without any of the frills funded by management fees at the establishments she'd visited with Alice. There was no warden here, no medical care and no hall carpet. Her footsteps clicked along the lino as she walked towards the sound of a door being opened. Despite her decision that it might be best to leave the past undisturbed, she remained curious about the Garrolds and needed to know more about them to decide how to handle Richard.

'Mr Jones, it's lovely to meet you.' Caroline extended her hand to the small, bald man in the doorway. 'Thanks so much for letting me visit.'

'No, thank you for coming over, and call me Geoff, please. Come in, come in.' He ushered her into his living room.

'I brought you these.' Caroline handed him the pack of chocolate-coated biscuits and sat down in the chair he directed her to.

'A little birdy must have told you they were my favourites. I'll put the kettle on.' He stepped into the kitchen that was no more than an alcove off his tiny living room. This flat would be no more suitable for Beth than any of the others Caroline had seen. It wasn't a disappointment of course. The text Peter had sent from the hospital had expressed his dismay at how ill Beth was and it was becoming increasingly unlikely that she'd be leaving hospital any time soon.

'I think I might be wasting your time, Geoff,' she said, smiling to cover her guilt. 'My nan probably needs somewhere a bit bigger than these flats seem.'

'Never mind, love. We can still have a cuppa and a chat, can't we?'

Caroline decided to be direct. 'Actually, Bill did mention that you and I might have something in common. You used to work at Farlane's, didn't you?'

'Well, I never saw you there!' Geoff brought two mugs of tea through and placed one on top of the pile of folded newspapers on the table in front of her. 'And I was there every day for the best part of forty years.'

'That's impressive, not many people can say they've been with a company that long any more. But no, I never worked there. I think I might be related to the Garrold family. Don't they own it?'

Geoff slurped his tea and nodded. 'Here, let's try these biscuits.' He tore the packet open and offered it to Caroline. 'It was Jim Garrold who took me on as an apprentice and Richard Garrold who gave me my cards. After the downturn in the nineties he just couldn't keep things going. Last I heard from one of my old mates there, it's all but closed.'

'That must feel strange when you worked there for so long.' Caroline nibbled at her biscuit before taking a sip of tea. She held the liquid in her mouth for a moment as she realised it had been heavily sugared. Geoff obviously wasn't used to catering for strangers. She forced herself to swallow.

'All things come to an end, don't they say? Might be good for your relations anyway, Jim Garrold always said the firm brought nothing but trouble to the family. Course he said it as he drove off in his Jaguar.'

Caroline smiled and wished Geoff's son was as good humoured as his dad. It would cheer her own workplace up a bit if he were. 'What do you think he meant by 'trouble'?' She kept her voice light and hoped Geoff would just consider her a gossip. The fact she had a mug in one hand and biscuit in the other helped contain her overwhelming urge to grill him for details and get out a pen to take notes.

'Well he'd had the firm from his dad before him, but he always said it was bad luck. It was a bit awkward you see. They'd managed to expand during the war and I think his dad felt guilty about that. He'd done something in the Navy in World War One and then spent the second war making money. And he died soon after it. They had this sign up by the main door with the managers' names on it. The Garrolds took over from the Farlanes about the turn of the century,' he leant forward to tap Caroline's knee, 'last century. Jim was the third Garrold to have it and that was when he was barely eighteen. He made himself sick over it and passed it to Richard about thirty years ago. And he wasn't best pleased.'

Geoff leant back and drained his mug before selecting another biscuit.

'I'm impressed you remember so much about it,' Caroline said.

'Our Bill's not the only historian.' He winked at her as he pushed the packet towards her. 'And Jim was an odd one. You'd remember the things he said. It was like he was brain-washed about it being a family firm, kept saying 'it's been handed from father to son, father to son...' as if that would keep the orders coming in.'

'I was doing some research into the family,' Caroline said, 'and came across William Garrold's name.'

Bill nodded. 'He was the first of them. Farlanes had it before him. There was some kind of rumour about his son, Thomas, that'd be Jim's dad, how he was forced to carry it on. Made him bitter, then the war profit drove him loopy and Jim was landed with it. Give me a heartless multi-national any day.'

Caroline smiled. 'You must have liked working there though, to stay so long.'

'Yes, me and plenty others. They treated us well enough you see. Not like some other firms. It was as if it wasn't just a family firm, but the firm was the family. Lots of Birmingham companies were like that though, weren't they? Cadburys and the like looking after their employees. Philanthropy and all that.'

It wasn't the impression Caroline had formed from her limited exposure to William Garrold. Philanthropy wasn't a characteristic she'd have attributed to him, based on his letter to his daughter. 'That's interesting,' she said.

Geoff drew a hand across his mouth to wipe away some crumbs. 'I think it was Jim though, he sometimes said his dad wouldn't have liked the way he did things: employing women, giving us more holidays - stuff like that.'

'There weren't any women there before?'

'No, but most of the work was too heavy for a girl. Then Jim made a point of employing some. I don't know who he was making the point to. Himself, probably. Like I said, he was an odd one. So how are you related to them?'

Caroline realised she was still gripping the now-cold tea and put the mug down carefully. 'Oh, some kind of cousins I think. We're not in touch. I stumbled across the name.'

'Well, Richard Garrold's decent enough. Now, would you like another cuppa?'

Caroline leapt up. 'Let me make it,' she said and took the mugs through to the kitchen. As she waited for the kettle to boil she concluded that while Geoff might consider Richard 'decent', she remained convinced of the need to treat him with extreme caution.

Chapter Fourteen

Beth's appearance didn't shock Caroline when she visited the next day. She'd already replaced her mind's-eye stock image of her bustling, vibrant nan with a vision of this prone, shrivelled body. Beth's eyes seemed to reproach Caroline for her thoughts as she sat down beside the bed.

'I'm sorry, Nan. I'd have been here yesterday but I had a few things to do.'

Beth turned her head on the pillow as though the view of the ceiling fascinated her. 'Your day off, wasn't it?'

Caroline nodded; working occasional weekends was a minor inconvenience compared to how useful free days during the week could be, but it was still nice to get both Saturday and Sunday off. It had worked out to have Olly come over on Saturday morning after he'd mentioned the rest of his weekend would be busy as it was his turn to have his children. 'I've done something you might not be pleased about,' she said.

'Oh.'

Beth's voice didn't give away any emotion but that didn't stop Caroline's guilt intensifying. 'Well, perhaps I've done a couple of things…' She told Beth what Olly had said about the paintings, and also admitted she'd looked through the box of Susannah's possessions.

After a pause, during which Beth apparently concluded her study of the ceiling and closed her eyes, she said, 'Tell your man that Susannah went to the Art School. See if that makes any difference.'

'You don't mind me finding out about her then?'

'I won't mind if the pictures turn out to be worth something.'

'But, Nan, they're worth something to you, to us as a family. Would you really want to sell them?'

Beth moved her hand towards Caroline, who leant across the bed to hold it. 'Listen,' Beth said, 'Aunt Susannah was headstrong and difficult, not unlike some other members of my family. But she acted on her principles. So do I. And so do you.' Her hand twitched inside Caroline's grip.

Caroline sighed and looked down at Beth's hand in her own. Lumpy joints and veins protruded against wrinkled skin in painful contrast to her own smooth, warm and stronger-looking hand. 'There were terms in her will which might be a problem. But I called your solicitor and she's going to come in to see you,' she said.

'Make sure your mum's not here at the same time.'

Although aware Beth couldn't see it, Caroline nodded. That wouldn't be an easy thing to arrange. Since Beth's health had worsened, Alice had stopped talking about future living and care arrangements and Caroline had only seen her if they overlapped during their visits to the hospital.

'Do you know anything about the furniture, Nan? Olly seemed to think some of it might be valuable.'

Beth drew in a breath as though hoping to find strength in it. 'Quite likely. Some of it came with the house. Get him to value it.'

Her clipped sentences and weak voice gave away her exhaustion. Caroline wanted to drop the subject, to smooth things over with small talk, to cheer Beth up and make her feel better. Ask what gossip Peter had shared with her. Maybe even share her own gossip that Olly wasn't just an expert but also wasn't quite just a friend. Something about the pallor of Beth's skin and the lack of emotion in her speech made Caroline pause though. She realised there might not be time enough for small talk.

'I don't feel comfortable not telling Mum about this,' she said.

During the pause before Beth answered, a woman in a neighbouring bed began to cough. At first it sounded like throat clearing before escalating into a hacking rattle which shook her body and summoned a passing nurse to take an interest. The curtains were whisked around the woman's bed as the sound subsided.

Beth's closed mouth moved as though she was considering forming words but needed to try them out before committing to the effort of saying them. Finally she said, 'Alice doesn't understand about principles. She'll only think of the money. You know the worth of something isn't just in money, it's in meaning.'

It was a garbled message, but Caroline understood what Beth was telling her. History was worth understanding so the same mistakes weren't made again. Comprehension of that was only one aspect though; acting to protect one's family was also important. 'I'm going to see Richard myself,' she said. 'I need him to convince me that you're doing the right thing, Nan.'

Beth nodded. Her eyes had been closed during most of their conversation and Caroline realised it was time to let her rest.

'My professional opinion is that Susannah's possessions might have historical significance and I wouldn't like to see the collection broken up,' she said. 'But my personal opinion is that I want you to do what you think best, regardless of what anyone else in the family says.' She stroked Beth's arm as she stood then bent to kiss the dry skin stretched tight over her forehead. 'History doesn't matter that much. Not compared to the present.'

'Or the future,' Beth murmured.

*

First thing on Monday morning, Caroline paused before she went into the museum and tried again to call Richard. After watching Beth sleep through most of the time she'd been at the hospital the day before, she saw that Peter and Alice weren't overreacting with their concern. She tapped on her phone's screen and dialled Richard's number from her Contacts list. It rang five times before a woman's voice answered, 'Richard Garrold's phone. Can I help you?'

The voice sounded young, and Caroline paused before speaking, suspicious that Richard might have persuaded a child to play at impersonating his secretary. 'May I speak to him, please?' she said.

'I'm afraid he's not available at the moment, can I take a message?' The singsong voice didn't falter. If it was a set-up, Richard had rehearsed the girl well; she sounded very business-like. Caroline stated her name and was immediately interrupted. 'Oh, Miss Hipkins, he did say that if you called he'd like to arrange a meeting. Are you free to come by the office any time tomorrow?'

*

Back at home that evening, Caroline sat at her dining table to review Susannah's scrapbook and the cuttings it contained. She turned to a fresh page in her spiral-bound notebook and clicked the top of a propelling pencil to ensure a sharp point for clear note taking. This was the kind of activity she felt confident with: dates, facts, and evidence. While the newspaper reports were bound to have put some sort of political slant on the stories they told, Caroline didn't expect the experience of reading them to trouble her emotionally.

She'd never researched into topics or people she felt a connection to before though. As she read the reports Susannah had collected, Caroline began to imagine how it must have felt to be involved. The earliest cutting came from the Birmingham Gazette in 1909 when Susannah couldn't have been much more than eighteen years old. It related the disruption to a meeting in Birmingham at which the Prime Minister was speaking. Some women had thrown stones while others climbed on the roof and dropped slates. The reporter seemed scandalised at the unladylike behaviour, his disapproval was evident as he recorded that the women 'misguidedly screamed their motto 'Deeds, not words' at the assembled crowd'. Ten women had been arrested.

Caroline smiled; like the defaced coins, committing minor damage to property seemed worth it to make their point. These 'deeds' were victimless crimes compared to the oppression of half the population, denying them a voice. Susannah would have been living with her parents when she'd read and been inspired by this report. No doubt William Garrold didn't encourage political debate around the family dinner table. Turning to the notes she'd made at the library, Caroline cross-referenced the dates. The Birmingham Women's Suffrage Society was well-established, but the more militant Women's Social and Political Union who were known as the 'suffragettes' set up branches in the city from 1907. Interrupting the Prime Minister was probably their first high-profile activity in Birmingham, perhaps the first time Susannah might have heard of them.

As Caroline turned the pages of the scrapbook she found that not all the clippings were from newspapers. Some were from what must have been pamphlets or newsletters – cheap reproductions on flimsy paper. There were adverts for jewellery and hat bands in white, purple and green – the colours of the movement, notices for meetings at which prominent figures would speak in support of women's rights, and intriguingly a notice requesting members to submit recipes for publication in the 'Women's Suffrage Cookery Book'. The recipes were to be sent to Miss S Garrold and the book to be produced by the Birmingham Women's Suffrage Society. Caroline noted the dates. It was proof Susannah hadn't always been allied with the militant wing of the movement.

She shuffled through the correspondence to retrieve the postcard with the photo of Handsworth Park boat house and checked the message. The recipe referred to must have been for the cookbook. She annotated her notes, turned the page in the scrapbook and gasped. The next page held a clipping from the Birmingham Gazette with the headline 'Boat house blaze'. It reported that the boat house had been set alight and suffragette pamphlets found nearby. 'There is no end to the insane antics of these outragettes,' the reporter fumed.

Looking again at the card, Caroline read the post script she'd previously ignored. 'You MUST join us.' It appeared Susannah had started out as a moderate and perhaps been persuaded that the campaign would not succeed without direct action.

The next cutting confirmed that her mind had been altered. Small acts such as disobeying the census requirements hadn't been enough for Susannah. Caroline found she was holding her breath as she read the next report. It listed Susannah's name among the women arrested and taken to Winson Green prison following what were described as 'acts of sacrilegious vandalism' at Birmingham Cathedral. The date fitted with that of the letter informing Susannah she'd been dismissed by her employers. Caroline knew what had happened to suffragettes incarcerated at Winson Green. They'd gone on hunger strike in protest at being treated as criminals rather than political prisoners. They'd been brutally force fed. Many had suffered lasting physical effects.

Overcome by a mix of horror and pride that her great-great-aunt felt so strongly she'd risk her health and reputation in this way, Caroline sat back and pressed a hand to her mouth. It was humbling. At a time when other women of a similar class were at home undertaking 'improving' activities such as embroidering table linen, Susannah had been on the front line of political protest. Caroline couldn't help wondering if, were she in Susannah's place, she would have acted so bravely. She hoped she would, but had to swallow her discomfort that actions such as daubing graffiti on the cathedral and committing arson were getting more aggressive and violent. She had to admit that, had she been there, she'd probably have stopped at the cookbook and not progressed to setting fires.

There was one final page in the scrapbook. Even before she began to read, the words 'Birmingham Museum and Art Gallery' registered in Caroline's peripheral vision. She had to force herself to go back to the top of the cutting to read the short article through in order. It told of the events of the 8th of June, 1914 when an unnamed suffragette had attended the gallery, appeared to admire an oil painting, then took an axe she had hidden inside her clothes and slashed an incision across the canvas. Caroline gasped.

She stood and grabbed the other piles of Susannah's papers, searching for anything dated later than that last newspaper cutting. The carefully arranged piles of letters and documents slid into a haphazard patchwork covering the table, but there was nothing there, nothing to confirm to Caroline that it couldn't have been Susannah who slashed the painting. Desecrating the Cathedral was serious enough, but Caroline didn't want to believe that her talented, passionate relative could have gone so far as to destroy a fellow artist's work.

The picture involved wasn't named. Caroline had no way of knowing until she got back to work and could look through their records whether it was chosen deliberately because the subject matter was offensive, or if there had been intent to upset the artist. Her earlier research suggested the targets of the suffragette's actions were usually chosen not only for their ability to make headline news, but also to hit at establishments most opposed to the cause. An attack on the museum had certainly been high profile but Caroline couldn't help her reaction. Reading that last report made her queasy and she stepped away from the table leaving the papers in a mess and unprotected.

The women's actions had gone too far. It had become personal.

Chapter Fifteen

Caroline yawned as she descended steps to the canal towpath for the quickest route to Hockley. She'd gone to bed physically exhausted then lain awake unable to sleep as her mind worked through what her response to Susannah's actions meant. It was hard enough to empathise with decisions others made in the present day, without also expecting to understand why someone in the past acted the way they did. As a school girl, Caroline had imagined she felt so strongly about women's rights she would have stood alongside the suffragettes had the choice been hers. But the reality of their actions revealed at least one of them had taken a step Caroline herself would have refused.

It implied she lacked both courage and conviction, but then, the easy option had always been her preferred choice. Her footsteps clicked against the laid brick path as she counted off the recent occasions on which she'd decided not to speak out, let alone take action. There was her lack of resistance in the face of requests from Alice, her reluctance to challenge Bill about his behaviour at work, and, most shocking perhaps, her decision to let her marriage go rather than take a risk. She frowned. Disappointing other people was one thing, being a disappointment to yourself was rather more serious.

In a brighter mood she might have heard an echo in her footsteps of the ring of horseshoes which would once have sounded on the path as barges were heaved along the canal. That morning though, the click of her smart, hard-soled shoes reminded her she'd chosen her outfit as armour in the hope it would protect her from whatever she might find at the Farlane factory.

The brick path became broken and finally gave way to mud as she got further from the city centre and into what had once been a thriving industrial area. Some of the buildings looked to be occupied by newer, lighter industries judging from the signage – internet sales, media and even a gym. Others still leaked the clangs and metallic hammering of manufacturing, although the smoke which had blackened the brickwork no longer belched from chimneys.

She'd asked to meet Richard early so she could arrive at work late, but not so late it would attract comment. As she climbed up from the canal to street level and found the entrance to the factory it seemed that not many Farlane's staff had arrived yet either. She rang the bell and seconds later a harsh buzz let her know that the door would open if she pushed. Inside Caroline was distracted by the wooden board Geoff had mentioned. The managing directors' names were inked in gold lettering at the top of a mahogany panel which had been designed for longevity. Richard Garrold's name was at the end of the list, but over half the board remained blank.

'I don't think there'll be names to fill the space now.'

Caroline turned and found Richard had joined her in the hallway. She held out her hand, keen to be civil if not actually friendly. 'Hi, it's good to see you again.'

'Your message worried me. How is Aunt Beth?' Richard held on to her hand and kept eye contact, a sincere frown wrinkled his forehead.

'I'm afraid the news isn't good. She had a blood clot and...'

Richard interrupted her. 'But surely they gave her blood thinning drugs, had her in compression stockings? Why weren't they checking for it?'

Caroline took a step back, surprised by his vehemence. 'Yes, but it still happened. No-one's to blame.'

Richard shook his head and asked, 'How is she now?'

'Still weak. I'm worried, to be honest.'

'I see. That's bad news.'

Richard led the way into his office past filing cabinets and a desk where a secretary might sit. As she sat down, Caroline looked around and registered the atmosphere of decay which hung over the room. A bulky computer monitor took up half Richard's desk and a glass fronted bookcase held lever arch files whose spines listed dates from the 1980s onwards. Even the museum was more up to date than this.

'I'm sorry I've missed your calls. I've been busy in meetings – shuttling between my bank manager and accountants.' Richard's leather chair creaked as he sat down and smoothed his palms over a manila folder on his desk. 'I've been unsure whether it would be appropriate for me to visit Aunt Beth.'

'She isn't really up to chatting at the moment so it might be best to wait,' Caroline said. She didn't add that Beth had implied that she didn't want Alice to get to know about Richard's existence. 'Um, could I ask why it is you've got in touch with her now?'

Richard nodded, but didn't reply immediately. He opened the folder, looked at what was inside, then slid it across the desk towards Caroline. 'I pulled out some information for you. I thought you might like the details.'

Caroline hesitated before taking the file. She could see it was thick with papers but knew she needed to resist getting drawn into a research project, tempting though it was. 'Perhaps you could tell me the highlights?' she said.

'This firm was founded by George Farlane in 1872. It grew quickly and he took William Garrold on as an assistant. William met Annie, George's daughter and married her – either for love or because he saw the firm's prospects and wanted to get on board, who knows? Of course George promoted his new son-in-law and made him Managing Director when he retired as well as leaving him the firm when he died. He didn't have any sons of his own. Annie was a favourite though and he left her the house he'd had built in Edgbaston – the house Aunt Beth lives in now.'

Caroline nodded. 'I see.' So far this hadn't added much to the information Geoff had supplied.

'William and Annie had two children – a son, Thomas and a daughter, Susannah.'

'I've heard about Susannah,' Caroline said, 'and found out a little about William. I gather they weren't close.' She glanced at the wall behind Richard's desk where a strange work of art hung. It was formed of bolts and screws in all sizes arranged in an almost floral pattern around the company name and she wondered why William Garrold hadn't been tempted to rechristen the firm after himself.

Richard shook his head. 'Thomas, my grandad, didn't help matters. He also had a son and a daughter, my dad and Aunt Beth. And he repeated what his father had done and passed the only asset the family had – this firm – solely to his son. Aunt Beth was expected to marry for her living. It wasn't something my dad, James, ever felt comfortable about.'

'Not so uncomfortable as to change things though?'

'Well no. The thing is, you see, my great-aunt Susannah had done that for him. She'd inherited the Farlane house from her mother and passed it to Aunt Beth. So the house stayed with the women, the factory with the men.'

Caroline picked up the file and flicked through the contents. None of the photocopies of title deeds, company accounts and wills caught her attention. She decided to assume it was the evidence which would corroborate Richard's story. 'That sounds almost fair; I mean it was George Farlane who made the family some money in the first place and then the assets were shared between his grandchildren.'

'The values were never equal though, which led to some friction. Property prices have increased of course and Aunt Beth's house must be worth more than George Farlane could ever have imagined. But the firm boomed. William Garrold turned the machinery over to munitions in the First World War and made a lot of money by so doing.'

Caroline guessed that might not have sat comfortably with Susannah's politics. It would have been another cause for argument between herself and her father. The outbreak of war was one of those times when principles needed to be compromised though. She gazed down at the final page in the file. The headed paper showcased the Farlane's name in decorative script across the top of the page and in smaller print below it read 'Est. 1872. Birmingham.' There was an elegant simplicity and confidence in those facts. It was a shame everything else had become muddled.

Richard went on, 'He needed to raise capital to expand and had hoped to sell the house after his wife died in 1917. But the deeds to the house were in her name and she left the house directly to Susannah.'

'I know.' Caroline nodded. 'But these decisions were made the best part of a hundred years ago. We can't presume to know what anyone intended.'

'Look, the thing is, this is all about the past. The firm expanded in the twentieth century but it's failing in the twenty-first. My order books are empty and I've had to let most of the staff go. I had a temp in yesterday to help get some papers in order, but couldn't even afford her for more than one day.' He shook his head as though bewildered at what had happened.

Caroline shifted in her seat. Here comes the sob story, she thought. 'Don't tell me,' she said, 'you need capital and the thought of the house crossed your mind.' Her voice was brittle. She wasn't surprised kind-hearted Beth had given in to Richard's persuasion but she knew history had to be interpreted with care.

Richard stood and came around the desk to stand by her side. 'You've misunderstood, although I don't blame you for being suspicious. Aunt Beth offered to help, but the firm can't be saved. We went into administration yesterday.'

'Oh. I'm sorry to hear that.'

'The world's changed; it can't be helped. But there's something else, which is what I was actually talking to Aunt Beth about.'

Caroline turned to watch as he walked away from her towards the back of the office where he stopped and looked up at the large oil painting hanging there. She stared at the picture. It showed the Farlane's factory in its heyday with workers bustling about and canal boats drawn up outside and, for a moment, she forgot to breathe.

*

As the bus carried her back to the city centre, Caroline gazed out the window. The red-brick buildings and hand painted signs on the small firms of Hockley were replaced by the premises of household names with plate glass windows, slick lighting and corporate branding. The short walk from the bus stop in the heart of the financial district back to the museum didn't give her enough time to think or adjust.

'Afternoon,' Denise said as Caroline walked into their office.

Caroline shrugged. While they worked flexitime, this was the first time she'd arrived so close to ten o'clock, but it was something Denise made a habit. Bill also looked up and raised an eyebrow at her but didn't pass comment.

Denise held out a slip of paper on which she'd scrawled two messages. 'So good of you to arrive before I had to tell the next person who rang that I am not your secretary,' she said.

'Thanks. And sorry. I got held up, family stuff, you know,' Caroline replied.

Denise's tone changed instantly. 'Oh, not your Nan? How is she?'

Caroline looked straight up from the note. 'Oh, um, no better really.' She sat down and swallowed the guilt created by Denise's concern. Her visit to the factory was with the intent to protect Beth's interests after all.

A glance at the phone messages didn't soothe her. One was from Olly, who asked her to call back, and the other was from someone called Phil, who'd left a mobile phone number. 'Any idea who 'Phil' was?' she asked Denise.

'Nope. Brummie accent, asked for you by name, didn't want to say anything more to me.'

'OK. Thanks.'

She pressed the power switch on her computer and checked the details she'd noted down the night before as she waited for the machine to request her password. Once she'd logged in she searched on the date of the suffragette attack in the museum's filing system. A brief entry about damage to a picture which had been on loan from a private collection came up. The artist's name was George Romney and the picture was described as 'Oil painting of Master Thornhill'. She ran an internet search on those details and stared in surprise when it returned a result.

She clicked through to a site which held images of thousands of paintings and scrolled quickly through those attributed to George Romney until the right painting came into view. It was a typical nineteenth century portrait in oils. The boy was shown leaning against a rock behind which an idealised backdrop of trees and sky had been hinted. He was shown full-length to display the fine clothes he wore – a frilled collar, white stockings and a chocolate-coloured suit whose lustrous fabric and ornamental buttons the artist had caught to perfection. He was clearly a member of the upper classes, painted to be admired, as was the artist's skill. The boy's languid eyes and smug pursing of his lips were enough to make

Caroline dislike the picture. His arrogant pose conveyed contempt for the observer.

The website listed the current owner as a gallery in America so the painting had survived the attack, but the nature of the protest still appalled Caroline. She needed to know who'd done it because, if it had been Susannah, it would be difficult to accept. There'd been no indication from her papers whether Susannah stopped adding items to the scrapbook because she'd arrested for committing the crime, ended her involvement with the suffragettes because she also felt they'd gone too far, or if it was just that World War One started just over a month later and other priorities intervened.

The museum's electronic record revealed no further details and Caroline shoved her mouse away in frustration.

'Where could I look up full records of old exhibitions?' she asked Denise.

'How old?'

'About a hundred years.'

Denise frowned. 'Well, you know all those filing cabinets in the corridor? They're full of old papers but I'd have no idea where you should start. There's a lot of old records over at the archives in the library too. You might find something there I suppose.'

'Thanks,' Caroline grabbed her notebook and put her jacket back on. 'Then that's where I'm going.'

Bill looked up. 'Hang on,' he said, 'I was planning a visit myself. I'll come with you. Might as well before they move everything to the new building and we've further to walk.'

Caroline drummed her fingertips against the cover of her notebook while Bill searched his desk for the papers he needed. It wasn't ideal to have his company when the trip wasn't entirely on museum business. On the other hand, a male perspective on the incident might be interesting.

'I'm following up the story of a painting that was damaged by a suffragette in our galleries,' she said as they left the museum and walked towards the library.

Bill nodded. 'I've heard about that. Not one of our pictures though, was it?'

'No, it was on loan.' Caroline fiddled with the strap of her handbag. 'Do you think it was a step too far?'

'As a political protest, you mean?' Bill was quiet as he thought. 'Well, I don't know. I suppose they felt they needed to do something dramatic to get attention. It's an interesting philosophical question: when is it ethical to break the law?' His tone was offhand, not shocked.

Caroline had to slow her pace to match his. Her impatience to get to the archives made her want to run. 'Imagine it happened today - say someone came into the museum and trashed our Staffordshire Hoard displays to protest about government cuts or something.'

Bill shook his head. 'I'd be devastated. The public would be appalled. It wouldn't be a good way to go about making your point.'

Caroline looked at the other pedestrians around them: young mums pushing buggies, elderly couples and a group of Asian youths. Would they be appalled? It was true the public appeal to collect funds to keep the Hoard in the West Midlands had been hugely successful - obviously people cared about their history and valued their treasures - but one oil painting? Would the public reaction to that match her own distaste?

As they stepped onto the escalator in the library Caroline asked, 'Don't suppose you know the name of the woman who did it?'

'The suffragette?'

Caroline nodded.

'No. It'll probably be mentioned in the records. Or the newspapers from the following day perhaps. I guess she was arrested,' Bill said.

'Yes. Of course.' Caroline stuffed her hands into the pockets of her jacket and tried to walk at a normal speed towards the duty librarian's desk. She cut short his pleasantries.

'I need to check something in the museum minute books, please,' she said and grabbed a request form to scribble down the details, 'and these newspapers.'

'OK, OK, there's no hurry. They're not going to change in the time it'll take me to get them,' the man replied. 'Take a seat, why don't you?'

She couldn't and instead paced the carpet between the desks and shelves, which earned her a loud 'tut' from a woman who'd covered the surface of a nearby desk with old maps and a puzzled glance from Bill as he completed his own request form. Caroline stopped walking and returned to loiter by the librarian's desk to wait. She pulled out her phone and repeated the internet search which had found the picture.

She raised the phone in front of her face, trying to imagine the painting hung on a gallery wall before her. Disliking a work of art was one thing, daring to damage it was quite another. She felt Bill hovering by her shoulder, also studying the painting.

'Is that it?' he asked. 'The one that was damaged?'

'Yes. What do you think?'

He took the phone and tilted the screen to see the image without reflections. 'Well, it's not really my kind of thing. I wouldn't give it wall space.'

'Could you have damaged it though? Could you have reached out and slashed the canvas?' Even to her own ears Caroline's voice sounded strangled.

Bill handed the phone back and opened his mouth to reply but they were interrupted.

'Here you go.' The voice startled her and she turned to find the librarian had returned with the bound volumes she'd requested.

138

'Thank you.' She carried the heavy books to a nearby table.

She started with the minutes from meetings at the museum. The pages gave off a musty scent and seemed to crackle as she turned them in search of the record she needed. Eventually she found the date and ran her finger down the typewritten text on yellowed paper to scan for references to the incident. The brief entry began with a description of what had happened which added nothing to her knowledge and went on to confirm that nothing could have been done to prevent the attack. As she turned the page though, it was heavier than the previous ones because a photograph had been pasted to the reverse. The picture was of the bottom of the painting, the positioning of the boy's legs carelessly crossed at the ankle were recognisable from the image she'd just seen online. Unlike the online image though, this picture showed three clean cuts slashed into the canvas, one of which bisected the boy's calf. Caroline squinted, seeing the damage inflicted didn't revolt her as much as she'd expected. She reached for her phone and held the two images next to each other. The online reproduction was less sharp than the old photograph, but its colours were bright. The painting had been fully restored. There were no obvious scars.

Caroline sat back and regarded the pictures. She imagined herself in the gallery, standing before the intact canvas and daring to raise a blade to damage it. She swallowed hard. It was no good. There was no way she could have done it. It would have felt like attacking the child himself.

'Why this picture do you think?' she asked as Bill joined her at the table with the file the archivist had retrieved for him.

He looked over, scanned the page and shrugged. 'I don't like the picture, but I can't see anything offensive about it.'

Caroline considered. 'I suppose it could have been an attack on patriarchal, privileged society. A challenge to the assumption that boys like this could confidently expect to inherit the power their fathers held, while women were silenced. Yeah, that would be enough to make any woman angry.'

Bill shook his head and sighed. 'You women do like to overreact.' He tapped the facing page of the minute book which recorded the next meeting. 'It says here the damage cost £50 to repair. That was a lot of money in those days.'

Caroline glared at him and moved away slightly. Looking back at the report, she took a slow, deep breath and ran a fingertip over each of the three slash marks in the photo, then shuddered. She almost expected to see blood drip down the child's white stockings. Her modern sensibilities would not allow her to accept the idea of such wanton damage to a work of art. All her training as a curator was to protect, to preserve. This was more than a political act. It was vandalism.

She stood and reached for the bound volumes of newspapers and turned the broadsheet pages over in chunks until she got close to the date of the incident. Then she turned each thin page individually, checking every headline until she found a longer article from a later date than the one Susannah had preserved. Holding her breath, she read the opening paragraphs which reported horror at the fact the museum and gallery would remain closed for six weeks in response to a scandalous event. Frustrated by the reporter's outrage and obtuse language, Caroline scanned the report to see if Susannah's name was included. She reached the end of the article and exhaled. That name was not there.

She returned to the top of the column and forced herself to read it slowly. A lone woman, the 'known suffragist' Bertha Ryland, had entered the gallery and stood calmly before the painting before reaching into her 'outfit' to retrieve a blade with which she inflicted gross damage upon the work. Other visitors had restrained her until the room attendant took control of the situation and led her away. Caroline was used to the impartiality of reporting by the BBC or the liberal approach of the newspapers she chose to read. The tone and style of this reporter's piece offended her almost as much as the slashed canvas.

The report focussed on Miss Ryland's actions, barely mentioning her motivation. As a means of spreading the message, perhaps the action hadn't been entirely successful. A letter to the editor had been printed below the journalist's report which suggested that "ladies should change into special light costumes like bathing costumes when they wanted to look at pictures".

'Ridiculous,' Caroline muttered and pushed the newspaper away. The child portrayed was innocent perhaps, but his family who'd dressed him for display and paid an artist to immortalise him were not. The history of their wealth would be bound to reveal unsavoury details of exploitation which the society of the time would have happily ignored. Her own instinct to defend an artist's moral right not to have his work interfered with began to seem an affectation compared to human rights. What was one unremarkable portrait out of thousands compared with giving a voice to millions?

The protest wasn't as high profile as the defacing of the Rokeby Venus at the National Gallery which she'd heard about before. She knew that picture was a national icon having been the subject of an appeal to save it for the nation, and was attacked because of its portrayal of women as passive. But this happened in Birmingham, to a less important picture; the incident had probably gone unreported in the national press. It was slightly more surprising it wasn't discussed more at the museum, but then security was tight these days and the likelihood of a political protest at the gallery reduced.

Bill had finished with his own documents and leant over to read the article she'd found. 'Well, it's not an impartial report, is it? What are you looking for?' he asked.

'I wanted to know who it was,' Caroline said. 'I wanted to understand how angry that woman must have been to have done it.'

'I see. Sometimes even recent history feels a very long time ago, doesn't it? Hmm, Bertha Ryland. I bet she was related to the Mrs Ryland who ran a campaign in the 1880s to make the art works in the museum more accessible to the masses. I've read some reports on that.'

'Bertha's actions can't have gone down well at home then.' Caroline scribbled a note to look the details up; it seemed the Garrolds weren't the only Birmingham family affected by the politics of women's suffrage.

'I wonder if they were any relation to Louisa?'

Caroline straightened up. 'Of course! That's why the name rang a bell. Louisa Ryland's the one who gave the land for Cannon Hill Park, isn't she?'

'Among other philanthropic gestures,' Bill said. 'She's one of my dad's favourite figures from local history.'

Caroline nodded, gathered up the materials she'd used and returned them to the librarian. She'd written an essay on Louisa Ryland for her History GCSE. Louisa's father must have been among the same set of wealthy Victorian industrialists as the Farlanes and Louisa inherited millions which she'd put to good use. She'd acted on admirable principles, much as Bertha Ryland did, but her methods were very different. These Ryland women might turn out not to be related to each other - it was a common enough name that there'd been one of them in Caroline's own school year - but they made an interesting contrast.

'All done then?' Bill asked as he stacked his own papers.

Caroline nodded and began to walk towards the exit. There was no question in her mind that if she believed something needed to be changed she'd step up and do something. How far she'd go was another matter and she felt tension drop from her shoulders with the relief that it hadn't been Susannah who slashed the painting.

'Anyway, there was all the trouble in Ulster at the same time, wasn't there? And rumblings in Europe.' Bill was puffing as he spoke from the slight exertion of rushing to catch up with her. 'The suffragettes didn't pick their timing very well.'

Caroline stopped, forcing Bill to turn and look at her as she said, 'What, you think they should have waited until it was convenient before having their say? You think they should have waited their turn?'

'Calm down. I'm only saying it wasn't ideal, was it?'

'Nothing's ideal, Bill. Nothing.'

*

Back at her desk, Caroline returned the calls she'd missed. First she called Olly.

'How's Beth?' he asked.

She paused before replying, but knew she couldn't start questioning everyone's motives. 'No better, I'm afraid. She did tell me that Susannah trained at Birmingham Art School though.'

'Ah, yes, that was why I'd called. I managed to ferret out a reference to her exhibiting some work. I know the archivist at the Art School and wondered if you'd like an introduction? We could go along and see what records they've got.'

Caroline thanked him and he agreed to call back once he'd arranged the meeting. She pressed the button to end the call before dialling the mobile number Denise had written down for Phil.

'Who's this?'

The abrupt method of answering startled her, but she decided to plough on politely. 'Hello, my name's Caroline Hipkins, from the museum. You called me earlier?'

'Yeah. Hold on.' There was a cracking sound as the man must have put his hand over the phone but Caroline could still hear him moving and a door being closed. 'It's me, the bloke who found the thing.'

She smiled; such a vague description could only be one person. 'Of course, how can I help you?'

'I want to talk.'

Chapter Sixteen

As she waited by the steep steps of the Art School's entrance for Olly to arrive, Caroline admired the building's ornate brickwork and tiled frieze. Unlike the classical design used in the smooth stone construction of the Museum and Art Gallery across the road, this building advertised its Victorian origins. It was more beautiful, she thought, and sadly lost from public view by being hidden in a side street. Ahead of her, a pair of carved wooden doors blocked the arched entrance while decorative stonework lined the walls of the stairwell. She climbed half way up the steps to read the gold lettering on a commemorative panel set into a recess.

It stated the building had been erected in 1884 using funds and land donated by some eminent industrialists and Louisa Ryland. Caroline smiled. The list didn't include either of the names Farlane or Garrold and she wasn't surprised the fashion for philanthropy had passed her relatives by. Benevolence was not a characteristic she'd associate with William Garrold.

The pressure of Olly's hand on her arm made her jump. 'What are you smiling at?' he asked as he bent to kiss her cheek.

'Oh, nothing really. Thank you for coming up from Stratford again, and for setting this meeting up so soon. You really didn't need to.'

'Always worth it to see you.' He smiled and squeezed the arm he hadn't let go. 'Shall we?'

Caroline pulled back and walked quickly up the remaining steps to put some distance between them. The weight of the door delayed her though and he was right behind her again as they entered the building's foyer.

Olly paused to ask for directions at a wooden reception desk, while Caroline moved forward into an open hall which enhanced the cathedral-like feel of the building. Although the walls were practical bare brick, the arched ceiling was supported by marble columns with carved stone arches stretching between them. Modern sculptures, obviously work by current students, were placed where a more sacred building would display religious statues, or other symbols. She paused to look around before following Olly across the mosaic-tiled floor.

'What a lovely building,' she said.

'Is this your first visit? I'm surprised.'

Caroline shrugged. While the Art School stood right next door to the museum she'd never had cause to think about it before. 'Neither the present nor the future are my field, are they? I'm not that interested in what today's art students are doing.' She tipped her head and grimaced towards a picture in which a fantasy landscape had been constructed using images torn from magazines. Olly smiled back.

'Let's hope Susannah's work is more to our taste,' he said.

As she followed him into the dark stairwell and placed a hand on the wooden bannisters to climb the stairs Caroline felt a connection with Susannah she hadn't experienced before. Although she'd been through the box of Susannah's possessions and spent hours in Susannah's home, knowing she'd also climbed these stairs made her seem more real. Caroline looked down at her feet. The staircase was made of iron and faced with wooden treads cut with deep grooves to ensure a non-slip surface. On the edge of each step, the metal was embossed with the words 'Hawkesleys Patent Step'. The only thing which had changed since Susannah had used the stairs was a few more layers of varnish on the wood.

'Everything OK?' Olly asked from the landing.

Caroline nodded and hurried to join him.

Away from the ecclesiastical design of the main entrance, the building was more functional. They walked along bare floorboards and glanced into white-washed studios where windows were set high in the walls to allow natural light to illuminate the rooms. In one, students in paint-flecked overalls were constructing a strange installation from strips of carpet and bicycle wheels.

'Here she is,' Olly said as he knocked at the door labelled 'Archives'.

He opened the door to a room in which the floor space was restricted by the number of filing cabinets, bookshelves and tables on which portfolios were stacked. Caroline breathed in the familiar, dry scent of the past, such a contrast to the rest of the building where fresh paint, chemicals and the waft of coffee aroma hung in the air.

'Thanks so much for seeing us,' she said as she shook hands with the archivist, a woman Olly introduced as Evelyn.

'No problem at all. To be honest, it was a treat for me to look at Susannah's work. Shall I show you?' Evelyn turned to one of the tables and opened a portfolio. Caroline and Olly drew closer to look as she moved a sheet of tissue paper to reveal a page of drawings, some coloured in watercolour. 'She submitted this for an exam,' Evelyn said, 'and was awarded a distinction.'

The drawings were nature studies: leaves, feathers and butterflies. Each was an exquisite miniature, life-like in proportion and colouring, fantastical in juxtaposition with the neighbouring item. 'May I?' Caroline asked, picking up a pair of cotton gloves Evelyn had left on the table.

Evelyn nodded and Caroline moved the sheet of drawings and lifted the next layer of tissue to reveal the page below. The tissue paper rustled in her hands and she realised how much she was shaking.

'Well, well,' Olly said, 'now that is interesting.'

The picture Caroline had uncovered was a watercolour scene. It appeared to have the same dimensions as the framed pictures from Beth's hallway. Caroline blinked a few times and looked closely. The subject matter matched exactly that of the picture she'd seen in Richard's office. She couldn't speak.

'The missing link?' Olly said.

Caroline licked her lips and nodded. 'In more ways than one.'

She ignored the questioning glance on Olly's face and turned to Evelyn. 'Can you tell us anything in particular about Susannah's time here?'

'Of course.' Evelyn pushed the portfolio aside and placed a handwritten ledger in front of Caroline. 'Here, you can see the record of Susannah's registration and,' she turned a chunk of pages to a marker inserted deeper in the book, 'here it shows her final marks.'

Caroline smiled to see that Susannah had passed her course and noted the date was immediately prior to the first record of Susannah's involvement with the Suffragettes. 'Would the students here have been politically active, do you think?' she asked.

'No, that's something which has really changed,' Evelyn said. 'Students today might be known for radical views and pushing boundaries, but it certainly wasn't like that when Susannah was here. The Art School was founded to provide training for designers who'd go on to work in the local industries. Many of them were here on a sort of day release from their jobs in manufacturing.'

'Not Susannah though?'

Evelyn smiled. 'No, the School also catered for middle-class ladies taking classes for leisure. They wouldn't have mixed with the industrial students; they were just a useful extra source of income. You're related to her, aren't you?'

Caroline nodded.

'You should see this.' Evelyn turned and took a slim, red leather covered box from the desk behind her. It looked similar to one from the box of Susannah's possessions, but this one was stamped in gilt letters 'Board of Education. South Kensington'. 'Susannah may have been here only for interest rather than career purposes, but she was one of the most talented students in her year.'

Caroline took the box and opened the lid, pushing against the stiffness of the hinge to reveal a medal set in a blue velvet-lined recess. She rubbed a gloved finger across its face and traced the embossed laurel crest encircling the stamped words: 'National medal for success in certificate awarded by the Board of Education'. Olly leant over her shoulder to see. 'And what were those awarded for?' he asked.

'That's a bronze medal and they tended to award them for outstanding performance in some aspect of art or craft. Read the back.'

Caroline eased the medal from the box and held it in her palm feeling the weight and solidity of it before gripping it between finger and thumb to view the reverse side where the words, 'Awarded to Susannah Garrold for watercolour work', were etched. She didn't want to look at Olly, certain she'd be able to see the recalculation about the value of Beth's pictures on his face.

'Why do you have it, if it was awarded to her?' she asked.

'Well this is where it gets interesting,' Evelyn said and placed a leather bound book with worn corners on the table before opening it at another marked page. 'It seems Susannah was a little ahead of her time in terms of being a radical student. These are the minutes of the School's Board meetings. Look.' She pointed to a passage written in clear black ink, the Secretary's careful, evenly formed handwriting stripping some emotion from the words.

'It is noted with regret that Miss Susannah Garrold has returned her Board of Education medal and certificate stating that she had no respect for an Institution which treats women as second class citizens. The Head of School confirmed that this was an isolated incident and that Miss Garrold had left her course. Other members of the Ladies' Classes have stated their satisfaction with the lessons and there is no cause for further action.'

'Poor Susannah,' Caroline said.

'But what a great story,' Olly replied. 'You know what this means...'

Caroline interrupted him. 'Yes. That Susannah was even braver than I thought she was. Thank you so much for your help, Evelyn.'

'It's been very interesting. I could pull a short report together if it would help? Olly told me you have some of Susannah's paintings in the family.'

'Yes. We do. That would be a great help, thank you.'

Caroline didn't speak as Olly led the way back down the stairwell and out to the street. He tried to interest her in discussing what they'd seen, but she wouldn't be drawn into conversation. She was aware how little of Susannah's story she'd revealed to him and was reluctant to increase his enthusiasm about the value of the pictures even further. Everything would have to be revealed to Beth first.

'Have you got time for a drink?' he asked as they walked away from the Art School. 'I don't have to get back for anything.'

'OK.'

Caroline told herself she was grateful to Olly for the introduction to Evelyn and that was why she agreed to his suggestion. At the very least she owed him a coffee. And his company was preferable to going back to the office.

'How's your nan getting on?' Olly asked once they were seated in a café with drinks in front of them.

Caroline frowned. The text message she'd received from Alice that morning hadn't sounded positive. 'Not good, actually. She's worse if anything.'

She didn't mind when Olly placed his hand on her arm that time. The warmth and pressure of the physical contact was welcome. What she really felt like was a hug, but perhaps he wasn't the right person. She changed the subject. 'How are your kids?'

He smiled. 'They're great, although they exhausted me at the weekend. Toby's five and I'm convinced he'll be a politician. He can already twist every subject in his favour. Emily's two and, without wanting to sound like a besotted parent - she's gorgeous.' His smile faded.

'It must be hard not living with them anymore.'

He nodded. 'My ex has a new man in her life. I'm trying to be very mature about his involvement.'

Caroline pressed her lips together. Perhaps Olly was equally in need of a hug. 'Maybe we should talk about something brighter? How's work?'

'Hmm, I'm still waiting for the provinces to reveal their artistic wealth to me,' he said and pulled a face to let her know he was teasing. 'I have seen some rather interesting watercolours recently though...'

'Well that case might have to go on hold until their owner has been apprised of recent developments.' Caroline sipped her tea and wondered where that formal language delivered in a mock-serious tone which mimicked his had come from. It could be interpreted as flirting.

He smiled. 'So, how's work for you?'

She couldn't help being honest. 'Not great.'

'I'm sorry to hear that. Why?'

'I just can't find the enthusiasm lately.' Caroline shrugged. 'I used to love handling items from the past. When I touched a comb, a bowl, an item another human being made use of perhaps thousands of years ago it was a privilege, like getting an insight to another life. I felt so responsible for the items and as if my role as their guardian really mattered.'

Olly put his cup down and pushed the saucer aside. 'What's changed?'

'I think I started to be more interested in people than things.'

With his head tipped to one side and his mouth slightly open as though he was about to speak, the scar across Olly's cheek was more noticeable. Caroline's gaze was drawn to it and she blushed as she made eye contact with him again. She wondered if he'd realised what she was looking at, or whether he'd assume she was distracted or if it seemed natural for her focus to wander like that. She wasn't thinking about his scar, or its cause, or his body in any way. She just wasn't sure he knew that.

Olly's words brought her back into the present, 'But the role of a curator is to educate, to share, to interpret for those who don't have your knowledge, to make the connections for them – isn't that a good thing? You enhance someone else's appreciation, give them a context or guide their thinking. Surely you do it for people?'

With her mind still partly elsewhere, Caroline spoke without thinking. 'Why should I?'

'Hey.' Olly reached across and took her hand. 'It's a difficult time at the moment, that's all.'

'No. It's not only the stuff with Nan. I walked through the Pre-Raphaelite gallery on my way to meet you today and it really irritates me - all that romanticising of mediaeval times and we're still clinging to it today. The pictures are all languid ladies lolling about the place. I want to do something which actually makes a difference, not just tell stories people think are cute.'

'Well I don't personally have a problem with a little languid lolling about.' Olly squeezed her fingers. 'Frivolity can be fun, wouldn't you agree?'

Caroline held his gaze. She didn't take her hand back straight away.

*

As soon as she entered the ward that evening, Caroline knew things weren't right. Beth looked as though she was asleep, although her skin was so grey it was only the slight movement of the blankets over her chest which confirmed she was still breathing. Alice stood by the side of the bed, her shoulders hunched and her hands in fists by her sides.

'Mum?' Caroline said.

It took a moment for Alice to turn her head to meet Caroline's eyes and her fierce glare made Caroline take a step back. 'What did you think you were playing at?' Alice asked. Her volume was pitched just above a whisper but her words carried the force of a slap.

'What?'

Alice grabbed Caroline's arm and dragged her back to the corridor. 'You sent that solicitor here.'

'I only did what Nan asked me to do.' Caroline jerked her arm out of Alice's grasp and rubbed away the pain. 'She's entitled to carry on with her life, despite being in here.'

'Her life? Not when it involves someone profiting from her death. She told me it was about her will and I can assure you she did not need the stress of thinking about that today. She's too weak to be making decisions. Too weak.'

'Is that what the solicitor said?' Caroline knew she'd explained everything clearly to the woman who'd agreed she'd assess how Beth seemed before taking any instructions. Beth had dealt with the firm for years. There was no reason to mistrust them.

Alice folded her arms and sniffed. 'I don't know what cosy chat she'd been having with your nan before I got here. I do know I sent her packing, although she claims she's drawing up the papers 'as requested'.'

Caroline took the few steps to a row of plastic seats and sat down. She covered her face with her hands and tried to think clearly. 'Mum, let's take things in order. Tell me how Nan is.'

Alice lowered herself into the neighbouring chair, her rigid spine releasing into a slump as she allowed the tension in her body to dissipate. 'The nurses won't say it, but I can tell they're worried she hasn't improved. If anything, she's a bit worse. She's been asleep since the solicitor left. Or maybe she just didn't want to talk to me.'

Caroline hid a smile. She'd been known to feign sleep to avoid talking to Alice herself.

'But you should have told me about the solicitor,' Alice went on. 'I knew your nan wasn't up to it; it's far from the best time for her to be thinking about her will.'

'She asked me not to tell you. She's entitled to privacy and still capable of making her own decisions.' Although her voice was neutral, Caroline knew Alice would leap on the criticism.

'And she thought I wouldn't let her?'

Caroline didn't reply.

Alice relaxed her posture further. She placed her handbag on the floor by her feet and leant back so her head rested against the wall. 'Tell me what's going on.'

'What did the solicitor say to you?' Caroline was unwilling to share any information Beth might still prefer to be kept private.

'That in her opinion Mrs Dabbs was of sound mind and that unless I had a power of attorney she couldn't discuss anything with me at this stage.' Alice repeated the legalese in a parody of a posh voice. 'She's changing her will, isn't she?'

Caroline avoided the direct question. 'Have you heard of the Garrolds, or the Farlane family?'

'We're related to some Garrolds,' Alice said and turned her head to look at Caroline. 'Not that I've seen them recently. It's a long story best saved for another time.'

'It is a long story but I've dug some of it up. You don't think I'd have just let Nan go ahead and do things without keeping an eye out for her, do you? As soon as she told me she wanted to change her will I tried to find out why.'

'And?'

'Remember they're her possessions, Mum. And, to be honest, a lot of the money came from the Garrolds in the first place.'

Alice gave a sharp laugh. 'A family she's had little to do with for fifty years! I take it she's decided she wants to give them something back?'

'I don't know what she's decided. But it's not what you think. I met your cousin Richard Garrold and he told me what he'd suggested to her.'

Alice's rage flared again. 'Suggested! A man we don't know comes out of the blue and tries to tell my mother what to do! I can't believe you didn't tell me about this straight away.' She sat up straight and turned her full attention to Caroline. 'You'd better start explaining things right now. Neither you nor your nan can be trusted to manage things on your own.'

*

With twenty minutes before the end of visiting time, Caroline lowered herself into the armchair by Beth's bed. She'd persuaded Alice to go home and decided to sit with Beth for a few minutes before leaving herself. Although she'd explained only the bones of the story of the Farlanes, the Garrolds, the politics and the money, Caroline was drained and disheartened. Alice had questioned every fact, disputed all the evidence and doubted Richard's motives. Responding to all of that while also wondering about her mum's own motives had depleted what energy remained after everything else Caroline had been through that day. Letting Alice take over would be a relief but she knew it wasn't what Beth wanted.

'Hello, love.' Beth's voice was a dry croak.

'Oh, Nan, I thought you were asleep.' Caroline stood up so Beth didn't have to twist her neck to look at her.

Beth closed her eyes again and nodded once. 'Did you see your mum?' she asked.

'Yes, but you're not to worry about any of that. Just rest and get better, OK?' Caroline took Beth's hand and stroked it as she rested her weight against the side of the mattress. 'I went to see Richard myself this morning and I don't want you to rush into anything.'

'But...'

'There are a lot of things I need to tell you. I've found things out about Susannah and her dad and where the rest of her pictures are. But this isn't the time.'

Beth opened her eyes again but seemed unable to focus. 'He'll be bankrupt unless I help. I can give him the pictures now and some money when the house is sold.'

Caroline laid her hand flat against Beth's arm. 'No, Nan. You're not well enough for this.'

'It might be my last chance; don't you think I should do something?'

The sudden clarity in Beth's voice caught Caroline off guard. 'No, Nan, you're going to get better...'

Beth interrupted her. 'I might not.' She paused before adding, 'Surely you of all people understand. I can change things; I can use Susannah's legacy to improve things for my relations.'

'I do understand, but you're rushing into this. Richard didn't ask you for money.' Caroline laid her palm across Beth's dry forehead and was surprised to feel the ridges of her skull so prominent through the thin skin. 'You don't have to do anything right now. I want you to make the right decision.'

'I might not have time.'

*

By the time she got home, Caroline's tiredness had intensified into an almost trance-like state. The knowledge she'd acquired in the past days had changed too many things. No matter what interpretation Alice put on events, it wasn't that Richard was trying to take things from their family; Beth wanted to be generous – to right some wrongs from the past.

Richard's trawl into the depths of the paperwork at Farlane's had uncovered a document relating to the oil painting which hung on the back wall of his office. It was a letter from Susannah in which she had given the picture on loan to the firm, but the terms of the loan were unspecified. From her work with loans for the museum, Caroline knew it was essential to tie down every detail regarding ownership, length of the loan, who was responsible for the item at each stage and what would happen in the event of any changes. This letter covered none of that. It stated only that Susannah Garrold sent the painting on loan to the firm of Farlane's. There were big questions: should the picture have been returned to Susannah's estate on her death or did it stay with the firm while it remained in existence? And what would happen when the administrators wound up the firm?

Richard was certain he had a matter of weeks before that happened. His creditors were being paid by selling the assets of the firm: machinery and materials. All he was left with was the building. George Farlane had constructed it back in 1881 and the deeds were now in Richard's name. There were many empty industrial buildings in Birmingham so this one was unlikely to sell for much if at all.

Caroline had taken some photos and she flicked through them on the screen of her phone. A red brick wall on the outside of the factory had been painted with the firm's name, the lettering now weathered and hard to read. Richard had told her the sign was last touched up in the 1970s and the photo showed the factory with all its pride drained away. Weeds grew in the guttering and broken window panes had not been replaced. She'd taken the photo because it so closely matched the subject of the painting though and she swiped back to the previous photo.

It didn't capture the painting well. The lighting in the office was poor and the canvas too big really for the camera in her phone to do it justice. The conditions hadn't been ideal for storing the picture either; it was covered in a layer of dust, nothing which couldn't be remedied though.

'It's this,' Richard had said as she turned to look at the picture. 'I wanted to give it back to Aunt Beth before the administrators decided to sell it, that's why I went to see her. It should probably have been returned a long time ago.' He explained that Susannah had sent the picture to her brother, Thomas Garrold, when he inherited Farlane's from their father. 'Neither my dad or I knew though. I suppose I thought someone commissioned it.'

Caroline had needed to pause, to reassess what was happening: that Richard hadn't been asking Beth for money after all. 'What did my nan say?'

'I told her I was winding up the firm and she replied that she doubted that was what Susannah would have wanted and that I should sell the painting if it would help. I explained things were really beyond that but she said she'd look out Susannah's things and see what could be done. She asked me to visit in a few days when she'd had time to find the paperwork, which is when I met you.' He sighed. 'I was humouring her really. Farlane's can't be saved and I'm only sorry that this rift between her and my dad meant I didn't meet Aunt Beth until now.'

Caroline rubbed her eyes and switched her phone off before heading to bed. She couldn't sleep. The events repeated through her mind, all the things Alice, Beth and Richard had said. Alice wouldn't believe Richard wasn't motivated by money and, with Beth so ill, this wasn't the time for any of them to be having these conversations anyway. Images played like a slideshow through her mind: the oil painting, the factory building, the watercolour at the Art School. What could Susannah have meant by painting that scene and sending it on loan? Was she trying to build bridges? And was it too late for Beth to build them now? To try would mean to fight against Alice. Caroline did not feel she had the strength for that.

She turned over, plumped her pillow and tried to put the puzzle out of her mind. She had the meeting with Phil to look forward to the following day. That would require enough mental energy for one morning.

Chapter Seventeen

The purple latex gloves snapped as Caroline tugged them on and watched Phil unwrap the package he'd brought. She'd shown him into a small room off the entrance foyer rather than any of the meeting rooms. Despite the lack of windows or comfortable furniture, she didn't want to risk bumping into Bill or Denise in a corridor, or intimidating Phil any further.

'I hope I haven't damaged it. I didn't have any of them gloves,' Phil said as he unwound the final layer of cloth and placed a metal object on the wooden table.

Despite her gloves, Caroline didn't touch it straight away. She looked for several moments before lifting it to view the reverse. It was obvious why Phil had brought it to the museum. Superficially, to a lay person at least, it appeared similar to the treasures from the Anglo-Saxon Hoard, photos of which had hit every newspaper. In reality, it didn't excite her. Without the coating of mud to lend the piece its air of intrigue, she could tell that while it might be old, perhaps even Anglo-Saxon, it could only be classed as junk. It was not a museum-quality artefact, not an advance in historical understanding nor a change in direction for interpretation of the past. It was only a broken bit of metal, dropped or discarded by its owner centuries ago and dug up by a modern-day fortune hunter, another piece of flotsam washed up on history's tide.

'Well?' Phil asked. He leant forward with his elbows on the table and flicked his staring eyes between the item and Caroline's face.

Caroline realised she hadn't spoken or moved for several minutes and her mouth had gone dry. She swallowed and turned the metal over in her hands to view it from all angles as though she were interested. It was no good though; she couldn't find any enthusiasm. 'I'm afraid I'm going to disappoint you,' she said. 'It's not gold, more likely to be bronze. This entwined abstract decoration was used in the Anglo-Saxon period so I see why you thought it might be like the materials on display upstairs, but I'm afraid it's really not the same quality. I'm not sure what it is, or was rather. Perhaps some kind of buckle or tab? The damage means it's impossible to tell and the quality of the decoration suggests it wasn't the property of anyone of particular wealth.'

'Oh.' Phil slumped back into his seat.

'I know, I'm sorry. But if you do much metal detecting you'll know most of what you find turns out to be nothing.' She finally managed to look at Phil, but he wouldn't meet her eye.

'I only just started. I thought maybe it was beginner's luck.'

Caroline put the item down. 'It was really; you found something this interesting rather than a modern coin after all. I'm afraid it isn't going to make headlines or your fortune though.' She didn't add that it wasn't going to make her career either but felt her disappointment might be equal to Phil's own, even if she'd been the more foolish one to allow her hopes to be raised. 'Look, I'll put you in touch with the Finds Liaison Officer. He'll record the details but it's likely you'll get to keep this.'

The chair legs scraped across the floor as Phil stood, grabbed the strip of metal, wrapped it loosely in the cloth and stuffed it back into his pocket. 'Right. Thanks.' He let the door slam behind him.

Instead of returning immediately to her office, Caroline walked through the reverse chronology of the fine art galleries to get things straight in her mind. The whole incident had been futile. Phil was an idiot, but it was unfair to blame him. She slumped into a vacant room attendant's chair positioned by the carved black marble door case of the seventeenth century art gallery and rubbed her eyes, not yet ready to face the reality of the present day. As the expert she should have known better than to think the opportunity to impress in her new job would be delivered to her as though by courier. Risking a rift with a new colleague had been stupid as well. She took a deep breath to calm herself and looked around.

A single visitor walked a slow circuit around the strip of carpet protecting the room's worn floorboards and looked more as though he'd come in to get out the rain rather than be enlightened. He paused near her, seeming to study a large painting. Only the calm hum from an air conditioning unit disturbed the reverent silence.

Not wanting to move and break his concentration, Caroline remained seated and glanced at the pictures hung on the room's mustard coloured walls. The majority were heavy framed oil paintings. Those to her right were domestic scale interiors or still lives. In one a young woman seemed to be having a lesson at a virginal while her tutor flirted with a maid, and in another two women worked to prepare a cornucopia of luxury food for a feast. Typical representations of gender roles. She sighed and wondered how much food the cooks got to eat themselves.

The man left the room and she stood to view the picture he'd paused by. It was by Rubens and showed a violent scene in which scantily clad Amazons lay slain while armed and armoured men rode into battle against them and in the background a city burned.

'Ah, I'm glad I've bumped into you.'

She forced a smile and linked her hands behind her back as she turned to look at Gerald, the Curatorial Manager - her immediate, although infrequently seen, boss. 'Hello. How are you?'

'Yes, yes, fine. I wanted to ask: how do you feel you're getting on?'

Caroline paused. The diplomatic wording of the question triggered an alarm bell. It wasn't a polite enquiry; she was trapped in an unscheduled performance appraisal. 'Ah, um, OK I think. Keeping busy. Getting involved.'

Gerald nodded and sunk his hands into the pockets of his jacket. 'Good. Yes, good. I just wondered if I might have heard more from you. Perhaps some new ideas?'

She felt her cheeks go warm in response to the injustice of the accusation. What did he think the suggestions she'd made in the last team meeting had been if not proposals for a different tack? While she thought about how best to respond, she glanced at the painting behind him. She didn't immediately recognise the artist and her impression was of a bland canvas depicting a scene of a pale, mountainous landscape. One side was sunlit although a storm was raging on the horizon. She squinted and could just make out two seated figures and two captured in motion: one chasing the other. The subject wasn't obvious and she couldn't read the small print of the title from where she stood. It didn't provide the needed inspiration.

'I am working on something,' she said, 'an exhibition proposal. I just need to think through some details before I'm ready to bring you an outline. Other than that, I've been getting heavily involved with the events and educational programme...'

'I see,' Gerald said, although his tone suggested he didn't. 'Well, I'll look forward to hearing your ideas.'

Caroline watched him walk away, annoyed he'd caught her in the galleries behaving as though she were a visitor rather than a member of staff. Better to have been found deep in research at her desk, or looking down a microscope to analyse new acquisitions with the conservation team, or fully in control of a tour group: all things she could and did do well. And, she realised, all things she'd avoided or been resentful about recently. Perhaps it was only that she hadn't settled into the job yet, perhaps it was the return to Birmingham which had unsettled her.

She approached the picture and bent to read the label. It seemed there was uncertainty about the date and attribution: it could have been painted by one of two men sometime in the sixteenth or seventeenth century. The subject was certain although the picture didn't immediately give up its story, instead putting the drama into perspective by siting it within a vast landscape. It showed the Roman goddess Minerva as she expelled Mars to protect Peace and Plenty. Caroline bent to look closely at the figures. The two seated ladies who appeared to be having a nice chat must represent Peace and Plenty, while Mars, god of war, fled before the raised arm of Minerva, goddess of wisdom, clad in her armour. Well done that woman, Caroline thought. Keep up the good work.

She straightened and closed her eyes as a rush of recollections and inspiration stuck her. Minerva was the Roman equivalent of the Greek goddess Athena, as depicted in the museum's reproduction Parthenon frieze. She was the goddess not only of wisdom, but of arts and crafts, courage, strategy and just warfare and was every bit a worthy heroine around whom to build an exhibition.

Caroline hurried back towards the office, paying no attention to the religious art of earlier centuries but smiling as she pushed through a heavy wooden swing door and noted the Birmingham crest with its female art worker embossed on the brass finger plate, yet another icon for her proposal. She swiped her ID card to gain access through a staff door and took a deep breath as she reached her office, expecting that Denise would have more complaints about her absence and still unsure how to admit to Bill that their battle over the mystery object had been in vain. The office was silent though. Denise looked up as the door closed; Bill remained hunched over his desk. Caroline jumped in with an apology before any complaints could be made.

'I know: I was longer than I expected. I'm sorry. I hope you haven't had to take any more messages for me.'

Denise paused before she replied and her voice was calmer than Caroline had anticipated. 'Just one message: your dad called. He asked you to call back. It's urgent.'

Although she'd reached her desk while Denise had been speaking, Caroline didn't sit down. She registered that Denise's voice hadn't been calm, it had been sympathetic. She grabbed her bag and jacket and ran from the room, dialling from her mobile as she dashed from the building.

Chapter Eighteen

With the curtains drawn the space around Beth's bed had become intimate as though it was just the family sitting together behind closed doors. Caroline felt the need to stay close and stood with the front of her thighs pressed against the mattress. It no longer hissed or sighed. There was no further need to protect Beth from pressure sores and the chill of the metal bed frame digging into her legs gave Caroline something on which to focus.

She'd reached the hospital half an hour before Beth died earlier that afternoon. She, Alice and Ray were there. They'd been talking, quiet and calm although Beth seemed unaware of their presence. Her eyes had been closed and her breathing shallow until, finally, it stopped. The only drama had been from Peter, who'd ranted on the phone to know why they hadn't told him, why he'd been excluded.

'We didn't know,' Ray said, because it was the truth. Until that morning, there had been hope.

Peter was now on a train back to Birmingham and Caroline couldn't imagine how he would be coping. She was glad of the privacy behind the closed curtains and appreciated the tact of the nurses for giving them this time with Beth. A sob choked her throat. It was Beth's body they were spending time with. Beth herself was gone.

Ray stood at an awkward angle with one hand on his wife's shoulder while Alice hunched into the visitor's chair and covered her face with both hands to catch her tears. Caroline couldn't look at either of them. We all failed you, Nan, she thought. We all failed.

A quiet cough from outside the curtain indicated one of the nurses was about to join them. She drew the curtain aside enough to slip in and with a sympathetic smile said, 'Would you come through to the family room now? I'll bring you some tea.'

Caroline moved towards the head of the bed and laid a hand on Beth's cheek. The skin was cold and seemed to hang differently from the bones so that Beth already looked unfamiliar. Without that unconscious muscle control which expressed her thoughts and feelings her face was blank; the features by themselves did not look like Beth.

'Bye, Nan,' Caroline said. 'Thank you.'

She didn't register the tears which were beginning to soak into the fabric of her blouse until she'd stepped out of the curtained-off area and the nurse handed her a tissue.

'We'll take Beth down to the mortuary now,' the nurse said. 'You come and sit down for a bit.'

Caroline nodded. She could hear Alice's sobs and Ray's voice gently consoling her as they said their goodbyes to Beth. Caroline left the ward and went to the family room across the corridor. Vinyl-upholstered chairs stood at angles to each other, a box of tissues had been left on the coffee table and a rack on the wall was cluttered with leaflets. Although the room had been decorated to mimic the comforts of a domestic lounge, it didn't work. She walked straight to the window and looked out across the city from the room's seventh floor vantage point. Beyond the hospital car park everything seemed very green with patches of allotments and clumps of trees which shielded all but the tallest buildings.

The view disoriented her. Roads didn't seem to run at the angles she anticipated. Landmarks appeared too close to one another. Nothing was quite in its expected place. She wouldn't have recognised she was in Birmingham; it didn't look the same as from ground level.

She turned away from the window as Alice and Ray joined her in the room.

'Come and sit down, love,' Ray said to her. 'You've been standing for hours.'

Caroline pushed away from the window ledge she'd been leaning on and perched on the edge of one of the armchairs. 'The nurse said they were going to move Nan's body,' she said.

Alice emitted a squeak and both Caroline and Ray turned to look at her. She'd clasped a hand over her mouth and stared wide-eyed at Ray as he moved to put an arm around her shoulders. 'They have to, you know,' he said. 'We've got time though. No need to rush anything.'

'We have to get a funeral director,' Caroline replied.

'Don't worry, love. I'll sort it all out.'

They exchanged a brief smile before Caroline slumped back into her seat. With Alice usually domineering, and Peter so loud, it was easy to forget her dad was so capable and reliable in a crisis.

The nurse brought a tray of mugs into the room. 'Take your time,' she said. 'Let me know if you need anything.'

Ray stood to hold the door open for her. 'Thank you.'

He passed one of the mugs to Caroline. She looked at the weak, milky tea it contained and waited for Alice to comment. She didn't. They all drank the tea in silence.

'I'll go and see what we need to do,' Ray said and left the room with the empty mugs.

Alice dabbed her mouth with a tissue before blowing her nose. 'That's it then,' she said. 'She's gone.'

Caroline looked up to see that her mum was staring out the window although her gaze seemed unfocussed. For the past few hours she'd been quiet, subdued by grief, but now her voice sounded firm.

'I can't quite believe it,' Caroline said. 'We'll all miss her so much.'

'And there's so much to do.'

'Yes, but like Dad said, there's no immediate rush.'

'The funeral, I don't know where we'll have the funeral. And I'll have to call people, call everyone.' The pitch of Alice's voice increased and her words speeded up. 'They'll all ask me how it happened. How it could possibly have happened. Somebody must have done something wrong.'

Caroline moved so she could take hold of Alice's hands. 'There are a lot of questions, but let's not panic.'

Alice turned to look at Caroline. 'My mother had nothing but hassle from doctors and lawyers in her last few days. Do you think that's what she deserved? Do you? What I know is that someone is to blame. No-one dies because of a little fall. She should be coming home with us today, not being taken to the morgue.'

The force of Alice's words stung Caroline like a slap and she took her hands away and sat back. Was Alice really suggesting Caroline herself might bear some blame because she'd called the lawyer? She wanted to defend herself, point out that she'd been following Beth's wishes and protecting her throughout. Alice was acting under shock and grief though. Caroline bit her tongue, sat back and waited for her dad to return with instructions about what she should do.

*

Caroline let herself into Beth's house, dropped her bag and lowered herself to sit on the bottom stair. Although light from outside still illuminated the hall, the day had been too long; too much had happened. As she leant against the bannister, Caroline wished for nothing more than to turn the clock back two weeks so that Beth would bustle out of the kitchen to offer a cup of tea, a nourishing meal or wise words. Tears came back to her already sore eyes with the realisation that she'd never see or hear Beth again.

Her final task for the day was to inform Beth's neighbours and collect the address book so Alice could start sharing the news of their bereavement. Caroline could see the book from where she sat. The faded floral print of its hardback cover stood out against the dark wood of the console table where Beth had kept it, placed neatly in front of the telephone. It had been a present from Caroline and Peter for a long gone Christmas. She leant over, picked it up and began to turn the thick pages. Beth's expressive handwriting filled the cream pages with loops and curls of information, sometimes crossed through where an updated address or phone number required an amendment.

As she ran her index finger over a well-used page to trace Beth's hand, Caroline felt jealous of all the people who didn't yet know Beth had died although she didn't envy Alice the job of informing them. She herself had deferred knocking on the neighbours' doors. She didn't have the words to start the conversation.

The shrill ringtone from her phone punctured the silence. She put the address book down on the stair while reaching into her bag to answer it. It was Olly.

'I thought I'd call to see how you are,' he said. 'You seemed a bit down yesterday.'

'Things have got worse. My nan died earlier today.'

She heard him take a breath before he spoke again. 'I'm so sorry to hear that. I hadn't realised things were so serious.'

'Neither did I.' Caroline held her free hand over her aching eyes as she pressed the phone to her ear. 'I'm not really sure what I'm meant to feel or do.'

'Grief is a funny thing. There isn't a 'right' way to go through it and it's no surprise you feel confused. You've had a shock so give yourself time.'

She didn't reply.

'Caroline? Are you there? Look, this must be inconvenient. Are you with your family? I'll call another time.'

'No, it's fine. I'm on my own. At Nan's. It's so strange to think she'll never come back here.'

'I can imagine. It's such a homely place.'

Caroline removed the hand covering her eyes and looked around. Two of Beth's coats hung from the row of hooks on the wall beside the front door, their shoulders drooping as though they knew their owner no longer needed them. The rug showed the wear of a pathway between the living room and kitchen doors. Her own face smiled down at her from happier days immortalised in family photographs. Olly was right: it looked like a home. It just no longer had an owner.

She slipped the address book into her handbag and stood up. 'We'll have to leave the stuff about Susannah for now. Thanks for your help though.'

'That's OK. Listen, I'll let you go but you must call if I can help at all.'

'OK. I will.'

Caroline watched the illuminated screen fade as she ended the call. Getting into the research about Susannah with Olly had been fun – more interesting than anything else going on in her life. But it wasn't important now. She picked up her bag and braced herself to speak to the neighbours. She lacked the vocabulary to explain what had happened and the strength to deal with their shock and sympathy, but there was only one way to start the conversations. She had to ring the doorbells.

Chapter Nineteen

Caroline wondered if there had been any point turning up for work. She wasn't exactly being productive but the death of a grandmother didn't qualify her for compassionate leave. The policy judged on legal definitions, and she wondered if human resources staff based entire conferences on their attempts to measure degrees of distress. They didn't always appreciate those 'resources' were actual people.

She hadn't turned the page of the document she'd been staring at for half an hour, and wouldn't have been able to answer questions on the content. As she gazed at the type on the page, different words ran through her mind. Alice's suggestion that the stress of the lawyer's visit had tipped Beth towards death couldn't be excused as owing to bereavement. The accusation that Caroline was in some way responsible was unacceptable.

At least Denise had offered to take the tour group Caroline had been scheduled for that afternoon, and Bill was keeping quiet. She knew she should share the news with him about the mystery object being worthless, but wasn't in the mood to talk and frowned when her mobile began to ring.

'Don't mind me,' Bill said. 'In fact, I'll give you a minute.' He stood up and left the office with his empty mug in hand.

Caroline raised an eyebrow at his uncharacteristic compassion and reached for her phone. An unfamiliar

Birmingham number was shown on the screen. 'Hello?' she said.

'Hello, Caroline. It's Mary Fisher here, Mrs Dabbs' solicitor - we spoke a few days ago. My condolences on your grandmother's death; your father called me with the sad news.'

'Um, thank you.' Caroline pushed the documents away from the front of her desk and leant her elbows there so she could cradle her head.

'As you know, Mrs Dabbs had asked me to draft her new will but as it was unsigned at her death, the old will remains valid.'

'Oh.' Caroline's eyes tingled with tears again at the frustration. If Beth had been stressed by speaking to her lawyer it had turned out to be futile anyway.

Mary's voice was brisk and coolly professional. 'You are nominated as sole executor and I wanted to check how you'd like to proceed. Should I apply for the grant of probate for you?'

'I'm sole executor?' That was a surprise.

'Yes, although I'm afraid there may be some delay. The death will be referred to the coroner because Mrs Dabbs died in hospital.'

Caroline swallowed. 'Coroner?'

'It's usually a formality, but occasionally checks have to be made about the cause of death.'

'I see.' Caroline leant back in her chair and rubbed her free hand across her eyes. 'So what happens until then?'

'It would be useful for you to come in to see me. We can read the will so you can understand the clauses and confirm the identification of all beneficiaries. When would you be able to come in to the office?'

They set the appointment for the following morning and Caroline dropped her phone back into her bag. It didn't seem right that Beth had chosen her to be executor. Alice wouldn't be pleased and Caroline wondered if Mary had shared any details about the will when her dad had called. Probably not, she'd come across as very formal and well, solicitors had to do everything exactly by the rules, didn't they? Which meant Caroline would have to break the news to Alice. She couldn't see that going well.

The office door opened and Bill returned carrying two mugs, one of which he placed on Caroline's desk. 'Here, I thought you could do with a cuppa as well.'

This time she couldn't stop the tears falling. 'That's kind. Thank you.'

He shook his head. 'No problem. Oh, and no sugar, was that right?'

'Perfect.' Her voice cracked and she gulped against a sob.

Bill began to back away. 'Right then; no rest for the wicked.'

Caroline reached across and stole a tissue from the box on Denise's desk feeling bad her tears had made Bill uncomfortable. Making her a cup of tea was more than she'd ever expected from him; he couldn't be expected to handle her emotions as well.

'I need to take tomorrow morning off,' she said once she'd blown her nose. 'Do you think Gerald'll understand? I know we're supposed to give more notice.'

Bill pulled his chair out from his desk and swivelled it to face her as he sat down. 'As long as you make arrangements for any cover you need, it shouldn't matter.'

'No, but...' Caroline paused. Their manager had made it clear he needed her to impress him. Bill wasn't in that position; he was, in fact, the competition. It would take more than a cup of tea to change that. 'It's fine. I'll ask him.'

*

As she walked into her parents' house Caroline noticed the runner protecting the laminate floor in the hall lay askew rather than exactly parallel to the skirting board. Alice couldn't have walked through recently. It was her constant adjustments to correct imperfections which made Caroline aware such imperfections existed. She glanced into the empty living room and eventually found Peter in the kitchen. They hugged for a moment.

'I'm making you a cup of tea,' he said.

She hid her surprise at yet another man acting out of character. 'Thanks. Where's Mum?' She slung her coat over one of the stools at the breakfast bar and watched as Peter poured boiling water into a bone china mug. The sound of Alice's disapproval about the lack of a teapot rang in her mind.

'Upstairs. Having a lie down. I've already taken her a drink.' He removed the tea bag, sloshed some milk in to the mug and pushed it along the polished granite work surface towards her. It left a wet trail across the gloss.

'How is she?'

Peter paused for a moment before answering. 'Quiet. Very weird.'

She turned the handle of the mug to face her and raised an eyebrow to prompt Peter to elaborate.

'She was talking about hymns,' he said.

Caroline frowned. 'For the funeral?' She hadn't begun to consider the details of the burial arrangements and wondered if there might be something about Beth's own wishes in her will. He nodded. 'How are you feeling?' she asked.

Peter plonked the milk back into the fridge and let the door fall closed. 'Angry. Frustrated. Mum's right: this shouldn't have happened. And what now? What are we going to do without Nan?'

Caroline gazed out the patio doors to the garden and cupped her hands around the mug. She remembered how harsh the rectangle of turf and recently erected fencing had looked when they moved in. She hated it at first sight. The house, the garden, her new bedroom: all of it was too stark, too rigid, too great a contrast to their old home. Now the lawn was softened with borders, mature shrubs screened the fence and she'd moved out years ago. She hadn't forgotten the dislocating impact of the change though and could still recall Alice's lack of sympathy to her young daughter's distress when she couldn't get to sleep in the new room. That memory was still raw and the pain reignited by recent events. Everything was changing again.

She looked back to Peter. 'Did Mum tell you what she said to me?'

'To you? No.'

'She said it was my fault, because I sent the lawyer in to see Nan. She thinks it was too stressful and that Nan wasn't strong enough to be disturbed.'

Peter met her gaze and held it. 'Do you think Nan was too stressed?'

'No. I think she knew her mind and would have been more upset if I hadn't done what she asked me.'

'Your conscience is clear then.' He reached for the dishcloth and wiped the counter.

Caroline clenched her teeth. That wasn't the support she was looking for. 'I'll go and see Mum,' she said and carried her drink upstairs.

She knocked on the bedroom door before opening it and found Alice sitting on the bed with a photo album on her lap. 'Oh, it's you,' Alice said.

Caroline forced herself to speak in a calm and sympathetic tone. 'How are you feeling, Mum?'

Alice shrugged and pulled her cardigan across her body as though she felt cold. Caroline placed her drink on the bedside table and sat down on the bed. 'May I see?' she asked and reached for the photo album.

'We have to decide how to dress her,' Alice said.

Caroline looked at the snaps from recent Christmases and birthdays which filled the page Alice had been looking at. Beth's face smiled up at her, delight at being surrounded by her family evident in her expression. 'Dress her?'

'For burial. We have to choose an outfit.'

Caroline gulped. Alice hadn't been reminiscing; she'd been using these pictures in which Beth was full of life as a sort of clothing catalogue for the funeral. She circled Beth's face in one picture with her fingertip. The clothes didn't matter, surely? It was the fact Beth was gone which she couldn't reconcile. The realisation that next Christmas they wouldn't gather as a family to recreate the image in the Edgbaston living room hit Caroline and her eyes filled with tears again.

'Yes, I thought that dress too,' Alice said and took the album. 'She loved that lilac print.'

Caroline brushed the tears away. Alice appeared too calm, as though she wasn't allowing herself to react to the photos. She kept these albums of carefully selected and ordered prints shelved on the landing, about a dozen books with matching spines and catalogued entries documenting the family from Alice's own youth through Caroline and Peter's. Fewer pictures had been added in recent years; there hadn't been so many occasions worth recording. Caroline rarely saw her mum looking at the photos anyway, they were just there: preserved as evidence that a family life existed. But now Beth, a key player in the drama, was gone and it was odd that Alice showed no distress.

'What do you think about funeral hymns?' Alice asked.

'Hymns?' Caroline stared out the window. 'I don't really know. It feels a bit hypocritical, I mean, none of us actually go to church.'

'So you think she doesn't deserve a proper funeral then? Well, of course, you'd know all about how things should be done these days. Where we should all live, when we should see our lawyers, and so on.' Alice's voice was crisp and she stood and walked to the bedroom door.

Caroline gasped. 'Mum, don't say that. I've only done what you or Nan asked me and of course she should have a proper funeral. I'm just not sure it would feel right if it was too religious.'

'What, then? What should we do – bury her in the garden while we sing pop songs? Would that be more appropriate?'

'Of course not.' Caroline stood and walked across to Alice. 'I don't know what to suggest, Mum.'

Alice sighed and her shoulders drooped. 'No,' she said. 'Your generation are still having weddings and christenings, not funerals.'

Caroline reached out and managed to give Alice an awkward hug which wasn't returned. She was unable to speak. All words seemed inadequate. Alice had lost her mother and, no matter how difficult their own relationship, Caroline couldn't imagine losing Alice. She was unable to find the vocabulary to express that, and decided not to argue if Alice wanted to lean on traditions and religion to get through the ordeal of burying a parent. Beth's death had brought the rest of the family's relationships into perspective and Caroline needed to prioritise: Alice came first.

'Although,' Alice said, 'by your age I did already have you, your brother and this house to look after. I wasn't entirely useless.'

Caroline sagged, clinging on to Alice as much to keep herself standing in the face of that attack as to continue comforting her mum.

Alice sniffed and pulled away. 'There's so much to do. We need to talk to the lawyer about the will…'

Caroline choked.

'What?' Alice asked. 'What's wrong?'

'She called me, the solicitor,' Caroline said. She paused as Alice's expression hardened. 'I was going to tell you another time, but Nan named me as her sole executor, on her previous will – the one that's still valid.'

Alice opened the bedroom door and stepped onto the landing. 'I see,' she said. 'Well, I'll wait for you to tell me what to do then.'

'Mum,' Caroline said and reached out to touch Alice's arm.

Alice moved away. 'Peter and I are going to talk about the funeral arrangements. If you haven't anything to add, perhaps you should leave us to it.'

Caroline dropped her hand and used it to steady herself against the doorframe. Her mum's words stabbed her heart. She followed Alice down the stairs as she replied 'Leave? Are you asking me to leave?'

Alice reached the hall and turned, the jerk of her foot twisting the runner even further awry. 'Perhaps that would be for the best. After all, I'm sure you're busy.'

Caroline descended the remaining steps slowly, weighing her options with each one. Alice was grieving. Alice was upset because Beth hadn't chosen her to be executor. These were excuses, but not explanations. Alice's behaviour was irrational. And hurtful. Caroline was also grieving but in any situation she was generally the one to back down and try to appease. Her instinct was to smooth things over, to offer to do anything with regard to the funeral and the will if Alice would speak to her kindly again. But that would mean letting Beth down.

The choice hung before her just as it had when Matt asked her to go with him to New York. Again Caroline had to decide whether to act in line with her instincts and risk hurting people or whether to follow the easier path. 'OK,' she said, and left.

Chapter Twenty

The litter of balled up tissues on the floor around Caroline's dining table betrayed how many tears she'd already shed. Her shoulders were hunched and she cradled her head in her hands. As she massaged her temples to relive the pressure of an aching head, she became aware of the buzzing vibration of her mobile ringing.

It was bad timing. She didn't want to talk to anyone and if, as was most likely, it turned out to be one of those call centres offering assistance with a spurious legal claim, she knew she'd say something unnecessarily cruel. She delved into her handbag with the intention of silencing the phone, until she saw it wasn't a withheld number. It was Olly.

She answered on impulse but found she couldn't speak.

'Hello? Caroline, are you there?' The tone of his voice fed concern into her ear. His sympathy was all too welcome.

'Yes. Sorry,' she said.

'No need to be sorry. Is this a bad time?'

She sighed.

'I'm an idiot,' he said. 'Of course it's a bad time. After our conversation last night, I wanted to make sure you were all right. I wanted to ask how you're getting on.'

It was the sort of thing Beth would have done: ring to check up on her. Tears leaked from Caroline's eyes again. 'Thank you,' she managed to say.

'You don't sound as though you're OK at all. Is anyone with you?'

She sniffed hard. 'No. I'm on my own. There's been a bit of a row.'

'Oh, I'm so sorry to hear that. It's such a difficult time for you all, I suppose.'

'Hmmm.' She didn't have any words to explain her feelings or what was happening. It was probably not something she should discuss with him anyway, not that there was a close friend she'd prefer to share her troubles with.

'I wish I was with you,' he said, and then paused as though he regretted vocalising the thought. 'I'm sorry. It's just that you sound as though you need a hug and all I can do is spout irrelevant platitudes from a distance.'

She allowed herself to smile and pressed the phone harder to her ear as she leant back in her chair. With her eyes closed to stop the tears she was more aware of his presence on the line from the slight sounds of his calm breathing and a low rumble of traffic noise in the background.

'Where are you?' she asked.

'At home, in Stratford. And you?'

'In the flat.' Her voice caught in her throat as she realised that 'home' was a word which used to have many connotations, but now only conjured an image of Beth's empty house.

'I see,' he said. 'What are you up to?'

'Just sitting here.' The question alarmed her with its suggested intimacy and she stood up in the hope she'd gain some control of the conversation. 'What was that noise?' In the lull while neither of them spoke she'd heard a ceramic clink. 'Are you eating?'

'No, sorry,' his voice had changed, as though he had cradled the phone against his shoulder rather than holding it in his hand. 'Just taking my cufflinks off. Was it this sound?'

The clink came again and she visualised a gold cufflink, probably monogrammed, as he dropped it onto a tray on a dressing table. Olly would have the best of both household and wardrobe accessories she was sure. Her thoughts followed the trail: if he'd taken off his cufflinks, he was undressing. She held her breath and her ears were alert for the sound of a rustle of cotton to indicate he was removing his shirt. The intimate atmosphere of them being alone although connected so closely by wireless signals became charged and she flushed as she realised how inappropriate her thoughts were.

'Yes, um, that was it.' She strode to the window and opened it to let fresh air cool her face. 'I have to see Nan's lawyer tomorrow. I need to sort a few things out but I probably will need a written valuation on those watercolours.'

'Of course, anything to help. I hope everything goes smoothly with the will. From my own experience, I know it can difficult.'

'Yeah, I'm not looking forward to it.'

'What about tomorrow afternoon, will you be working?'

Caroline looked down at the reflection of lights winking from the surface of the canal below her. The interiors of houses, hospitals and the museum were suffocating her. She wanted to be outside. 'No, I've taken the whole day off.'

It was as though he could read her mind. 'Why not come to Stratford for the afternoon? I'm working in the morning but we could take a walk by the river perhaps? It might do you good to have a break.'

She was in no position to resist temptation. 'Thank you. That would be lovely.'

*

The motorway was clear and the ease of cruising between white lines as tarmac slipped under the tyres left too much of Caroline's mind free to review the events of the morning. She'd woken with a jolt in the early hours, confused until she realised it was her ringtone which had disturbed her rather than any of the incomprehensible images from her dream. She ran her tongue around her teeth in an attempt to prepare to speak, but her voice still croaked as she brought the phone to her ear and said, 'Hello?'

'Oh, crap. I've woken you, haven't I?'

It was Matt, her ex-husband, his voice still distressingly familiar even though she hadn't heard it for months and he'd picked up a slight American inflection.

'I just got your message, about Beth. I'm so sorry, Caz. You must have thought I didn't care.'

Caroline closed her eyes again. Her whole body remained heavy with sleep and she was loath to shake it off. It hadn't occurred to her to wonder about the lack of response to her emails in which she'd broken the news of Beth's illness and then death. Matt and Beth had got on well, but once she'd sent the messages to acknowledge that, Caroline hadn't thought more about it. She hadn't noticed that she didn't know his reaction to the news.

She swallowed, to loosen her voice. 'No, it's fine. You must be busy. I just thought you'd want to know.'

'Of course, thank you. I, um, don't think I'll be able to get back for the funeral though.'

'I wouldn't expect you to; it's too far.' The formality of their conversation bored her. She wanted to slip back into sleep and the longer he stayed on the line the less easy that would be. 'Perhaps we can talk another time, maybe when it's not the middle of the night?'

'Yes, yes, I'm so sorry, for everything. Good night.'

She'd switched the phone off and dropped it on the bedside table. As she turned over in hope of sinking straight back into the embrace of sleep, it occurred to her that the sound of Matt's voice on the line had nothing like the same effect as speaking to Olly the previous evening. Both men were concerned about her, but she was far more open to sympathy from one than the other. One had become largely irrelevant after playing a huge role in her life, while the other had returned from her past to stir up a not entirely unwelcome frisson. She supposed she'd felt like that about Matt once. So much had changed that it was hard to recall.

The visit to Beth's solicitor hadn't eased Caroline's confusion. The terms and endowments of the will were clear but that didn't make things simple.

'What had she changed in the new will?' Caroline asked.

Mrs Fisher lined up the pens and papers on her desk. 'I'm afraid that's confidential.'

'But your client is dead, and I'm her representative.'

'The will we've just read is the legally binding one. That's all I can tell you, I'm afraid.'

As she drove away from Birmingham, Caroline was aware of the legal paperwork as a burden carried in her handbag. There was so much to do, so much to be decided. She wasn't sure she had the strength for it.

*

The bustle of the Dunnant's auction room was a welcome distraction. Caroline looked at the buyers gathered around her, some perched on the assortment of chairs which must form lots for the current sale or one to come, others leaning against items of antique furniture. Many looked bored and she assumed they were dealers rather than ordinary shoppers. The auctioneer was addressing some of them by name in an attempt to encourage sales.

He pointed his gavel at the latest lot, a collection of porcelain dogs which Caroline thought particularly hideous, as he scanned across his audience to identify a target. 'Nice item for you here, Bruce,' he called.

On entering the room she'd spotted Olly sitting at the desk behind the auctioneer. He appeared to be responsible for taking telephone bids. She glanced at him again and caught his eye as the start price for the dogs dropped. He raised his eyebrows and grimaced. The general opinion on the quality of the lot appeared to match her own. The collection sold for £10, to the man the auctioneer had appealed to and Caroline glanced down at the catalogue she'd been handed, wondering if he'd spotted something everyone else had missed and was about to turn them round for a decent profit.

From the listings, Caroline could see that there were still over a hundred items to get through before the end of the sale, although with the relentless pace being maintained she didn't imagine it would take too long. The auctioneer was a large man in a shiny blazer, pink shirt and clashing tie in stripes of lurid green and yellow. The speed and eloquence of his spiel were assured but Caroline found herself letting vague descriptions of items, sales patter and lot numbers race past her without registering them, as though he spoke a foreign language. The sounds lulled her into relaxation. She sat very still, careful to make no stray gestures which could be interpreted as bids, and watched the crowd while tension slipped from her muscles.

She saw Olly lift his phone and speak to a caller, his voice too low to carry over the auctioneers' but he was poised, ready to attract attention to his bid as soon as required. There was other bustle behind the main desk as porters prepared items and Olly's colleagues manned further phone lines or laptops. All the men wore the same tie and Caroline looked to see what item of uniform the women were issued. It took a while to spot. Most of the women were young, with only their smart clothes and glossy hair to distinguish them from the female buyers who mostly favoured Barbour jackets. Finally she found it though: looped about the neck of a more mature woman who seemed to be directing the porters was a scarf in the yellow and green stripe.

She smirked as she imagined the young women's reaction to being presented with the logoed silk square. They all looked the type to have said 'thank you' very politely while suppressing the desire to recoil and Caroline wondered how long Dunnant's would hang on to that vestige of their traditions.

She leant away from her neighbour as he began to bid for a lot with extravagant waves of his auction catalogue. By shrinking into her chair she hoped to disassociate herself from his taste. The lamp base he was bidding for was vile. Online bids seemed to be popular with the auctioneer often turning to liaise with Olly and his colleagues behind those desks. What did reassure Caroline was that the market for the antiques they were selling still existed. The size of the numbers being called and frequent punctuating knocks from the gavel against the auctioneer's desk proved that deals were being done. It wasn't fine furniture or exquisite artworks that were being sold, but items which would add grace or character to homes. She wasn't the only one to value the past.

With the final item sold, the noise level in the room rose and Caroline sat up straighter in her chair. The crowd were comparing thoughts and moving towards the exits. She looked around to find Olly. He was standing in a knot of his colleagues, listening to what she supposed must be some kind of final briefing but he turned to smile at her and raised a hand to gesture that he'd be with her soon.

She picked up her bag and wandered to the back of the room where a display of hideous paintings lined a breeze block wall. The lack of finesse in the décor amused her. It was a long way from the London auction rooms where Olly worked before.

'I can assure you these aren't fair representation of our business.' Olly's voice was close to her ear, making her jump.

She smiled. 'You won't be disappointed I don't want to bid for any then?'

'Not in the least.' He bent to kiss her cheek and placed a hand between her shoulder blades. She shivered against its warmth. 'How are you?' he asked.

She found herself unable to break the eye contact despite fearing that he'd be able to feel that her heart had begun to beat faster. The heat of his hand on her back could have been branding her. She forced herself to look down and mumbled, 'Better for getting out of Birmingham. Thank you for suggesting it.'

He shook his head to dismiss her thanks. 'It's lovely to see you, as always. Now, may I show you something you might find more interesting than these?'

Caroline followed as he led the way out of the auction room and through the foyer where a queue of successful bidders waited to pay for and collect their items.

'I'm sorry the sale took so long,' he said as he held open a door discreetly marked 'staff only' and ushered her into the back offices. 'We had more than the usual number of difficult-to-shift items.'

'Don't worry; it was interesting. I haven't been to an auction for a while and it's fun to watch.'

'Not quite so much fun for the workers.' Olly smiled at one of the polished young women who came out of a door and walked down the corridor towards them. She returned his smile, but flicked an appraising glance over Caroline, who suppressed a smile.

'It must be hard to keep focussed. Do you have to work at all the sales?'

'Yes. With such a small firm it's very much 'all hands on deck'.'

She nodded, guessing that was another difference from his previous job. No wonder he was keen to hang on to interesting bits of work rather than delegating the research tasks. They probably fed his ego more effectively than sitting in the office doing admin.

A number of doors led off the corridor, most labelled with names and which were clearly offices but Olly paused in front of a blank door and tapped a number into a keypad to release it. He glanced at Caroline and smiled before he pushed the door open and invited her to enter.

While she'd been aware of the security features throughout the building – from displays of the pictures being recorded by CCTV on a monitor in the foyer, to iron bars across the windows where people were waiting to pay – the contents of this room were protected to an even higher degree. Olly turned to another keypad to disable an alarm and stepped forward to remove a padlock securing the door to a cage which filled most of the room.

Caroline followed him inside and looked around. The items stacked inside this room confirmed the sale she'd witnessed was not one of Dunnant's prestige events. To her right hand side were some crates which, from the markings stamped on them, she guessed contained a valuable collection of wine or port. Dominating the centre of the room was a large and ornately carved table to which her limited knowledge attributed seventeenth century origins. The wall to the left was lined with forbidding safes, sealed with a variety of knobs, digital settings or padlocks.

'This must be the treasure chamber,' she said.

'Not entirely.' Olly moved to the back of the room where a dust sheet was draped over an easel, concealing the picture below. 'We also have this. It's causing me considerable trouble.'

He lifted the sheet to reveal the painting and stepped back to stand next to Caroline. She looked at the picture and bit the inside of her lip, aware he was expecting her to say something. As the pause in their conversation lengthened she became anxious and her heart rate increased again. It was the classic nightmare of being examined on a subject she hadn't studied. She didn't recognise the artist, couldn't think of anything useful to say about the composition and, worst of all, didn't like it. If he was testing her knowledge and taste, she was about to fail.

She blinked and looked again, analysing the data as she'd been trained to do. It was a painting in oils. The subject matter was a seascape with a ship buffeted by waves, its sails swollen by wind. The frame was heavy with mouldings. Eighteenth century, perhaps? Nineteenth? Possibly British? She was relying on knowledge of similar pictures she'd seen but really was out of her depth. This was his area of specialism, not hers.

'I know what you're thinking,' he said.

She doubted it but held her tongue and adjusted her expression to an enigmatic smile.

'It's not quite right somehow,' he went on. 'The owner gives it that old chestnut of an attribution, 'Eighteenth century British School', but I'm not happy. Yes, the style says Brooking, but the quality doesn't.'

'No,' said Caroline as she wondered who on earth Brooking was.

'The frame's right, the canvas, paint, varnish, everything. There are labels on the back which seem to indicate a history.'

'And yet?'

'It's too good.'

Caroline frowned. Hadn't he just said the quality wasn't good? She watched as he stepped close to the painting and bent to peer at it. His movement seemed practiced, as though he'd looked at this painting in the same way several times recently. 'Too good?' she prompted.

He returned to stand next to her. 'The paper trail. I haven't seen pictures by Masters documented so well. That this could have survived with all its papers in order is unlikely.'

'Oh. So it's a fake?'

'Perhaps not, perhaps only the papers have been faked by someone who'd like an attribution to increase its value.'

Caroline nodded. It came down to provenance again: where something had been, and why. 'How will you list it in the catalogue then?'

'That is something on which I am still working. Any ideas? The client is understandably peeved by my caution. Apparently my predecessor in this role was not so careful in his analysis.' He shrugged and moved to draw the sheet back over the picture. 'I thought you'd like to see one of the mysteries we're working on here.'

'It's fascinating. Is this what you've been researching in Birmingham, then?' She turned to follow him out of the cage and waited as he fixed the locks in place and set the alarm.

'No, that one's definitely top secret.' He smiled. 'Come on, let's go and see what's happening in the present day.'

Chapter Twenty One

Men and women in bright holiday clothes wandered the paths which criss-crossed the riverside lawn. They licked ice creams or swigged soft drinks from plastic bottles. Caroline envied their freedom to take time out from their lives. She longed for the same opportunity – to leave her problems aside and enjoy the moment.

Beside her Olly stretched his arms along the back of their bench and turned his face up to the sun. His idea that it would be wise to get out of the city for a break had proved sound and he seemed to understand her reluctance to talk. She wanted to watch the parading fashion show which mixed tourists in modern dress with tour guides costumed in Elizabethan tunics and breeches, and to eavesdrop on conversations in accents and languages from all over the globe. It grounded her, fixed her position on a geographical and temporal scale, and provided much-needed contrast. She smiled as a child dropped his ice cream and ran back to his mother with a wail while a swan scrambled from the water to scavenge the molten chocolate mess from the pale stone paving.

None of it mattered; it was just life, mundane and repetitive. Drama was for the theatre. In the backdrop of real life the branded facades of chain stores shoved up against half-timbered neighbours who'd witnessed the changes of four hundred years or more, four hundred years during which families had always behaved as the stars of their own soap operas. Caroline yawned so widely she thought her hand probably too small to cover her open mouth. The perspective was exactly what she'd needed.

'Sorry,' she said.

'For what?' Olly's tone was lazy as though he also found the scene in front of them hypnotic.

'Being dull company.'

He laughed. 'It's never dull, believe me.'

'I could perhaps contribute more to the conversation,' she said.

'What conversation?' He squeezed her shoulder and smiled when she looked up at him. 'It's fine, I know you've got a lot on your mind. Although, if you're open to distractions, I do have a present for you.'

Caroline straightened up and turned slightly on the bench. 'A present? It's not my birthday.'

'No, but as I'm unaware when your birthday is, perhaps I'm allowed to give gifts on random occasions when you might need a little cheering up.'

He took a slim, square navy box from the inside pocket of his jacket and handed it to her. She paused as she held it, and breathed in the citrus scent of his cologne released by the movement of his clothes. 'Thank you,' she said.

The lightness of his words contrasted with the significance of him presenting her with a gift. It suggested she'd been on his mind, and the box seemed very much like the type which might contain jewellery. She considered the implications as she ran a finger over the textured lid. It was unbranded and made from heavy plastic with a straight border engraved upon it: quality, without ostentation.

'You are allowed to open it,' he said.

With the box flat on the palm of her right hand, she used her left thumb to ease the lid upwards to reveal a layer of foam padding. She glanced at him but couldn't read anything from his expression. She didn't know how she should react if he'd bought her a valuable item, and her training also restrained her. Look first. Think. Only touch once the initial evaluation is complete. She wished she had her latex gloves on before she went further.

She removed the padding to reveal a metal disc cushioned on a second layer of foam. She tilted it and found it was a badge with a rusted pin fixed to its reverse. Aware that he was watching her scrutiny she turned her attention to the picture on the face. In colours of purple, green and white it depicted a female figure pushing open iron gates. Around her, a banner unfurled to read 'Votes for women'. It was a suffragette pin; one of many she knew had been sold to raise funds for the cause. Over one hundred years old, the tinges of rust eating into the edges of the enamelled design betrayed its age and indicated it had been used, perhaps pinned with pride on a daily basis to a previous owner's lapel.

She traced her finger tip around the border of the image. White birds followed the figure as she stepped through the gates towards her freedom, ready to accept her power.

'Thank you,' Caroline said, her voice little more than a whisper. 'Where did you find it?'

'Contacts,' he replied and tapped the side of his nose. 'Finding out Susannah was a suffragette showed where you get your argumentative side from. I thought it was something you should have.'

'Yes. Yes, thank you. I love it.'

She looked again at the image. There was something familiar about the design and she tried to place it, perhaps she'd seen it in Susannah's papers, or in the books she'd read about the Women's Suffrage movement. She knew the colours were purple for dignity, white for purity and green for hope. They'd been used on everything from pins like this one to items of jewellery set with amethysts, pearls and peridots.

'It's only a trifle,' he said. 'There's quite a market for some of the suffragette memorabilia. A hunger strike medal recently went for seven thousand.'

She wasn't interested in the price, and it didn't actually matter whether or not she recognised the image; what mattered was that the badge was hers because Olly had found it for her. She tucked it back into its protective cocoon, clicked the lid securely in place and turned to him. 'Really, thank you,' she said and moved closer to kiss his cheek.

It was bergamot, the fragrance from his cologne. Close up it was unmistakeable. A Mediterranean scent which she knew was used even back in ancient times. A memory came back of some research she'd read where chemical analysis of the contents of perfume jars from an archaeological dig had identified the ingredients used. The dig had been on Cyprus. The populist headline suggested they might have found Aphrodite's perfume factory. She breathed in deeply. 'Can I be greedy – is that hug you mentioned on the phone still available?'

He turned to her and she circled her arms around his torso, keen to get as close to the warmth and solidity of his body as possible. With her face pressed against his shoulder and the slow rhythm of his hand stroking her back – down the length of her spine and up again in to her hair – her grief, stress and tension evaporated. Her skin tingled.

'Is this terrible timing?' he asked, his voice no more than a whisper against her ear.

She felt the trace of afternoon stubble on his cheek graze the tip of her nose as she turned her face towards him. 'No,' she said and pressed her lips against his.

*

With a smile Caroline plumped a pillow, leant back and savoured the illicit thrill of being in bed during daylight. She curled her knees into the warmth Olly had left on the other side of the mattress and looked around his bedroom while he fetched them some drinks.

The familiar cheap, modern furniture and cream painted walls were evidence he'd rented the flat furnished, although some traces of his personality had crept in to the room. There was the porcelain pen tray on the bedside table. Even without lifting it to view the makers' mark she could tell from the rich lustre, dark gilt edging and elegant design that it was an antique. Only one of his cufflinks currently rested in the tray. The other was most likely either lost on the floor or still attached to the shirt she hadn't troubled to remove carefully. Propped against the wall was a framed studio portrait of two blonde haired children - a boy and a girl with matching gummy smiles. Caroline turned away.

A pile of books stood on a chest of drawers across the room. She sat up and found that if she squinted she could make out the titles on the spines. They were mostly reference works – price guides and identification manuals relevant to Olly's career – but the topmost book she recognised because an equally pristine copy sat on her own coffee table. It was written by their university tutor who'd landed a book deal and also popped up as the tame expert on occasional television shows.

'Are we jealous?' she asked as Olly came back into the room and handed her a glass of wine.

He looked confused, then smiled as he followed the direction of her gaze to the book. 'Of his new-found fame? No. Of the money? Maybe.' He pulled at the duvet she'd tucked around her, slid back into bed and fitted his legs into the curve of hers. 'Fortunes aren't easily come by in our line of work.'

'Unless you find a treasure trove,' she said.

'Or take the fifteen per cent commission from selling one.'

Caroline laughed and flicked a fingernail against his shoulder. 'So mercenary.'

He pushed his shoulder back against her hand. 'What, and you care only for the artefacts I presume? Preservation is its own reward?'

She sipped at her drink. The chilled, dry white wine cooled her mouth and sharpened her thoughts. What he'd said wasn't true. Preservation was worthwhile, but it hadn't felt like any kind of reward for a while now. 'Do you ever wish you'd chosen a different career?' she asked.

'No, I think I'm quite well suited to my present field and it suits me.' He put his glass down and ran his finger along the line of her collarbone. 'I get to spend my time in the presence of beauty.'

She squirmed away from his touch. The past few hours had been a wonderful escape and Olly's attention a great confidence boost. But she had to address her problems, take action.

'Everything OK?' he asked.

'No, I need to, um…' She pushed herself into a sitting upright position, drew her knees to her chest and hugged them. 'I should…'

'Nothing. You should do nothing. There's time.' He began to stroke her arm. 'Look, Caroline, this is fine. We're fine. Just relax.'

'I should go.'

'You should drink your wine and stay the night.'

She took another sip. It was good wine. 'There are things I need to think through, stuff to sort out. And, ugh.' She covered her eyes with a hand and shook her head.

'What is it?' He sat up and put his arms around her. 'What can I help with?'

'You can't. It's not Nan, or Susannah. It's me. I don't achieve anything. I'm not productive or creative. The past doesn't change.'

He released his grip but took hold of one of her hands instead. 'Our interpretation of it does. You tell the stories of history, without which humanity would be destined forever to repeat the same mistakes. You save us.'

'That's ridiculous.' She took a deep breath. 'We assume people today are somehow 'better' than people in the past because we don't keep slaves, or make war in the same way. We think we're 'civilised' and the past was sometimes barbaric. But it's more complicated than that. It's our individual actions we're judged on, and individuals don't act in the same way as whole societies. As individuals we probably haven't changed much, even if the culture around us has. Culture puts a veneer of interpretation on events, and that's all I do.'

He leant away to retrieve his glass and a draught of cold air slipped under the duvet. Caroline was aware of the shrill and hectoring tone to her voice, aware that she was panicking, but couldn't stop. 'Look at Susannah's life – her talent, her actions – I feel inadequate. What have I achieved? What difference have I made? Preserving is not as fulfilling as creating or changing. That's what she did, wasn't it? And the rest of my family, they all make things or do things. Nan's house and that furniture you admired – funded by the manufacture of bolts!' She paused to take another gulp of wine and felt his hand on her arm.

'From bolts to balti; Birmingham's come a long way.' He laughed. 'Listen, do you think you might be feeling this way because you're under rather a lot of pressure? Bereavement is hard, and from what you've told me it sounds as if your family aren't making things easy for themselves.' He tucked the duvet back around her. 'And, when I called in to see you that first day at the museum, it looked as though you were embroiled in some office politics. It's all come at once, hasn't it?'

His proximity was too tempting and she slumped against his chest and closed her eyes. 'I need to be doing something,' she said.

He prised her fingers away from the stem of the wineglass and she heard a clink as he placed it beside his own. 'For tonight,' he said, punctuating each word with a kiss starting at her shoulder and working in towards her neck, 'all you need to do is stay here.'

*

Caroline suppressed a yawn and knocked on the panelled door to Gerald's office with her notebook in hand. The notes outlined her exhibition proposal but as her prepared spiel had been looping round her mind during the early morning drive back from Stratford, she doubted she'd need them. Whatever doubts she had about her commitment to her career, there was no excuse for being unprofessional. She'd put the work in, might as well give the presentation her best shot.

'Come in.'

She tried not to read anything in to the cool tone of voice, turned the brass handle and stepped into her manager's cluttered office. Piles of paper on his desk were weighted down with pots which could have been ancient, or could have been made by his children, there was no space for more books on his shelves so piles of them littered the floor and an oil painting stood on end leant against his desk.

'Good morning, Gerald. Can you spare a minute for me to run through the exhibition proposal I mentioned?'

He turned his head slowly towards her as though loathe to deprive his newspaper of his attention. 'A proposal? I'm afraid I don't recall your mentioning it.'

She returned his gaze without flinching but her confidence wavered. 'It won't take more than a moment. I'd, um, just like to hear your initial reaction before I work up the details. May I?' She gestured to the chair in front of his desk.

He nodded and leant back, eyes narrowed. The suspicion that he couldn't remember her name crossed Caroline's mind. It didn't help. She took a deep breath.

'What I think is lacking,' she said, 'is representation of the domestic work undertaken by women. The museum collections reflect Birmingham's industrial and trade

198

history, but the role played by women outside the factories isn't covered in detail.'

'Sounds fascinating.' His dry tone indicated he didn't mean it.

'Well, I think…'

'What period?'

The interruption unsettled her further. 'I'm sorry?'

'What period of history are you wittering about?'

She began to regret being there, it was clearly bad timing. And now he'd definitely remember who she was, for all the wrong reasons. 'Um, Victorian, Industrial Revolution, through to post-war I suppose.'

He picked up the newspaper and flapped it to straighten the broadsheet before folding the page to highlight an article he handed across the desk. 'There, you see that? National curriculum, Key Stages Two and Three. Tell me how your idea fits in.'

The text blurred as Caroline tried to scan read it. The implication of the headline was that government proposals were to change topics on education syllabuses, to redirect learning to a fuller appreciation of British history. Her mind raced but didn't deliver a solution. 'Perhaps I should do a little more investigation,' she said and pushed the newspaper back onto his desk.

Gerald rubbed his eyes. 'We will need to develop our education programme to meet any changes. Is that you?'

'Education?' Caroline shook her head. 'No, not me.'

He frowned and she spoke again in case he was about to ask what the hell she was doing there. 'I'm Antiquities, mainly, but you asked us all to chip in with proposals.'

'But your idea is regarding something less ancient?'

Caroline took a deep breath and launched back into her pitch. 'Yes. I believe museums have a role in speaking for individuals, not only entire civilisations or historical periods. We should also tell the every day, humane stories. And I particularly feel there'd be community interest in and relevance to an exhibition about the history of women's craft works and their impact on home life in Birmingham over the past two hundred years.' She speeded up as she spoke, gasping to get the last words out as she ran out of breath. The spiel she'd prepared sounded unconvincing even to her own ears.

Gerald drew the newspaper back towards him. 'I can't see that it would fit with our learning priorities.'

'Community outreach,' she said, grasping to respond to the criticism. 'Older people, links to immigrant populations, the city of a thousand trades in the home as well as the workplace.' She pressed her lips together to stem the gabbling and waited for him to speak.

He turned to look at the painting on the wall behind his desk. It showed the museum on its opening day with a crowd of citizens eager to enter. Caroline knew the history; she'd revised it for her interview and wondered how closely the founding principles still guided the museum's strategies. Birmingham's nineteenth century citizens demanded an art gallery and examples of metalworking had been gathered to inform and inspire those working in the industry. The collections expanded into ceramics and decorative arts, but the emphasis remained on applied skills and many of those skilled craftworkers were women who'd been busy with domestic crafts as well.

Gerald sighed. 'I'm not convinced, but still: work the idea up and keep the costs low. Then we'll see what other ideas you're competing against.'

She nodded and left his office. Hearing the idea out loud hadn't convinced her either.

Chapter Twenty Two

It was warmer outside than Caroline had anticipated and she unbuttoned her jacket and slowed her pace as she walked along the tow path. She ignored the nagging inner voice which immediately accused her of stealing time away from family and work responsibilities; it sounded far too much like Alice. A phone call would have been enough to tell Richard the details of Beth's funeral, but she'd found she wanted to see him. It was as though the Farlane's building drew her towards it.

The past few days had been difficult. Alice and Peter had asked for her input to the funeral arrangements, but without sincerity. She'd hardly dared state her preferences for the flowers and faked enthusiasm for the details Alice outlined. Work had been uninspiring. Despite Gerald's go-ahead to prepare her proposal, Caroline found that even she'd lost commitment to the idea. Could a celebration of knitting really change the world? Even Olly hadn't been in touch since she'd left his flat and she mentally kicked herself for even expecting he would.

She straightened her shoulders and turned away from the canal. This wasn't a good time to be starting things. She'd probably feel better after the funeral and no harm would come of keeping her head down for the time being. Stirring things up with the family while emotions were strained might lead to another rift like that between Susannah and William one hundred years before. Susannah at least had her convictions and friends within the

Suffragette movement to reassure her; Caroline had more to lose than to gain.

'Come on in,' Richard said as she arrived at the factory. 'Take a seat and I'll make you a drink.'

She turned the chair before sitting down. No point facing Richard's desk when he wasn't in the room and a decision still had to be made about the painting hanging on the back wall of the office. The legal implications of Susannah's loan had yet to be untangled.

As she studied the painting for a second time it triggered an odd sort of déjà vu. She frowned. It wasn't only that she'd seen the picture before; she knew she'd seen something else like it. Her mind raced to make connections. The tall iron gates to the building were captured in the act of being opened and the figure who pushed them seemed a smear of white paint. Caroline stood and squinted at the picture. There were other figures depicted: men in dark clothes with light coloured aprons approached the factory or were just visible inside the doorway. That figure holding the gate though, it seemed as though all the clothes were white. That was no apron. Caroline leant closer. The figure wore no cap and seemed to have flowing hair. It could almost seem to be female, or could it?

She stepped back as Richard returned and handed her a mug of tea. 'When did you first employ women here?' she asked.

'During World War Two. We changed more of the production to munitions again and there were plenty of takers for the work. My dad's decision, I think. We were lucky. Other factories were bombed.'

Caroline nodded. 'But this picture was painted earlier than that.' The symbols in the picture were clear now she'd studied it and Susannah's impudence made her smile. 'This image, of the gate being pushed open, it's not true to life is it?'

Richard shook his head. 'I took it for artistic licence. It looks like the machinery's operating inside, so the gates would be fixed open. I thought perhaps the intention was to invite the person looking at the picture in to the scene, but I'm no expert on art appreciation.'

'Perhaps it's to make a very specific point.' Caroline put her mug down and retrieved the small navy box from her handbag. She removed the lid, passed it to Richard and watched as he compared the image from the Suffragette pin to that on the painting.

He laughed. 'Well that's sneaky. Political propaganda dressed up as a pretty picture.'

'I think Susannah was teaching her family a lesson. Shame it was wasted on them really.'

She took the box back and lifted the badge out, holding it in line with the picture so the image overlaid the gate in the painting. It was all there: the suffragette's colours of pure white, hopeful green and dignified purple all present in the scenery around the edges of the picture. The splashes of colour surrounded the factory building and that female figure opening the gate as though she owned the factory made a fine punchline. Susannah hadn't ever given up trying to change opinions and her influence had made it through to the present day. The Garrolds did not ignore their responsibilities or convictions. They spoke up. Caroline wondered if she could be brave enough to do the same.

'Have you decided what we should do with the painting?' Richard asked.

She smiled. 'I think it deserves a wider audience, don't you?'

*

The microphone attached to the church lectern amplified the rustle as Alice smoothed out a sheet of paper. Caroline looked away and focussed instead on the mounds of floral arrangements which almost concealed Beth's coffin, unable to watch as her normally brisk and competent mother took time to get her voice under control before speaking.

'Beth, my mother,' Alice's voice cracked on the word mother and she paused before continuing, 'was a warm, welcoming and forgiving woman. At 85 years old she'd seen so many changes, but if anyone ever suggested that things are no longer like the 'good old days', she disagreed. 'The best time is now,' she'd say, 'because you and I are here together.' It was guaranteed to make anyone in her company feel special but I really believe she meant it.'

There was a pause, during which Caroline heard sniffs from the pews behind her. She glanced at Peter and could see his cheeks were wet. She reached out and took his hand, glad that he squeezed back.

Alice went on, 'Mum didn't make time for regrets; she preferred to focus on potential and she could see potential in the most unlikely places. Whether it was finding a new use for a jug with a chipped spout, or devising a solution for a family problem, she always had an interesting idea. I know I won't be alone in missing her because of that.' She paused again.

Caroline looked up, concerned delivering the eulogy was proving too painful. She watched as Alice dabbed at her eyes with a white handkerchief embroidered with blue flowers. Caroline recognised it. She owned some like that herself. Beth had embroidered them both a set - soft cotton squares edged with forget-me-nots - as a present on the first Christmas after Caroline left home for university. She wished she had one of them to hand herself, to dry the tears which ran down her cheeks.

'We've all got our own favourite memories of Beth,' Alice said eventually. 'Myself, I'll treasure some of the things she taught me, such as her special recipes with hidden vegetables that perhaps Caroline and Peter still don't know they ate. But there's one of her phrases in particular which I'll miss. I don't think she was aware of saying it, it had become a routine for her and I'm not sure when she started. The words must have come from half-heard road safety advice and she repeated them to everyone she said goodbye to. 'Take care then,' she'd say. 'Look about you."

Caroline gulped, the realisation she'd never hear Beth say those words again winding her like a punch. She closed her eyes and slumped against Peter.

Alice speeded up, obviously keen to finish. 'It's advice she took to heart herself. She was always so interested in other people, especially her family and friends. We no longer have her here to say so, but I hope none of us forget to look about us and remember her, with love.'

She stepped back from the lectern and walked quickly back to the front pew. Caroline's face was wet and she was grateful when Peter reached into his pocket and passed her a tissue. She didn't hear the vicar's closing words and stood on reflex when her dad and Peter stepped forward to help the undertakers bear the coffin out of the church. As they lifted it, she followed Alice to form a procession behind them, slipping her arm through Alice's as they walked. Alice wouldn't meet her gaze, but did squeeze her elbow against Caroline's hand.

The cortege drove along suburban streets to the red sandstone gateposts of Lodge Hill crematorium. The funeral director got out of the gleaming hearse and, carrying his top hat, walked in front of the cars to lead the way along a wide, smooth drive flanked by gravestones and memorial benches. They pulled up under a canopy fronting the brick chapel and the mourners stood aside as pallbearers carried the coffin inside. Birds sang from surrounding trees and the occasional shrill laugh from a member of the funeral party provided an inappropriate soundtrack. No one seemed sure how to behave. Caroline watched people adjusting unfamiliar formal clothes as they waited; catching themselves smiling at old acquaintances then realising it wasn't a happy occasion. After a brief, impersonal service, an automated screen slid around the coffin and the congregation filed outside.

A freshly block-paved patio had areas marked for the floral tributes of each cremation and Caroline left Alice and Ray talking to some of the mourners while she examined the flowers for Beth. A particularly garish arrangement arrested her and she bent to check the card, wondering who could have so little feeling for what Beth herself would have preferred that they considered sunflowers an appropriate tribute. As she reached to move the ribbon obscuring the attached card she noticed a woman approaching and withdrew her hand.

'Hello,' the woman said as Caroline straightened up. 'I hope you don't mind me being here. I wanted to share my condolences. I remember your nan so well. She used to make us ice cream sundaes in the summer holidays.'

Caroline looked at the woman's face in confusion, until recognition of her features fell into place. 'Steph? Is that you? It must be twenty years.'

'And I'm sorry to catch up with you again in these circumstances.' Steph put a hand on Caroline's arm. 'My mum saw the notice about the funeral in the local paper. I wanted to pay my respects and, of course, I hoped you'd be here as well. It's been about seventeen years, I think. Too long.'

'Gosh. Thank you so much for coming.' Caroline hesitated, but then reached out to draw her old school friend into a hug before holding her at arm's length. 'You look great, how are you?'

'I'm fine. Still in Birmingham - got a house in Hall Green. Married, two children. Nothing out of the ordinary. What about you?'

'Oh, um, well, back in Birmingham, working at the museum.' She grimaced. 'Divorced, renting, bored.'

Steph shook her head. 'And bereaved, so don't beat yourself up about any of that. We should get together and talk properly some time.'

'I'd like that. Very much.' Caroline became aware of someone else hovering near by and turned to find Richard waiting to speak to her.

'I'll leave you to it,' Steph said. 'There'll be lots of people you have to talk to today. I'm glad I got to say hello again though.' She passed Caroline a slip of paper. 'Here, I wrote down my phone number, call me when you get a chance. And don't worry - things may look bleak at the moment, but I guarantee they'll get better.' She kissed Caroline's cheek and turned to leave.

Caroline smiled. It was good to see Steph again and she couldn't now think why she'd let the friendship lapse when she'd gone off to university. It was only the difficulty of keeping in touch with people in the days before mobile phones or social networking which had come between them. Not a good enough excuse for not getting in touch as soon as she'd returned to Birmingham, especially when Steph had been such a close friend for so many years. For now though, she had relatives to deal with.

'Are you OK?' Richard asked.

Caroline nodded and followed his gaze up to the chimney rising like a steeple from the building behind the chapel. Pale smoke had started to emerge.

'I wondered if you'd perhaps introduce me to your mum?' he said. 'I'd like to meet her but didn't want to announce myself if you think this isn't the best time. Her eulogy was lovely, but very emotional and I don't want to upset her any further.'

'Of course she'll want to meet you. You're cousins after all.' Caroline started to walk back towards her parents but noticed the funeral director had already brought the car round. He held the door open as though he expected his passengers to join him imminently. 'You will come back to the house, won't you, Richard? Perhaps it would be better for me to explain things there.'

He nodded and she went to join her parents. 'Is there anything we else we need to do here?'

'No,' Ray said, 'the funeral director will pick up the ashes later and hold them until we've decided what to do. I've told most people to come back to the house with us, except that chap you were just talking to…'

'Don't worry, I've let him know.' Caroline didn't want Alice distracted by Richard's presence at that moment. 'Did you see Steph came? Wasn't that lovely of her?'

'Steph?' Alice asked. 'From school? That is kind. Your nan made such an impression on people.' She sniffed and dabbed at her eyes with her hankie again.

Ray led her to the funeral car and Caroline paused, distracted by the sight of Steph kneeling to lay flowers at a headstone in the middle of a nearby row before she joined her parents for the silent drive back to Beth's house.

The family had gathered there earlier to wait for the cortege to take Beth away for the final time. Ray had collected chairs from around the house into the living room and Alice had stacked the fridge full with clingfilm-covered platters of sandwiches. Peter had left rows of glasses ready for drinks to be poured.

Nothing was how Beth herself had arranged things on the occasions she'd hosted parties and Caroline found walking back into the house to find everything unfamiliar almost more upsetting than the funeral service. She glanced into the living room and her eye was immediately drawn to a framed photo of Beth smiling which Alice had brought from her own mantelpiece. She choked down more tears and backed out of the room.

As a distraction, Caroline tried to make herself useful. The kettle reached boiling point and she filled pot after pot with tea. Beth's house was full of people whose names she couldn't recall. Many of them were friends of Beth's from her time working in a local charity shop; others were from her book club. There were old and current neighbours, friends stretching back decades and even a woman who'd told Caroline she and Beth and been young mums together.

Not so well represented were family. She, Peter and their mum were the only immediate relatives Beth had, and Richard of course. But Beth had obviously nurtured a wide circle of friends. Caroline heard several stories of how Beth had been fondly welcomed into other people's lives, and would be sadly missed.

Once most people had left, she steered Richard away from the stragglers in the kitchen towards the living room. 'Come on,' she said, 'let's talk to my mum.'

They found Alice slumped on the sofa. The day had clearly drained her but she put her glass down and sketched a smile as Caroline and Richard approached. A tinkling chime as Beth's mantelpiece carriage clock registered a quarter hour broke the silence. Caroline checked her watch which disputed the time told by the clock. Interruption to Beth's weekly winding routine had obviously caused it to run slow. She smoothed the sleeve of her black jacket back into place.

'Mum,' she said, 'there's someone I'd like you to meet.'

Alice snapped her features into a polite expression. 'Hello, I'm sorry, we haven't had a chance to speak. Were you a friend of my mother's?' She leant forward to shake Richard's hand.

'Mum,' Caroline interrupted as their hands touched, 'this is Richard, Nan met him just before she died. He's a relative of ours. Your cousin.'

Alice's smile vanished and she dropped Richard's hand as her eyes widened. 'You? You're the one who wanted Mum to change her will?' She stood and Richard took a step backwards. 'I don't know how you dare show your face,' she said.

Caroline placed a hand on her arm. 'Mum, you've misunderstood. I've been trying to explain to you. Richard didn't ask Nan to do anything; he was trying to give her something…'

Alice was in no mood to listen. 'All that happened in the last weeks of my mother's life was stress and pain. If you had any motive but trouble, why didn't you get in touch before now?'

'Alice, please,' Richard said, 'I haven't been in touch before now because you know it was difficult. Aunt Beth and my dad lost touch a long time ago and I know it was entirely my dad's fault. But I assure you I only tried to give Beth what I thought belonged to her. I didn't upset her, I promise you that.'

'Ha! And I'm supposed to think a Garrold's promise is worth anything?' Alice shook Caroline's hand off her arm and raised a finger in Richard's face. 'Your family took everything. Everything!'

'Mum!' Caroline was shocked by the realisation that Alice had known all about their shared history with the Garrold family but couldn't stand by and allow her to berate Richard. 'None of this is Richard's fault. Everything that may have been done in the past was done by people who are now dead. Let's try to be civilised about this.'

Alice rounded on her. 'Civilised? Oh, yes. That would suit you. Why face a problem when you can back away from it?'

Caroline felt the sting of the words and for a moment couldn't breathe. Her mouth opened but she couldn't speak either.

'I think I'd better leave.' Richard turned and walked towards the door.

'Is everything all right?' Ray had come back into the room and furrowed his forehead as he looked at the three of them. He stepped towards Richard. 'I'm Ray, Beth's son-in-law,' he said. 'It was good of you to come.'

The stock platitude directed Alice's ire towards him. 'No,' she said. 'It was not good of him to come. It was not good of him to get involved in Mum's life at all.'

Caroline noticed her dad's eyes flick towards the table by the sofa and she also counted the number of empty glasses there. Was Alice drunk? It was a better excuse for her behaviour than anger and Caroline latched on to it.

'Mum, why don't you sit down? And Richard, please stay, just for a moment.'

Richard shook his head. 'I think perhaps there'll be a better time for this.' He clasped Caroline's hand. 'Thank you, and I'm sorry - not just for your loss, that's what everyone's saying. I'm sorry I didn't get to know my Aunt Beth sooner. Everything I've heard said about her this afternoon has convinced me it's my loss.'

As he left the room Caroline realised she was crying again. She turned to face Alice who had sunk back onto the sofa. 'He's not the enemy, Mum. It was Nan who wanted to do something for him, not him who asked for it. You know what she was like.'

'Come on, love.' Ray put an arm around his wife. 'Perhaps now isn't the time to talk about this?' His glare at Caroline told her it really wasn't the time for any more. Unfortunately Alice wasn't listening.

'Well the Garrolds will have nothing from us. They gave us nothing and they'll get nothing in return,' she snapped.

Caroline thought of Susannah and tried to summon some of her determination. 'I'm executor of the will,' she said, her voice quiet but controlled. 'I'm in charge of the disbursements and gifts. Nan might not have changed the text of her will, but I know what her wishes were.'

Alice looked up, her eyes glinting. 'If you do anything outside of the text of my mother's will, I'll take you to court.'

Chapter Twenty Three

The edge of each stone tread up the stairs into the museum showed the wear from generations of footsteps. Caroline studied each one as she climbed and thought about how every visitor took something away with them: knowledge, inspiration or time passed. Fortunately her day off had fallen on the day after the funeral so there'd been time to think before she returned to work. She hadn't left the flat and had barely eaten. Ideas began to germinate though and she felt stronger mentally now, if not emotionally.

Instead of going straight to her office, she took a detour into the seventeenth century gallery where the painting of Minerva hung. As she examined it, one of her ideas began to seem achievable. She straightened her shoulders and smiled.

'Bit insipid for my taste,' Bill said. She hadn't noticed his presence and wondered why he was in that room. He stepped forward to examine the label for the painting. 'I prefer a bit more blood and gore with my scenes of warfare and retribution. This is a bit tame and girly.'

Caroline laughed. 'I'm all for a bit of quiet myself. There are too many bloodstains across history.'

'Hmm, you do of course know that Minerva is a myth rather than an actual historical figure? You and I are in the business of facts, not fiction.'

'Of course. And why? Why do we do this?'

Bill frowned at her. 'Is that rhetorical or are you having an existential crisis? Wait there, I'll fetch Denise.'

Caroline shook her head. 'No need. No crisis. A moment of clarity, that's all. I'd lost sight of the reasons I got into this, why I love history. I mean, it's all about what's worth remembering, isn't it? Whether that's ancient skills and knowledge, the fall-out from political manoeuvring, or just the mistakes people made. The point is how we can use what people have learnt or done in the past to make life better today.'

'Very, um, worthy.' Bill's tone suggested he didn't entirely agree. 'So why were you grinning at this picture then? It's not the truth, or even great art.'

'It is the truth: some things are worth fighting for. That message is in myths, in Bible stories, in reported historical fact. You have to work out which side you're on in life and fight the right battles. And, whatever ails you, you generally find some ancient Greek or Roman worked out the solution ages ago.'

'Well, thanks for the pep talk. I'll leave you to it.' Bill turned to go and Caroline noticed the folder he was carrying.

'What's that?'

He lifted it as if surprised to find it in his hands. 'This? Oh, only my proposals for next year's programme. Just dropping it in to Gerald's office.'

She watched as he left the gallery before turning back to the picture. 'Minerva, goddess of wisdom, protecting Peace and Plenty,' she muttered to herself. 'Perfect. I've a lot to learn from you.'

*

Steph stirred her coffee and looked up at Caroline. 'So what are you going to do?'

They'd met in a city-centre café and spent the lunch hour catching up on the missed years of careers, romances and life choices. Now they were on to another round of coffees, family formed the topic of conversation and the problem of executing Beth's will intrigued Steph.

Caroline sighed. 'The right thing, of course. The problem is deciding exactly what that is. The law says her current will stands - no question. But I know she planned to change it, and I know the general direction of her thoughts, so it seems wrong to ignore those wishes.'

'But if your mum disagrees...'

Caroline nodded. 'Things could get messy.' She lifted her cup and glanced out of the window as she sipped. Up the road from where they sat were the Family Courts - an anonymous building she'd noticed only because of the numbers of ordinary people filing past security checks dressed in what were clearly bought-for-the-occasion 'best' clothes rather than standard office or casual attire. She had no desire to join them should Alice stand by her threat to sue over any divergence from the text of Beth's will. That left two options: forget the changes or persuade Alice they were the right course. Neither would be easy.

'Do you remember at school, in History with Mrs Hudson we wrote a play about Boudica?' Steph sat up straighter as she spoke and pointed across the table at Caroline. 'You're her. That was all about the terms of a will wasn't it? Ancient Britons versus the Romans. She fought to make sure the right thing was done. Go Boudica! Rule Britannia!'

Steph's loud enthusiasm attracted glances from the neighbouring tables and Caroline blushed as she shook her head. 'She was fighting because her husband's will wasn't respected. Instead of his land staying in the family like he said, the Romans grabbed it when he died. I'm not the plucky ancient Briton in this story; I'm assisting the Roman invaders. My mum's Boudica and there's every possibility she might replay history with battles ending in lots of futile death and destruction. Boudica was no saint; much innocent blood was shed.'

'Oh,' Steph said, 'silly of me to try to outsmart a learned historian.' She frowned. 'But the Roman occupation wasn't entirely a bad thing in the long run. There was a bit of civilising of the barbarians after all: plumbing, decent roads, wine…'

'So in about two millennia my mum might forgive me?'

Steph smiled. 'I wouldn't hold your breath.'

'I just don't know if the risk's worth it. I mean, I might get everything wrong, hurt everyone…' Caroline's throat tightened and she stopped speaking and concentrated on swallowing down her panic.

'You might. Or, you might get everything right. I wouldn't put it past you. I mean, look at you. At school you were always the one with aspirations, plans and ambitions. And you did it - you went off and got your degree, landed a fancy job doing something you love. I don't doubt you can do whatever turns out to be the right thing now.'

Caroline paused with her coffee cup half way to her mouth and stared at Steph.

'I don't doubt it,' Steph repeated.

Her words were the encouragement Caroline needed. She nodded. 'I'll let you know. But this is going a step further. I'm not happy any more only studying history. I need to do something, to get involved.'

'Do that. Also, keep me up to date on the latest about Olly, won't you?' She winked and laughed.

Caroline drained her coffee and, to cover her embarrassment, signalled to the waitress for their bill. 'I can tell you now. He's bad news.'

Steph grinned. 'Which is why he's so appealing, right?'

Caroline shook her head. 'You make me feel fifteen again. Although actually, thanks for that.'

*

Caroline flopped onto Beth's sofa and tapped her fingernails against the side of her mug as she looked

215

around. She'd already packed up lots of Beth's possessions and the room had lost all its familiar associations. 'Will it be worth it, do you think?' she asked.

Olly straightened up from the crouched position he'd assumed under the dining table and scrawled a note on his pad. 'That very much depends on how worried you are about the inheritance tax bill. This house must easily put you way over the threshold.'

Caroline groaned and wished again that she hadn't been nominated sole executor of Beth's will. Why was it these tasks never fell to Peter? 'It's all going to take months to resolve, isn't it?'

He clipped the top back on to his fountain pen and joined her on the sofa. 'These things do. And if you'll promise not to breathe a word of it to my boss, I'm going to recommend you send a couple of items to a specialist auction rather than considering a local sale.'

'You think there's something special here then?'

'You know there is. Why else would I have been so keen to assist you today if not to get a better look?'

Caroline hesitated. Without consciously admitting it to herself she'd hoped he'd been happy to help because he wanted to see her again. In a carefully neutral voice she asked, 'What do you think's particularly valuable then?'

'Well, there's this,' he said and placed a kiss on her forehead, 'and the sideboard. Possibly that chair.'

She blushed and looked at the chair he'd nodded towards to avoid having to meet his eye. Its seat was of woven rushes that had seen better days, but now she looked at it properly, she could see the frame was elegant. The struts of the ladder back were curved and increased in gradation up the back. The supports to the arms were shaped with simple decorative turning. As she thought back she could remember it always sitting in the corner of the room, rather than being drawn forward for every day use - as though Beth had treated it as special. She was surprised she'd never noticed it before; she'd always assumed it was set aside because it was a mismatch to the rest of the dining set. 'Who do you think made it then?' she asked.

'Potentially, but only potentially mind, Philip Clissett from the Cotswolds: much admired, much sought after and hence much copied. We need someone more knowledgeable than me to assess it. I think it's the finials on the ladder back that clinch it, but I'm not sure. I have seen them go for around a thousand apiece in good condition. The sideboard is Heal and Sons. No expertise needed, there's an ivorine label on the side of one of the drawers. I think it's an early piece though. Lovely styling.'

'And the rest?'

Olly shrugged. 'Mixed quality. I mean, obviously this sofa's modern. The dining table's nice, and that little oak writing desk. The clock - does it usually keep good time?' Caroline nodded and he made an extra note on his pad. 'Then there are the pictures…' The tone of his voice implied he was building up to reveal something exciting.

She turned to look at him. 'Do I need something stronger to drink than tea?'

'Don't worry; I'll catch you if you faint.' He reached over her head to slip an arm around her shoulders. 'All part of the service.'

Caroline glanced around the room. The pictures ranged from mass market prints to family photographs, but there was also a series of watercolour sketches framed and displayed in a row above the mantelpiece. They were very different from Susannah's paintings and used strong colours to fill square designs in which leaves and tendrils curled around fruits and flowers. Each element of the design was outlined with a thick black line. Caroline was surprised she'd not noticed their quality before, but then Beth had always placed cards and photos propped in front of them, or obscured the display with flower arrangements.

'You must mean those designs,' she said and nodded towards them. 'Nothing else in here looks significant.'

'Oh I don't know,' Olly replied and ran a hand down her arm. 'That photograph is particularly charming.'

He pointed and Caroline blushed as she realised he was indicating a family snapshot her dad had taken on a beach holiday. Her teenage self sat in the foreground of the photo, awkwardly hugging her knees to conceal a bikini-clad body. 'You looked very much like that when we first met,' he said.

'At no point during our time at university did I wear a bikini.'

'No? Must be my memory playing tricks with me. A little fantasising perhaps.'

He squeezed her again and she took the opportunity to nudge his ribs with her elbow while not actually pulling away from his embrace. 'Anyway, the designs,' she said, 'are you going to share your insight?'

'I suppose that's what I'm here for. They're cartoons, sketched proposals for stained glass panels, and they're by Florence Camm. They're signed. I imagine she and your great-aunt might have known each other; they probably overlapped at the Art School. Anyway, I have seen her pictures go for up to £500 a piece and you've got six there, of very decent quality. If we find the designs ever got made up - say in a cathedral or somewhere - the sketches would be worth even more. So it's all adding up.'

Caroline shook her head. 'I've heard of her. Some of her work's in the museum. I just can't believe I never noticed any of this stuff. With my training it's shocking how blind I've been.'

Olly pulled her against him. 'Don't feel bad about it. You were too busy living with it all, and lucky you to have had that opportunity. I imagine there were always other things going on when you were in this room so you didn't stop and really look at things.'

'You're being kind. It's unforgiveable. I should have made sure Nan had the correct insurance, asked her what she knew about the histories of these items. I should have done a lot more.'

Olly turned her face towards him and pressed his lips against hers whispering 'Sssh' in between kisses. She gulped against the panicky tension in her throat and focussed on the sensation instead. Hints of his citrus cologne tantalised her with erotic memories as she moved closer. Her fingertips slipped over the close-woven fabric of his shirt tempted by the warmth of his skin underneath and as she twisted her body to face his she began to think that perhaps the things she'd neglected in the past didn't matter after all. The present needed more urgent attention.

His notebook fell to the floor with a thud as he brought his other arm up to embrace her, and the sofa's springs creaked beneath them. She was lost in sensation until the sound of the front door slamming and Alice's voice calling, 'Hello? Who's there?' ruined the mood.

Caroline jumped up, straightened her skirt and smoothed her hair before calling back, 'It's OK, Mum. It's me and...' She trailed off as she caught sight of Olly smirking as he re-fastened the shirt buttons she'd undone.

'And what?' Alice asked as she entered the room. 'Whose car is that outside?'

Olly stood and extended his hand. 'Good afternoon, Mrs Hipkins. May I express my sincere condolences on your loss.'

Alice looked from him to Caroline and back again. Her eyes narrowed. 'Thank you,' she said.

'Mum, this is Olly, um, Oliver Mortimer. He's a friend of mine who's in antiques. I asked him to come and give us some advice on Nan's things.'

'Us?' Alice asked. 'I don't recall you mentioning it.'

Caroline flushed deeper. 'I didn't want to trouble you, Mum. Olly's doing this as a favour; it's nothing formal. Yet.'

'There are some valuable pieces here, Mrs Hipkins. I envy you having grown up among them.' Olly crossed the room to retrieve his jacket from where he'd slung it across the back of a dining chair and extracted a leather pouch from a pocket. 'I think Caroline's wise to get them properly valued.' He glanced at Caroline. 'May I take some photographs to go with my notes?'

Caroline nodded. 'Of course. Perhaps we should leave him to it for a moment, Mum?' She led the way into the kitchen and flicked the switch on the kettle. 'I'm sorry if you'd rather I'd told you I was starting to do all this, but I really didn't want you to feel any extra stress.'

'It was quite stressful to arrive here and find a strange car on the drive.'

'Mine's there too. Surely you knew everything was OK if I was here as well?'

Alice didn't reply, but looked away. Caroline sighed and opened a cupboard to get a mug for her. The thrill and embarrassment of almost being caught otherwise occupied with Olly had faded. Now she was irritated. What did Alice expect? That nothing would be done unless she herself was in charge?

In the pause after Caroline had finished scraping the tea bag canister across the kitchen counter and delving in the cutlery drawer for a clean spoon, Alice asked, 'What did the will say about Mum's possessions? Did she know some were valuable?'

Caroline took a breath. She'd hoped not to discuss specifics with Alice just yet. 'Not many items were mentioned. It's mostly covered by general bequests.'

Olly joined them before Alice could ask any other questions. He slipped his camera back into his pocket and said, 'I've taken all the details; perhaps I should write up my notes and let you have my guideline valuations?'

His expression was of purely professional interest and Caroline could have kicked him for being so smooth. 'Thank you, that would be great,' she said. 'I'll see you out.'

'It was good to meet you, Mrs Hipkins,' he said as he turned to shake Alice's hand. 'Once again, my condolences.'

Caroline took hold of his elbow and pulled him into the hall, closing the kitchen door behind him. 'You are infuriating,' she said.

'Me? Or her?' he replied and put his arms around her waist. 'Because my money would be on her really.'

Caroline squirmed away from him. 'Not helping,' she said. 'I mean, yes, obviously you are helping and I'm very grateful. Thank you for coming over and thank you for sharing your knowledge.' Her shoulders sagged.

'That's OK. As I said, I'll set this out in writing, follow up on a couple of queries and let you have my thoughts in the next few days.' He bent to kiss her, his mouth lingering on each cheek. 'And if there's anything else I can do, Aphrodite,' he whispered, 'you know where I am.'

Caroline closed the front door behind him and leant against it until her heart rate returned to normal. When she returned to the kitchen she found Alice had made tea for them both and set the mugs at opposite ends of the kitchen table. She sat at the head of the table, arms and legs crossed and a frown fixed to her forehead.

Caroline sat down. 'I'm a bit worried about the insurance,' she said, hoping she could distract Alice with a minor practical problem.

Alice looked at her. 'I take it your man thinks Mum's things are worth more than we knew then?'

Caroline blushed. 'Not 'my' man. He's just a, um, friend who's an expert at these things.'

'Shame,' Alice replied. 'He seems charming.'

Caroline took a sip from her cup and used it as an opportunity to suppress her grimace. It was typical that Alice would be impressed by Olly's manners and accent. She herself was finding the emphasis they were both putting on the financial value of Beth's things distasteful. It wasn't the money she wanted to think about, she wanted to consider the meaning of it all.

'Very nicely dressed, didn't you think?' Alice said.

'Mmm, I suppose.' Caroline leant back in her chair and screwed up her eyes. Seeing Olly through her mother's eyes abruptly robbed him of his allure. In person, and as a reminder of simpler times, he was compelling. She'd been receptive to his looks, his charm and confidence. As usual though, Alice's opinion triggered a knee-jerk rebellion. If Alice thought he was a good thing, then Caroline was over it. No matter how tempting the memories proved to be.

Chapter Twenty Four

'You did go home last night, didn't you?' Denise asked as she entered the office.

Caroline glanced up. 'Yep. Got to leave early today,' she replied, 'but I want to get this done.' She resumed typing the document which outlined her proposal for an exhibition in liaison with the Art School. All her recent thoughts and ideas clicked together so well she kicked herself for not focussing on them sooner. The role of women in the Arts and Crafts movement would tie in with the museum's own collection of Pre-Raphaelite paintings and industrial design, while the social history of the suffragette movement in Birmingham would develop the materials already included in the new local history displays about the city. The words flowed as she tried to collate her enthusiastic ideas into coherent paragraphs, only pausing to nod affirmatives whenever Denise offered cups of tea.

Once satisfied she clicked to save and print the document then crossed the office to deal with the flashing red lights which appeared on the printer whenever she expected it to live up to its name. As she stabbed at buttons and opened and slammed paper trays, she asked, 'Denise, do you remember that chap Oliver Mortimer who came in to see me?'

Denise looked up. 'The posh one?'

'Ah, that answers my question. I was going to ask what you thought of him.'

'Well, I spoke to him for all of about two seconds so,' Denise paused and stared at the ceiling, 'posh as a general categorisation, polite as an observation on character.' She smiled. 'Any particular reason?'

The printer finally whirred into life and began to deliver the pages of Caroline's report. 'I knew him at university,' she said. 'I'm not sure if I've changed my mind about him.'

'That can happen. As further discoveries are made, initial hypotheses may have to be rejected.'

'He isn't a topic for historical research.' Caroline picked up the bundle of pages and tapped them against the top of the printer to bring them into alignment. 'He's just a bloke.'

'A bloke you're sleeping with.'

Caroline flushed and lied. 'No!'

'Then a bloke you have slept with. It is about history, after all.'

'Sometimes I like the days when Bill's in,' Caroline replied. She clipped the printed pages into a cardboard folder and left Denise sniggering to herself.

*

Silence fell as Caroline looked around at the assembled members of her family. Alice and Ray sat on Beth's sofa, while Peter slouched on the matching armchair. Richard was sitting in the chair by the fireplace, the one Beth herself had used most often. Caroline had seen Alice scowl as he sat down, as though she considered it sacrilegious for him to have chosen that particular piece of furniture.

'Thanks for coming over,' Caroline said. She'd decided to behave as though she were in charge of a particularly acrimonious court case. 'I know there are a lot of things we'd all like to say, but I'm going to go first.'

She ignored the fact that Alice had turned the scowl towards her and picked up a pile of papers from the dining table behind her. 'I've made copies of Nan's will for us all -

her original will - and I'll talk you through the main points.'

The paperwork was passed around and Caroline began to talk again, glad that at least now everyone had something other than her to stare at. 'As you can see, Nan didn't intend this house to go directly to any of her descendants. We're to sell it and split the proceeds between Mum, Peter, me and several charities. She signed this will three years ago. It was drawn up by her lawyer who told me she'd given Nan some advice about how to minimise the inheritance tax burden - that's where the charity bequests come in.'

Alice sniffed. 'I wish she'd actually discussed it with me.'

'I wish she'd taken more advice about what her possessions were worth,' Caroline replied. 'I've been given an initial valuation on some of the furniture and paintings and it's possible that the remaining part of Nan's estate aside from the house, the chattels as the will refers to them, are actually worth more than you might imagine.'

'I assume that means a bigger tax bill?' said Ray.

'Yes, Dad, that's currently looking likely. However, it's only the house and how the proceeds from that are split and how she wants a few bits of jewellery to be passed on that are detailed explicitly. The division of her other possessions are at my discretion as her executor. I imagine she thought it would be a simple task.'

Alice folded her copy of the will in half and sharpened the crease by drawing her fingernails across it. 'So what is Richard doing here?' she asked.

Caroline glanced at him apologetically. 'Richard has in his possession a painting by Nan's Aunt Susannah which might really form part of Nan's estate - there's some doubt in my mind about its actual ownership. As there is in his, which is why he'd come to see Nan just before she had her fall. He was trying to give it back.'

Alice turned sharply to look at him. 'Give it back? Or ask to keep it? I know you're in financial trouble. Were you planning to sell it?'

Richard leant forward as he spoke and gestured with an open palm. 'Give it back, I assure you. It seems the painting was only ever meant to be on loan; it should probably have gone to Aunt Beth when Great Aunt Susannah died.'

'But the details are muddied by the time that's passed and the things that have happened,' Caroline said. 'And the fact that intentions haven't been clearly stated. Until now.' She looked around to make sure she had everyone's attention. 'At the hospital, Nan told me she wanted to change her will. She didn't get round to it before she died. Her solicitor had only just started redrafting the text, but Nan told me she wanted to include Richard in her bequests. She said that. Clearly. The fairest thing to do would be to allocate him an equal share.'

Peter uncrossed his legs, before recrossing them then speaking to break the tense silence which had descended. 'That's not what's written here.'

'No,' Caroline said, 'it's not. But it was stated as a clear intent.'

'To you,' Alice said. 'No one else.'

'No.'

Richard stood up. 'Look, I feel dreadful about this. It's not what I wanted. I planned to return the painting to Aunt Beth, not take anything from her and I can't stay here and be the cause of an argument between you.'

'Well your family have always been good at causing an argument,' Alice snapped.

Caroline stood as well and placed a hand on Richard's arm. 'What are you on about, Mum? You're as much a Garrold as Richard is. It's not your generation who caused any problems, or Nan's for that matter. This is our chance to change things. To bring the family back together.'

'And you implied something about the tax bill?' Ray said.

Caroline smiled at him in relief. 'Yes, that's the other thing. At the moment, it seems Nan might not have made enough charitable donations in her will to get below the inheritance tax threshold. It would depend on the sale price of the house. But I'd like us to discuss reducing the tax by allocating a larger proportion of the value of the house to her charities, and giving some of her possessions away - things such as the paintings.' She put pressure on Richard's arm to encourage him to sit down again. 'And while we're talking about varying the terms of the will, we could also agree to a more suitable distribution.'

Richard did sit down and Caroline took a deep breath while everyone considered what she'd said. The negotiation about reducing the tax bill was likely to be a quick win but adding Richard to the beneficiaries was a more difficult battle and the one thing she didn't want to get drawn in to was a discussion of which of their family had done what in the past. She certainly didn't want anyone else to look at what Susannah's will had actually said, not when it could possibly be interpreted as having the intent that the whole house went to Alice on Beth's death.

The temptation to destroy that document had been great but other copies of it could be found if anyone decided to dig. It didn't tell the story she wanted. She hadn't mentioned it to Beth's lawyer and was hoping not to have to show it to anyone at all. Denise may have reminded her that the discovery of more evidence could change the way history was interpreted, but this wasn't about history. This was about Caroline wanting to write the future.

Having let them think for a moment, she carried on talking. 'I've been looking into the split between our family and Richard's. It seems to have come about because of great-great-aunt Susannah's political beliefs and how various inheritances were changed as a result.' This was the risky part; she hoped no one would suggest getting all the old wills out for analysis. She moved on quickly. 'William Garrold, Susannah's father, married into the Farlane family and inherited their successful family firm. Because, in those days, things like that went to the men. Susannah's politics meant she was estranged from him and the firm has been passed direct to successive Garrold sons ever since. I don't think Richard's dad felt very happy about that.'

She glanced at Richard who confirmed it with a shake of his head. She went on, 'But now, the firm is no longer trading. Richard has had to wind things up and has managed that without dragging his family into debt.'

Ray raised his eyebrows and looked over to Richard, obviously impressed.

Richard cleared his throat. 'It's been terrible to have to close it down, after so many years. But things have changed beyond anything the Farlanes or William Garrold could have envisioned.'

'They certainly have,' Caroline said. 'And we've changed. Susannah campaigned for equality for women. Look at me: I have every opportunity Peter has. This is the modern world. But there's still some of the Farlane fortune and Garrold talent in it.'

'What about the Dabbs?' Alice asked, referring to her dad. She reached for Ray's hand, 'Or the Hipkins?'

Ray laughed. 'Come on, love. Neither the Dabbs nor the Hipkins ever came to much. Caroline's right, it's the Farlanes this all came from originally, and Richard's as much related to them as you all are.'

Caroline smiled at her dad, buoyed by his support. 'I've spent enough of my life preserving the past,' she said. 'But this, our family history, is my one chance actually to do something memorable. To change something, to be part of something. I want to do the right thing.'

Peter put down his copy of Beth's will and ran his fingers through his hair. 'So you're suggesting we change what Nan's said here, give more to charity and share the rest with Richard? And you think that's what Nan wanted?'

'Yes.' Caroline didn't dare say any more. Peter didn't reply. She hoped he was considering things.

Richard was shuffling his feet and frowning into the fireplace. 'I didn't want this,' he said. 'I didn't come here asking for anything.'

'But you could use it,' Caroline said. 'You told me you'd had some ideas for the future of Farlane's but been unable to implement them because of lack of capital.'

'I don't think we're really talking about those sums of money,' Richard replied. 'Manufacturing's moved on; we're not in the game any more.'

'There are alternatives. You own the building; you said you'd be sorry to see it go. It could be redeveloped into something else.'

He shook his head. 'To do anything would require significant investment.'

'Or partners.' Everyone turned to look at Ray as he said this. 'Business partners with investment capital.'

Caroline smiled. Her dad might describe himself as a boring accountant but she wished she'd got him on side as a negotiator from the start. He'd obviously guessed what she was thinking. 'It's a good point, Dad. I mean, what would I do with a chunk of money now anyway?'

Alice gaped at her. 'Buy a property? Set up your own business? Get yourself some security? Have you abandoned doing anything conventional in your life?'

'Maybe I'd like to invest in the family firm,' Caroline replied. She was enjoying the speed of the debate but a glance at Richard's wide-eyed stare made her realise things might be moving too fast to control. 'Look, I've made some pretty big suggestions. I think we should all go away and think about things overnight. We don't have to make any decisions immediately but I do want to get things

229

moving soon. Like putting this house on the market. There's no point it sitting here empty.'

Alice put a hand to her mouth and whimpered.

'Be realistic, Mum. It'll be for the best. Let's come over again tomorrow and think about a strategy for that. I think we're all agreed about increasing the charity donations though?' Peter and Alice nodded. 'So I'll start working on that and confirm the total value of Nan's possessions. If you don't have any objections, I'm going to suggest to the Museum and Gallery that some of the paintings would be of value to their collection. None of us want to go through the paper trail to unravel who really owns the painting Richard has, do we? So let's give it away.' She looked around again to make sure everyone was in agreement before carrying on, 'And you can get back to me in a couple of days about varying the will to include Richard, but you know it's what Nan wanted.'

*

Once the others had left Caroline flopped into Beth's armchair. She traced her fingertips over the shiny patch of worn fabric where Beth had always leant one elbow and whispered, 'I wish you could have sorted this out for yourself, Nan.' While the discussions had gone better than anticipated there was still much to do. Even gifting items to the museum wouldn't be straightforward. They'd want to see paperwork she'd rather keep hidden; they'd want assurances that they could legally take possession. She knew all this. She did all this for her living.

There was only one way to get round the truth. The idea crept up from the back of her mind, at first alarming to her professional ethics but then, as she tested it against the proofs of what Beth had wanted or what Susannah would have done, the dilemma shrunk. What was needed was obvious and easy in a purely practical sense. She had to destroy the historical evidence. There didn't need to be a paper trail about the painting of the factory. As Olly had pointed out, complete records were suspicious. It was

230

much more likely that papers would have been lost or agreements wouldn't have been written down. If she told them no documentation existed they'd have no reason to ask anyone else. Her conscience flared at the thought of destroying the letter, but really, there was nothing to it.

She stood and went around the house to turn off lights and check everything was secure. As she put on her coat in the hallway she smiled. The thought that perhaps Susannah had departed from there to go out into the world to make a difference, that Beth had returned there to do good for her family, was inspirational. Caroline was struck with a desire to celebrate them. She delved in her handbag for her phone and sent a text to Olly before she could consider it too carefully.

'Dinner at mine tomorrow? 7.30.'

His acceptance came back immediately and she smiled as she locked the front door and got into her car. As she reversed out the drive a thought struck her. There was a missing link in that chain of inspirational women: Alice. It made no sense. Why was Alice so intent to preserve the division in the family? What did she know that Caroline didn't, and why was she so keen to hang onto the money?

Chapter Twenty Five

Caroline pressed her lips together and held onto the edges of the chair as Gerald turned the pages of her report.

'That is fascinating,' he said. 'You think we could meet these dates?'

'Absolutely,' she said. 'The paintings could be brought in straight away and the other items are in our collection or elsewhere in Birmingham. I'm certain we could get loans organised. As you can see from the final page, my estimate for the costs is very low.'

He turned to the back page and a slight twitch of his mouth suggested he'd considered smiling. Caroline bit her lip and wondered if his reactions were ironic. Perhaps he didn't like the idea at all. She folded her arms and kept quiet.

'Well, as I say, it is fascinating; and the suffragette link certainly adds value.' Gerald closed the folder and looked at her. 'This is your family history; are you sure about putting it on public display? I imagine you'll be proposing articles for publication and I'd want you to be interviewed for the publicity materials. Would you feel comfortable with your personal life becoming public?'

Caroline smiled. 'I doubt there'll be paparazzi camped outside my apartment. It's fine. I'm passionate about this project because it's about real Brummies, the real Birmingham. I don't have anything to hide and, actually, a little bit of celebrity might make it even more appealing to my family.' She couldn't tell him she didn't have approval from the rest of the family yet, but telling them he was keen on it would definitely impress them.

'All right, well, I'll certainly consider it. Leave it with me for now.' Gerald's expression conveyed that it was time for her to leave. She did, and felt more positive than in a long time as she strode down the marble-floored corridor. In Susannah's footsteps, the simple act of asking for something, stating a demand, had brought her a long way. Caroline hoped it was the first step in the right direction.

'Anyone for a cup of tea?' she asked as she returned to her desk.

Bill looked at her, eyes narrowed. 'You're in a good mood.'

'Which is lovely. Yes, please,' Denise said.

Caroline crossed the office to collect her mug. 'Am I not always in a good mood?' she asked.

'Well, mostly, perhaps.' Denise paused. 'Actually, not always, no.'

'Then I apologise and will mend my ways forthwith.' Caroline chinked their mugs together and headed for the door.

'Is there, um, any particular reason?' Bill's voice was hesitant.

Caroline turned to him and grinned. 'Revelation, inspiration and perspective. Decisions and achievements.'

'Any we should know about?'

'Sure, if you're interested. You see I always knew curating isn't about controlling people's responses to what's displayed, it's more about making them think. But I hadn't applied that knowledge recently. I got confused and thought preserving the past is most important when really it's the future we should be concentrating on. Understanding history is brilliant as long as you act on it and never ever make the same mistake more than twice. And I intend to take that advice.' She let the office door slam shut behind her not caring if they thought her mad.

*

233

As she flicked through the floral wallpaper-covered exercise book Beth had used to copy down favourite recipes Caroline's eyes filled with tears. With the tip of her index finger she traced the familiar handwriting on each page, almost hearing Beth's own voice speak each word. The grease-spotted paper was evidence of how well used the book had been and each page sparked memories of meals in that kitchen throughout her life.

'Are you making progress?' Alice asked as she carried a cardboard box and a roll of bubble wrap into the kitchen. 'Put any open food into this. Wrap the jars first. I'll take them home and see if I can use them. I know you don't cook.'

Caroline blinked the tears away and stepped down from the stool she'd used to reach the top shelves of Beth's cupboards. She passed the book to Alice. 'Look, Nan's recipes.'

'Oh,' Alice gasped as she took it. 'I haven't seen this in years.' She pulled out a chair from the kitchen table, flinching as its legs screeched against the tiled floor.

'And I do cook,' Caroline said. 'Sometimes.' She turned back to the cupboards and placed part-used jars of herbs and spices, plastic containers holding decanted rice and pasta, and packets of stock cubes into the box. She ignored a memory of Alice lecturing her on how to pack toys for the move to the new house, with strict instruction to throw out anything not played with in the previous six months, and considered again which of her small repertoire of meals she could reasonably serve to Olly. It was perhaps a good job the food wasn't really what the evening was about.

It was only when that cupboard was empty that she noticed Alice's silence. 'Everything OK, Mum?'

Alice sniffed. The recipe book lay open on the kitchen table in front of her and her hands were over her eyes. Caroline pulled over a chair to sit beside her and squeezed her shoulders.

'That was my dad's favourite,' Alice said and pointed to the open page.

Caroline pulled the book towards her and smiled when she saw how Beth had annotated the title for Dundee Cake with a sketched heart and the name George. 'I don't really remember Grandad,' she said.

'You were a baby when he died,' Alice replied. 'I can remember, sitting here after his funeral with you in your pram and mum just here,' she pointed across the table, 'and my Uncle James, Richard's dad, making mum cry even more.'

'You met James Garrold?'

'Of course, he was my uncle.'

'But, you and Nan never mentioned them. Pete and I didn't know they existed until I met Richard. Why didn't you tell us?'

Alice took a tissue from the pocket of her cardigan and blew her nose. 'You didn't miss anything. I didn't see James Garrold after that day and hadn't met Richard before now.'

Caroline wasn't prepared to let the subject drop. 'Why didn't you see them?'

Alice frowned and smoothed a strip of yellowed tape which, until its sticking power failed, had held a recipe clipped from a magazine onto a page in Beth's book. The sound of the dry tape crackling filled the pause until she replied, 'Before Dad died, Mum hadn't seen Uncle James for the best part of thirty years - since my grandad died and left everything to him. Then James had the cheek to come to Dad's funeral, sit in this kitchen and offer Mum money. As though my dad hadn't been able to provide for his family. As though nothing could work unless a Garrold had his say in things. Well, we told him what he could do with that opinion.' Alice's face flushed and she thumped the table. 'George Dabbs put his family first, not some stupid firm.'

Caroline reached across to stroke Alice's arm. 'I see,' she said. 'But this house…'

'Belonged to the Farlanes, not the Garrolds. That firm was successful long before the Garrolds got their hands on it.' She closed the exercise book and slapped her hand down on the cover. 'I suppose you think it was easy for my dad because we had this place and he didn't have to worry about keeping a roof over his family's heads. Well nothing was easy after the war. Unlike James Garrold, my dad fought for his country.'

Caroline tried to calculate the dates. 'Umm, wasn't James too young to be in World War Two?'

'Lucky for him.' Alice found her tissue again and wiped her eyes. 'Dad never let us down. Never. And Mum and I were in no need of handouts from the Garrolds.'

Caroline paused. She couldn't help thinking Alice's strident words put her most in mind of those letters from William Garrold - the pride, belligerent tone and refusal to allow family ties to water down opinions clearly ran in the family. 'What about now though, Mum? Richard's your cousin, not your enemy. Nan wanted things to change, not stay the same.'

Alice lifted the recipe book and stood up. 'I assume it's OK for me to have this?'

'Of course, but Mum, listen…'

'No, you listen,' Alice tucked the book into the cardboard box before turning to Caroline with her arms folded. 'The reason I didn't tell you about our relations is because they've caused nothing but problems. Even Susannah, who you seem to have taken to heart, was essentially a criminal who brought shame on her family. I thought you historians agreed Suffragettes didn't help women get the vote; their stunts actually made women look stupid. It was sensible women knuckling down to work during World War One that did more for women's rights than them.'

Caroline opened her mouth to disagree - that conclusion was not agreed by all historians. Alice wasn't finished speaking though. 'Anyway, when you were little, your Nan and I decided we wanted only to look forward, not hang on to old feuds. That's why we never spoke of them. Our family is what matters. You and Peter should start behaving like adults and use your inheritances from Nan to set yourselves up. That's what she would have wanted.'

'She'd changed her mind.'

'No. She hadn't.' Alice turned and left the kitchen.

'Well, if that isn't hanging on to an old feud...' Caroline returned to packing up the kitchen.

It could never be known what made the greatest contribution to achieving votes for women. The Suffragettes had reinvigorated a tired campaign, raised awareness and encouraged debate about the ideas while World War One had given women opportunities to prove themselves. In the end all anyone could truly say was that things had changed because brave women took action.

She yanked open the drawer Beth had called the 'useful' one, its handle festooned with a garland of rubber bands. The force of the movement shunted the contents to the front of the drawer revealing a jumbled mass reminiscent of a pirate's treasure chest. She reached in and pulled the pile apart, finding batteries, screwdrivers, a tape measure and pencil stubs. Every item in the collection had a value, some residual use, had been deemed worth keeping - except perhaps for the old coins Caroline took for foreign currency when she first picked one out, but which closer inspection confirmed as half-pence pieces. She smiled, and lifted out a flat green tin which had once held toffees. She leant against the counter as she prised open the hinged lid to reveal a stash of odd buttons: plastic, wooden, brass, some fabric-coated and others leather-wrapped. They clicked and tapped against each other as she stirred them with a finger tip and recalled being handed the tin as a small girl. She'd knelt on a chair at the kitchen table, tipping the buttons onto a metal tray to play at sorting them by colour, by size, arranging them into patterns and selecting favourites. She could still hear the sound they'd made. Probably my first curatorial experience, she thought.

A stray item in the tin caught her eye. She lifted the small metal object and recognised it as the miniature iron which was one of the playing pieces from a Monopoly set. It had probably been dropped when she and Peter got the game out to play one school holiday afternoon when Beth was looking after them. Caroline had always insisted on playing as the little dog, while Peter chose the top hat. Beth must have found the iron after they'd left and popped it in the tin for safekeeping. She'd always encouraged them to play that game, probably because it kept them occupied for hours as Peter indulged his frivolous streak to buy streets in his favourite colours while Caroline practised business strategies and won every game. She smiled at the memory. 'Probably missed a vocation there,' she murmured, dropped the iron back in the tin and threw the tin in the bin. It was bric-a-brac now. She didn't have time or space for keepsakes.

She moved to the final cupboard and pulled out a dusty stack of cookbooks, clearly not ones Beth had found much use for. As she hesitated and wondered whether to dump the entire pile into the recycling box or whether they were worth adding to the charity shop donation, the word 'suffrage' leapt out from the spine of the bottom-most book. She shoved the other books aside to reveal a red, board-backed book called 'The Women's Suffrage Cookbook'. Caroline's mouth dropped open. This must be the book Susannah helped collect recipes for. A wood-cut image of two children below an apple tree decorated the cover and she carefully lifted its worn edge to read the title page. Susannah's name wasn't listed, but the trail of connections was intriguing and some of the recipes sounded enticing. The pages felt fragile and she only turned a few before her caution about handling a historical artefact stopped her. The page lay open on a recipe for pineapple pudding which referred to tinned pineapple as though it were a luxury item suitable for a dinner party. It reminded her she needed to be elsewhere. Taking a linen tea towel from one of Beth's well stocked drawers, she wrapped the book and carried it carefully out to the car.

*

She was staring into her own kitchen cupboards a few hours later when her mobile rang. 'Hi Olly,' she said. 'I hope you aren't especially hungry.'

'Ah, I'm afraid I won't actually be able to make it I'm afraid. Something's come up with the kids.'

Caroline closed the cupboard door. 'Oh. I hope they're OK?'

'Yes. I just need to stay here for now. With them.'

There was something about his tone which seemed strange. His voice was quiet, as though he was trying not to be overheard. Perhaps the children were in the room with him, she thought. 'Of course. We'll get together another time.'

'Yes, yes, that would be good. I've sent you an email by the way, have you seen it?'

'Not yet. I've been battling my mother all afternoon.'

'Right, well it's a listing of my initial valuations for you to start thinking about. I'd total the items we talked about from the house as potentially up to thirty thousand, but then there's the large painting you say is at the factory and you mentioned some suffragette memorabilia? Without seeing those I can't say for sure, but really, the total could go higher than fifty thousand.'

Caroline took a breath. 'Right, thank you. I'm not sure how to feel about that.' She also wasn't sure how to feel about his manner. She couldn't detect paternal concern, or the sound of a man disappointed to be breaking a date. He sounded purely professional.

'Well don't do anything hasty. There are some significant items there.'

'Items? I'm still thinking of them as my nan's possessions.'

'Hmm, yes, but everything has a price. Look, I have to go but I'll be in touch again soon.'

No, Caroline thought as she hung up, not everything has a price; some things are worth more than money. She dropped the phone onto the kitchen counter and returned to the perusal of her cupboards. If she wasn't cooking for him then beans on toast seemed a reasonable choice. She just had to forget Alice's jibe about her cooking abilities, and not remember that cookbook of Beth's filled with nutritious and delicious ideas, and then she wouldn't feel inadequate or guilty.

She lifted the ring-pull to rip the lid from the can of beans and stopped. That was what was wrong with Olly's tone of voice. He sounded like neither a concerned father nor an apologetic lover because what he had sounded was guilty.

*

The meeting of the curatorial services and exhibitions teams had been scheduled to start five minutes before Caroline slipped into a seat towards the end of the table. She was surprised they hadn't started without her. Gerald shuffled his papers and called the meeting to order. Caroline intercepted a glare across the table from Bill. Perhaps he felt she'd let the team down.

'Right, we'll start with the plans for next year,' Gerald said. 'Thanks to all who submitted exhibition proposals; there were some interesting ideas.'

Caroline noticed Bill sit straighter in his chair and leant forward herself.

'Unfortunately,' Gerald went on, 'we don't have resources to do everything and I'd like a couple of the proposals worked up further, although I hope we can do both. Priority area one is the contemporary art collection

240

so I'd like to see detailed costs for the suggestion in that area, please.' He glanced towards the modern art curator, who nodded eagerly, then looked around the table until he caught Caroline's eye. 'Priority area two is diversity. Caroline proposed something about women in Birmingham's history, politics and culture with potential to acquire some important objects which will increase our representation of local, female artists. I'd like a full plan drawn up for that before the next acquisitions meeting, please. As I said, the other ideas were interesting but those are the two we'll run with this year. Right, next on the agenda is our strategy and policy for collections and acquisitions looking ahead to 2020.'

Caroline dipped her head to hide the flush in her cheeks, surprised to find her reaction was embarrassment at being singled out rather than delight at her success. She could tell Bill was glaring at her and didn't want to catch his eye. She missed most of the other business of the meeting as she was busy mentally listing what needed to be done to flesh out her proposal and panicking at the prospect of doing it. Long hours at her desk no longer appealed.

'So,' Bill said as they walked back to their office, 'what are these important objects you've uncovered. Don't tell me it's anything to do with that dodgy character with his photographs of mud.'

'No, you were right about that. It turned out to be nothing special.' Caroline reached out to touch Bill's arm, to force him to turn and look her in the eye. 'I'm sorry if you feel I've trodden on your toes or kept things from you. My exhibition idea only came together in the last few weeks. It's based on my great-great-aunt Susannah who was an artist and involved with the Suffragettes; I've just found how much of her work is around. Her pictures really are ideal for the collection and my ideas fill out a bit of the city's creative history that's not much known.'

'And it'll be a nice bit of income for your family to sell them to the museum, I suppose? You don't think it's any kind of conflict of interest?'

'Absolutely not. I need to work out the details but they'll probably be a donation in lieu of tax. There are some documents, bits of suffragette memorabilia which I'm going to have to consider carefully because I am executor of the will and have to make sure that doesn't conflict with my role here. But you know how tough the acquisitions committee are. The paperwork and everything will have to be exact, clear and beyond reproach. I wonder if I could ask you for input? Your experience would be a great help.'

Bill was silent for a moment and Caroline feared she'd come across as patronising rather than conciliatory. Finally he sighed and said, 'You know how I feel about paintings, but I suppose I could help.'

'I promise you hers are nothing like the average painting we get brought in from family collections. I guarantee you're going to like the story which goes with them as well. It might make your dad smile too.'

Chapter Twenty Six

Caroline smiled at her reflection in the mirror as she fastened her jeans. No point dressing smartly for the occasion although, unlike Alice, she was looking forward to it. Alice's reaction had made Caroline glad she'd chosen to give the invitation by phone rather than in person.

'You're doing what?' Alice had said.

'Going into business with Richard,' Caroline repeated. 'Sort of a family firm, I suppose. We might call it Farlane's.'

The phone line remained quiet as she'd waited for Alice to decide on a response. It was a while in coming. She leant against the window ledge in her living room and gazed down the canal. A thin line of smoke rose from the chimney of a narrow boat moored upstream, incongruous among the glass and steel buildings and neon adverts - someone living in a traditional way, although probably for a holiday rather than a lifestyle.

'Farlane's?' Alice said eventually. 'And what is it you plan to do?'

'Redevelop the factory building into workshops, meeting rooms, perhaps a café, gallery, even a guest house or hostel. You know how that part of town has changed. There's a market for all sorts of alternative uses. We need to work out a plan and invest in the changes.'

'Which will cost how much, exactly?'

Caroline shifted the handset to her other ear. It was easier to be vague over the phone. 'Not as much as you'd

243

expect. Not to get up and running at least. We're drawing up the plans but it's down to Richard's good management that he's wound up his firm without many debts and selling the remaining machinery will give him a little capital. Obviously I have my share of the inheritance to invest.'

She heard Alice's intake of breath and paused to see what she'd say.

'You'd do that? Give the money your nan intended for you to the family which abandoned her?'

'No. I'm making an investment in my future. We'll need to apply for a loan but,' Caroline paused before dropping the final bombshell, 'Peter's thinking about coming in with us as well.'

'I see.' Alice's tone indicated that she did not see. 'Neither of you considered discussing this with me?'

Caroline moved the phone so Alice wouldn't hear her sigh. Then she said, 'No, Mum. This is our decision, our future. We can't worry about what happened in the past. Look, I was ringing to invite you down to the factory tomorrow. Meet us there; we'll talk you through the plans. Maybe then you'll understand.'

As she drove towards the factory to meet everyone the next morning, Caroline had a sense of a fresh start. It was as though she'd finally taken the right course of action.

*

Peter scrutinised the exposed timbers of the factory roof. 'They'd clean up a treat,' he said. 'Forget rustic charm, industrial chic is what everyone wants from a mini-break these days.'

Caroline tried to rein in his enthusiasm. 'None of us have any experience in running hotels. I prefer the idea of diverse uses for the building. Maybe we could put some apartments for short-term lets into a mezzanine floor and make a feature of the architecture, but I would like to spread the risks a bit.'

'And I'd like there to be some manufacturing somewhere on site,' Richard said. 'George Farlane put this building up to make products, not breakfast.'

Peter nodded. 'With these big windows I can definitely see the space working for artists. In fact, I might be tempted myself. We could hark back to the thing about Birmingham being the workshop of the world in our marketing stuff.'

Caroline glanced at Alice. She'd said nothing since arriving at the factory and her lips were pursed almost as tight as her arms were folded. She'd listened to their plans and followed Richard on a tour of the building but, unlike Ray, she'd asked no questions, passed no comment. 'What do you think, Mum?'

Alice looked at her and then looked away. 'What I think doesn't matter. As you've pointed out the money will be yours to invest how you see fit.'

'We'd rather have you on side.'

Alice dropped her arms to her sides, hands clenched in fists. 'Neither of you have ever made it easy for me to be supportive. You couldn't make ordinary, traditional choices, could you? I'm not allowed to say I'm disappointed by your decisions; I just have to accept them. You won't settle down, I should forget about grandchildren, you're going to risk your money on this idiotic idea. Why worry what I think?'

Caroline took a breath. Retaliating in anger would not be a sensible move but Alice's bitterness was unfair. She glanced at Peter's stunned expression and recalled Alice's question to her after Peter had told them about his sexuality, 'Is there anything we can do?' she'd said.

Caroline had dismissed it at the time as an inappropriate response motivated by shock; she'd just been pleased how well Alice seemed to have taken it, but now she wondered. Alice may have been more deeply wounded by her children's unconventional lives than they'd guessed. She shook her head; neither of them were deviant by the standards of the twenty-first century. Homosexuality and divorce were commonplace among her friends. Not so common among Alice's though. She appeared to consider those concepts as odd as the idea of women with votes had been to William Garrold a hundred years before.

Caroline frowned. 'It does matter what you think, Mum. I'm sure Peter agrees we don't want to do anything you'd be upset about. But Richard isn't the enemy, you know. He's your cousin.'

'Family doesn't matter,' Alice snapped.

'History doesn't matter,' Caroline replied. 'This is about mine and Peter's future. We have to make our own contribution.'

'You're repeating history - feeding money into this place, upsetting people.'

Peter stepped across and put his arms around Alice. 'There's one sure way to stop history repeating, Mum: do things differently.' He hugged her but she remained rigid in his arms.

'He's right,' Caroline said. 'There's no point clinging to the past. We have to learn from it. And one thing I'm sure of is that I could do with a change.'

'You're planning to give up your job to do this?'

'No. Not necessarily. I'm sure I can do both for a while and I do like my job; it's just not quite enough. This isn't an unnecessary risk, Mum. I need something else in my life. I want to build something, make some kind of legacy for Nan.'

Alice gaped. 'Your security should be her legacy. She'd have been proud of that.'

'I disagree. I'm doing this.' Caroline folded her arms.

Alice pushed Peter away, turned and rushed out of the factory. Ray patted both his children on their shoulders without speaking then followed his wife.

'Oh. Oh, dear.' Richard's voice was quiet as he stepped towards Caroline and Peter. 'This was the last thing I wanted.'

Caroline shook her head. 'Don't blame yourself and don't feel bad.' She linked one arm through Peter's and reached out to Richard with a smile. 'Look about you,' she said. 'We've got work to do.'

*

Later that evening Caroline leant against the frame of the door to her balcony and gazed out across the canal. They'd stayed at the factory discussing plans until it got dark and her mind buzzed with potential and ideas. Reflections of coloured light glared against the water and she could hear the siren of a vehicle responding to an emergency on a nearby street. The city view was alive and vibrant. Only a few months ago the flat had seemed unhomely, not a suitable refuge, but now she was glad it had challenged her. Different paths lay ahead and returning to Birmingham finally felt like the right decision. She wanted to share her news with someone, but wasn't going to be first to break the silence with Alice. She considered calling Steph but realised there was one thing she had yet to resolve.

She stepped back into the living room and reached for her phone. Some things didn't need to be curated or invested in; they needed to be deleted.

'Caroline.' Olly sounded pleased to hear from her, but she also noted the click of a closing door in the background. He needed privacy to speak to her.

'Hi, Olly. Can you talk?'

'Yes, of course. Look, I'm so sorry to have let you down the other night. Can we make plans for another time?'

She noted his voice was quieter and somehow less confident than previously. 'Well, that depends,' she said. 'Are you free to make plans, or do you perhaps have other commitments?' She poured a glass of wine and put her feet up on the coffee table while he worked towards what he had to say.

'No, well, of course, I mean, I'd love to see you.'

'But…'

'But, well, I do have to think of my children.'

'And…'

'And, um, yes. It's Sarah, you see. She's changed her mind. Says she'll have me back.'

'Right.' Caroline was pleased to find she wasn't upset about his news. In fact, it was amusing to listen to him squirm.

'I have to do what's best for the children, I'm sure you understand?'

'Oh, of course I understand.'

'But I'd love to see you again. Perhaps we could get together, during the week sometime?'

'During which week?' She kept her voice light but it was anger which fuelled the teasing.

'How about next week? Perhaps Thursday?'

'Thursday?'

'Well, Sarah will be working; the kids will be at school…'

'So you'll have time to fit in a little infidelity dressed up as a business meeting?'

'Caroline, let's be mature about this. We're good together. Our history is worth something.'

Caroline swung her feet to the floor and sat up straight. She was in no mood to provide anyone else's ego boost. 'Not everything can be priced in pounds, Olly. Sometimes it's only worth remembering the past so as not to repeat the same mistakes.'

He lowered his voice, an attempt at either secrecy or seduction, she wasn't sure which. 'Aphrodite, please. This doesn't have to be over.'

'No, Olly, it does. I'm very grateful for your help with valuing Nan's things, and I'm happy to chat anytime on a purely professional basis. But for us as anything more than acquaintances in the same field, then yes, it's over. Put your wife and family first for once. It's the future which matters. Their future, not yours.'

She ended the call and drained her wine glass. Sometimes a mistake did have to be made twice before it was properly learnt, but she'd got it now. Olly was not the man for her. What they'd done didn't need fixing and was not worth preserving. Not all history was worthy of record after all. Most of it was background noise.

THE END

Author's note

The Museum and Art Gallery where Caroline works is a fictional place although it bears some similarity to the Birmingham Museum and Art Gallery. I've taken liberties with actual museum policies, procedures, history and geography for the sake of storytelling and can assure the staff of BMAG that all present day characters and events in this book are fictitious.

Thanks are due to: Julia Kirby for discussions about museums; Andy Pilkington for discussions about history; Andy Killeen and the members of the Pow-Wow Writers' Group for discussions about writing and for their feedback on extracts from an early draft; Anne D'Souza and Kirsten Lacey for supplying insightful observations; and Jane Dixon-Smith for the cover design.

Any historical inaccuracies are entirely my fault. If you'd like to read more about the Suffragette's activities in Birmingham the historian Elizabeth Crawford has an interesting website full of information at www.womanandhersphere.com.

I visited a number of locations in and around Birmingham to build up the settings for the book. If you'd like to pick up some of the atmosphere I'd recommend you visit: Birmingham Museum and Art Gallery, Birmingham School of Art on Margaret Street (I was lucky to get a tour during an Open House weekend; I'm not sure how accessible it is otherwise), The Pen Museum and the Museum of the Jewellery Quarter, and Winterbourne House and Garden.

I often find exhibitions a great source of story ideas and being immersed in Lundhal & Seitl's 'Symphony of a Missing Room' which visited Birmingham as part of the Fierce Festival in 2011 started me thinking about what is in museums and what should be there.

Birmingham is definitely a place where things happen. Some of them even make history. I consider myself lucky to live here.

Katharine D'Souza
2013

www.katharinedsouza.co.uk

Also by this author:

PARK LIFE
A tale of neighbours, cafes and cake in Birmingham.

Craig's ambitious. He wants promotion, recognition and to be one of the lads. Relationships and family don't feature in the plan; until he's given no alternative.

*

Susan's taken a huge step. She's walked away from the oppressive security of her marriage and moved to Birmingham for a fresh start – in the flat next door to Craig.

*

They're not friends. But maybe a neighbour can do more than keep an emergency spare key.

*

Life isn't a walk in the park. Perhaps taking one might help.